KING TIDE

A MIAMI JONES CASE

AJ Stewart

Jacaranda Drive Publishing

Los Angeles, California

www.jacarandadrive.com

This book is a work of fiction. Names, characters, places and incidents are either products of the author's imagination or are used fictitiously, and any resemblance to actual persons, living or dead, business establishments or locales is entirely coincidental.

Cover artwork by Streetlight Graphics

ISBN-10: 1-945741-04-X

ISBN-13: 978-1-945741-04-3

Copyright © 2017 by A.J. Stewart

No part of this book may be reproduced, scanned or distributed in any printed or electronic form without permission from the author.

Books by AJ Stewart

Stiff Arm Steal
Offside Trap
High Lie
Dead Fast
Crash Tack
Deep Rough
King Tide
No Right Turn

For Heather and Evan.

CHAPTER ONE

The weather guy was adamant we weren't going to see a hurricane. The computer models proved it. There was a US model that said the tropical storm would scoot up closer to the Bahamas, and a European model that said it would ride the Gulf Stream out into the Atlantic. The weather guy seemed particularly enamored with the European model, but I for one couldn't see what Europeans knew about Florida weather that Mick didn't.

Mick didn't agree with the models. I wasn't even sure Mick had seen the models. The television in the inside bar at Longboard Kelly's was on the Weather Network, and the graphics showed a half dozen lines sweeping in from east of Cuba and then sweeping out again farther north and east of South Carolina. Mick paid it no mind. He said it would make landfall in Florida, somewhere between Boca Raton and Cape Canaveral. He said by the time it did it would no longer be a tropical storm. Most definitely a hurricane, in Mick's opinion. Not necessarily a big one, not like Andrew, but more than a tropical storm. Enough to blow your house off its foundations if it were in a trailer park, and the fronds off a palapa if they covered your favorite bar.

Ron and I and a couple other regulars helped batten down the hatches at Mick's bar. It was my home away from home and to be fair, with Danielle away at the academy, it was closer to my actual home than I cared to admit. We pulled in all the chairs and umbrellas from the courtyard and stacked them inside, and then we lowered the shutters across the outside bar and locked them down.

Ron looked over the scene as if Mick was closing Longboard's for good. The sorrow on his face was palpable, as if he knew something. He didn't care for the weather models, either. Ron was an analog kind of guy. His silver mane and sun-splotched face made him look like he had been at sea all his life, rather than selling insurance before joining my mentor and friend, the late, great Lenny Cox, as a private investigator. Ron handled most of the corporate work, and spent a fair amount of time working with computers, but he never seemed to trust them. What he trusted was Mick's sixth sense about these things.

"Let's get these inside," Ron said, picking up the wooden bar stool that was his throne at Longboard Kelly's. I collected the stool next to it, the one with my butt print in it, and we stowed them behind the bar. With the shutters down and storm clouds circling it was dim inside. The only glow came from the television. I watched the light play across Ron's face. He was like a sunflower. The sun was his power source and without it he looked drawn and sickly.

"We best sort Miami out," Mick said, appearing out of the darkness. He was squat and broad, like a mortar round, and about as chatty.

"You think my place might get hit?" I asked him.

"Moon's your trouble."

"The moon?"

Mick nodded and then huffed like it was self-evident and not worthy of the extra verbiage. "It's a full moon, behind them clouds. Perigean moon. We got a perigean spring tide."

"A what?"

"King Tide. Moon is close to earth, so the high tide will be higher than normal. You know when Flagler Drive gets flooded?"

"Yeah."

"King Tide. Only add a hurricane. It hits north of here, there'll be storm surge in the IC. You're on the IC, right?"

I nodded. "Yeah, my place is on the Intracoastal."

"You want it to be there when you get back?"

"Probably."

"Then git goin'."

We left Longboard's behind and traveled up Route 1 to Singer Island. The traffic was heavy. Most folks didn't want to leave unnecessarily so they chose to believe the computer models. But most folks weren't stupid, so they were out stocking up on last-minute items, like water and bread. A drive-thru cigarette hut had a line like a buffet on a cruise ship.

I pulled onto the island and back around toward the Intracoastal Waterway. My house sat at the end, overlooking the water and city of Riviera Beach to the west. My seventies rancher was old Florida. All the new-build McMansions around it were new Florida. I had a pretty particular position on which architecture I preferred.

I slowed and backed my Cadillac SUV into the driveway. Ron jumped out and directed Mick's truck into the space beside. His pickup was older than the Union—more rust than steel.

But it held its share of sandbags, which we unloaded from both vehicles in a procession of trips with a wheelbarrow. Mick wheeled a hefty pile of bags around to the back of my house, and we set them across the patio. Already the water level was up, gray and ragged, pounding against the seawall and spilling onto the grass. Mick brought another barrowful of sandbags, and I tossed them into place with a sound like punching a muscular gut. The effort seemed futile against the power of the water.

Mick sensed my apprehension. "It won't stop it. But it might divert it a bit," he said.

"What's the difference?"

"New carpet versus a new house."

I nodded and scooped up another heavy bag. The humidity was stifling and I was sweating like a sumo, and the rain washed the salt from my skin.

Ron propped a lounger onto its castors and wheeled it into the garage and then came back for the second one. Beyond Longboard's, that patio and those loungers were my favorite place on the planet. It was where I sat and watched the world go by, the yachts and the gulls and the pelicans go about their daily grind. It was where Danielle sat and watched the world go by beside me, and it seemed somehow apt that the view had grown angry and the loungers had been wheeled away in her absence.

My shoulders burned by the time I dropped the last sandbag in place. Ron had secured the steel storm shutters across the windows, and the scene looked like Normandy, without the razor wire, or the massive human toll. I shook my head to swish away the ridiculous simile. Mick slapped my back as we surveyed the barricade.

"You do what you can," he said.

It wasn't exactly a Hallmark card, but it was Mick. It was as sugarcoated as he got. We stood in the rain for a moment, looking at the back of my house like patrons at The Met look at the art.

"We should get going," said Ron.

I could see he was getting antsy, so I nodded and we walked around the side of the house. We tossed a few last sandbags around the front door and then stepped to our vehicles.

"Where are you going?" I asked Mick.

"Longboard's." He looked at me like there could be no other answer.

"Will you be okay?"

He grunted. "This too shall pass." Mick pulled open the door to his truck and it screeched in anger, and then he dropped down inside and he revved the engine to life. Ron and I got in my SUV. It didn't groan or require revving. I simply turned the key. With the rain and the slap of the palm trees I wasn't even sure the engine had started, but I pressed the accelerator and we moved so I figured it had.

We followed Mick out and crawled along Route 1 until Mick pulled off for Longboard's with a wave of his hand. I continued into West Palm Beach. Flagler Memorial Bridge was being rebuilt, and had been closed due to the impending storm. Traffic was being routed south to Okeechobee Boulevard and across Royal Park Bridge, which made the usual traffic snarl in West Palm even more fun than usual. Cars were breaking down, tempers were fraying. Storms always brought out the best in folks.

Most of the downtown traffic was trying to get west on Okeechobee, away from the water and wind, which was the smart play. It was going to be our play too, once we had everyone on board. But first we were headed onto the island.

There weren't many with us. The traffic flow was definitely headed for the mainland, so we picked up speed as we rose over the Intracoastal. The water below looked like it was boiling. There were whitecaps and eddies and spray as if the water were being propelled from below. The water was the same heavy gray as the sky, and the rain hit the windshield harder now that we were in the open.

As we reached the crest of the bridge I saw down to the island. It wasn't the pretty tropical view that snowbirds traveled thousands of miles to see. The palm trees were bent over as if waiting for some kind of corporal punishment, and a line of cars stretched back into Palm Beach. Most of them weren't going to make it.

The surging Intracoastal had broken the seawall along the park and was rapidly spilling across Royal Palm Way. As it did so it cut access to the bridge. A Palm Beach PD SUV was stuck farther back in the traffic, sounding its electronic bleep into the wind, trying to reach the flooding water.

I looked at Ron and he at me.

"They're going to close the bridge," he said.

"Yes."

"We have to get Cassandra." There was a rising panic in his voice. Ron was a solid guy, Florida through and through. He loved everything about it. The sun, the sailing and even the tropical storms. But it had been stress that had driven him out of the insurance game, and whenever it rose its ugly head I worried for him. He didn't wear it well. I on the other hand had played professional baseball for a living. I knew a thing or two about stress. That wasn't to say I didn't feel it, or that I went looking for it. But when it came, as it inevitably did, I had a method that had always seen me through.

Breathe and keep true.

The water was cascading onto our side of the roadway as we reached the bottom of the bridge. I could see the police car on the other side pulling across the lanes, lights ablaze, stopping the fools trying to get off the island from attempting to drive into the torrent of water.

I took a deep breath, in through the nose and out through the mouth, and then like a fool I jammed the accelerator down and burst into the flood.

CHAPTER TWO

This wasn't my father's Cadillac. Not that my father ever owned a Cadillac. But there were plenty of men of my father's vintage driving around South Florida in two tons of fifty-year-old Detroit steel, and those babies were going down like the Titanic if they hit this water. But my Cadillac was a whole other generation, more Jeep than Caddy. It had all-wheel drive and traction control and goodness knows what else to keep us on the road. Still, when we hit the water the steering wheel was pulled from my hands. The water was only as high as the rims but it fought above its weight class. The Caddy jerked right and if there had been another car beside us I would have taken it out. But all the smart money was trying to get off the island, so I pulled hard on the wheel and kept my foot clamped down on the pedal and we pushed through the tide and burst out onto the island.

We drove on through increasingly deserted streets toward the ocean side of the island. As we reached our pit stop we were almost sideswiped by another Cadillac, a black Escalade, the bigger, badder brother of my vehicle. It was the kind of thing that looked like it belonged to the Secret Service, even when it was piloted by a petite Palm Beach housewife. I gave the driver a mental cussing and then followed the Escalade down the palm-lined driveway to the majestic steps of the hotel.

The Mornington was one of the grand old hotels from the age of railways and robber barons. It had begun life as a personal residence for a rich New York industrialist, a job title that I found covered a lot of territory. After the golden age of rail the building was sold by the great grandchildren to a Boston-based hotel consortium that specialized in boutique hotels, boutique being Palm Beach-ese for hotels that only rich folks can afford.

Ron and his partner, Lady Cassandra, lived in an oceanfront apartment in Palm Beach that was currently undergoing renovation, and because no one worth a bean actually lives through a renovation, they had moved temporarily into a suite at The Mornington. I had no idea why Cassandra was referred to as Lady, but I did know her late husband had done very well for himself, and according to Ron, Cassandra had invested the estate shrewdly. It was fair to say that she wasn't hurting for a dollar. But for all the trappings she was a down-to-earth woman who made Ron smile, and that was good enough for me.

I pulled in behind the Escalade at the base of the stairs that led to the hotel entrance. There was ordinarily a canvas awning to keep the hot Florida sun off the balding heads of the discerning clientele, but the awning had been removed in preparation for the oncoming weather. A big guy jumped out of the Escalade and pounded his way up the stairs. He carried an umbrella that he didn't open.

We got out into the downpour and charged up the stairs. The doorman was nowhere to be seen, and I pulled open the hefty glass door and let Ron through, and then dashed in myself.

It was like stepping through the looking glass. The glass door swung home with a suck and shut out the sound of the rain, leaving only the sound of classical harp music that echoed around the wide open lobby. It was a grand space: high chandeliered ceilings, gilded sconces and plush love seats. There were fresh flowers in crystal vases and the reception desk was dark wood, which reminded me of the New York Public Library.

There were people in the lobby, but not many. Clearly most of the guests had either checked out or never bothered to check in. Sitting in the middle of a tropical storm was very few people's idea of a swell time. I loitered by the concierge desk while Ron took the elevator up to collect Cassandra. The big guy from the Escalade was leaning over the check-in desk like he was in a serious hurry and an immaculately dressed guy behind the desk cradled a phone between his shoulder and chin and offered the big guy the kind of smile that only top-flight hospitality professionals can muster, something that says: I have no greater concern in the world than your welfare—it's just that I don't really give a damn about you.

"I'm afraid Mr. Walter isn't answering, and I don't have a spare porter at the moment," said the desk guy in a smooth English accent.

"Just give me the room number. I'll get their damn bags."

"I'm sorry, sir, you are?"

"I told you. EvacJet. We're here to fly the Walters to Atlanta."

The desk guy glanced toward the floor-to-ceiling windows across the lobby. On another day he would have seen blue sky and jaunty palms and a seawall that led down to the golden beach. Today it was dark and getting darker, and the palms looked like they were trying to touch their toes. It wasn't any kind of weather to take a flight. The commercial airlines had halted flights the previous evening. But it didn't faze the desk guy. He nodded and returned his impassive eyes to the big guy.

"Can one fly in this weather?"

"Not for long, pal. That's why we're in kind of a hurry here."

He nodded again, and then he tried the phone once more. The big guy threw his hands into the air and spun toward me.

"You believe this guy?" he said to me.

I shrugged. "You really fly in this weather?"

"We fly in anything. It's getting off the island that's gonna be the problem."

"EvacJet, hey?"

The guy nodded. "Five-star evacuation from danger. There's even champagne on board."

"A lot of call for that sort of thing?"

"You'd be surprised."

Fact was, I wasn't surprised. There were people in the Palm Beaches who visited food banks as a matter of survival, and I saw more than my share of young mothers swallowing their pride and using food stamps to buy baby food at the local Publix. There were also plenty of folks who owned twenty-million-dollar estates that they only visited for two weeks in the winter. I'm not saying one was related to the other, not necessarily, but there were few things that people did that surprised me anymore.

"Sir?" The desk guy was replacing the phone in its cradle. "Mr. Walter is awaiting you. Suite 202. Ocean side."

The big guy nodded and turned for the stairs by the elevators. I watched him hit the door to the stairs and disappear at a gallop, and then I glanced back at the guy behind the desk. He had swept-back brown hair and he was tall and lean in a way that was purpose-built to wear a suit. And he wore it well. The word that came to mind was dapper.

He gave me his concerned but not really face. "I'm sorry, sir, but the hotel is closed for the duration of the storm."
I grinned. I was impressed that he was prepared to even give consideration to the idea that I wanted to check in, given I was standing in the lobby in a pair of cargo shorts and a shirt covered in blue foliage. I was so wet a puddle had formed around my feet big enough to house a small alligator.
I said, "I'm not looking to stay."
"You shouldn't even be on this island," said the voice behind me.
I didn't turn. I didn't need to. I knew the voice well. And I knew it was going to drive Detective Ronzoni a little nuts that I didn't spin around in shock. I kept my eyes on the English desk guy until the detective came around from behind me.
"Rice-a-roni," I said.
"Ronzoni, smart guy," he said. Like me, he was wet to the core. Only he was wearing a JC Penney suit that hadn't fit well before it got drenched. Unlike the desk guy, Ronzoni had an unusual frame that didn't wear clothes well. He was thin in the arms and legs and chest, but he had developed a bulge of a gut that made it look like he had gobbled a watermelon whole. It was the curse of the cop. They didn't do as much running in real life as they did on television. The ones who kept trim had to work at it like everyone else. And like everyone else, if they didn't work at it, well, watermelons.
"Nice to see you, Detective."
"Why are you here, Jones? We're closing the island down."
"You are? Looks like Mother Nature's closing it down for you."
"Whatever. You need to get gone now."
"I'm halfway out the door, Detective."

He didn't answer. His attention turned to the desk guy, and Ronzoni flipped open his ID. "Ronzoni, Palm Beach Police Department."

"Andrew Neville, The Mornington Hotel," replied the Englishman with just the right level of sarcasm that it flew right over the earnest cop's head.

"We're evacuating the island," said Ronzoni.

"So I understand."

"You have any outstanding guests?"

"All of our guests are outstanding."

Again I watched the comment fly over Ronzoni's head. He was a good cop, not necessarily as honest as the day is long, but a good deal more honest than the gems of society he put away. He worked hard and was dogged. But wordplay was not really his thing. I wondered if it was the Englishman's accent that was confusing him, because everything that came out of the guy's mouth sounded superior as hell.

"How many guests do you have here?" Ronzoni asked as if the previous exchange had never occurred.

Neville clicked at his computer, and spoke as he looked at the screen.

"Ten, as of now. Mr. and Mrs. Walter are about to leave with an evacuation service. So, eight." He glanced over Ronzoni's shoulder at me. "And this gentleman, whose status is unconfirmed."

"I'm here to collect Ron Bennett and the Lady Cassandra."

"Ah, the Bennett party."

I shrugged at that. Ron and Cassandra weren't married, unless things had gone sideways overnight. Perhaps they felt it better to check in to a hotel as a married couple because Palm Beach was such a conservative place. Perhaps it made them giggle like teenagers. Perhaps it was just the Englishman's assumption.

"So that makes six."

"Where are they?" asked Ronzoni.

Neville sighed. "Mostly in the lounge."

"Okay. How many staff?"

"Myself, my assistant manager, one maid, the chef, and I think our groundsman is on his way in."

"On his way in? From where?"

Neville might have shrugged, or might have been my imagination. He didn't strike me as a shrugger. "I'd have to check the employee files to know where he lives, Detective."

"But we can assume he doesn't live on the island," said Ronzoni.

"Yes, I think we could safely assume that."

It was a pretty good assumption, unless he was the world's most highly paid groundsman. Palm Beach was an island separated from the mainland by the Intracoastal Waterway, and had become the winter retreat of choice for wealthy families from New York and Boston when Henry Flagler put the train line down from St. Augustine to Miami. But because it was an island the train had to stop on the mainland before the well-heeled made their way across to their estates. As happened all over the country a town sprung up around the train station, and became the imaginatively named West Palm Beach. The rich lived on the island; the help lived in West Palm. West Palm grew to dwarf its salubrious sibling, but some things never change. The help still came from the mainland—only now they came via bridges. Bridges that were rapidly disappearing under what Mick had called a King Tide.

Ronzoni nodded to himself. "If he's not here yet, he's not getting here. Do your staff have Palm Beach IDs?"

"Yes, of course."

"All right. Your groundsman will be able to help with the cleanup. Any staff who want out need to be here in the lobby in two minutes. I will lead them off the island. You say the only guests left are in the bar?"

"The lounge."

Ronzoni turned to me. "Be ready to follow me out of here in two."

"Yes, chief."

He nodded like he enjoyed being called chief and paced off toward the bar. I noticed a couple standing just outside the entrance to the bar. They were both young and blond, and the woman was slightly taller, but not particularly tall. Although I couldn't hear them, my mother would have said that they were having words. He wore the look of a scolded schoolboy and she was laying down some version of the law. When Ronzoni reached them he spoke, and the blond guy nodded and strode away, while the woman led Ronzoni into the lounge.

I heard the elevator ding and the doors opened to reveal Ron and Cassandra. They had less luggage than I would have thought. One small roller case each. Whenever I think of the kinds of folks who stay at The Mornington I always picture large trunks covered in stickers from exotic locales, but my source material might have been out of date.

Cassandra smiled in a fashion that looked designed to minimize the wrinkles around her eyes.

"Thank you for coming for us, Miami."

"Not a problem."

"I don't think the Camry was built for this kind of weather."

I nodded. Ron still drove the same beat-up Camry he had before he met Cassandra, and she didn't seem bothered by it at all. I actually thought she saw it as part of Ron's charm. But she was right—the Camry wasn't built for a tropical storm, let alone a hurricane. Ron had changed clothes, into chinos and a fresh polo. I didn't see the point. We were going to get drenched getting to the Caddy.

"You want to change?" he asked me.

I shook my head. "Slight oversight. I forgot my duffel at home. I'll get a new shirt when I get to Tallahassee."

The elevator let out another ding and the doors opened again. The big guy from EvacJet stepped out, carrying a proper Palm Beach amount of luggage. He dragged three large suitcases, two of which had Louis Vuitton duffels on top of them. Another duffel was strapped across his chest. An older couple dressed for a jungle safari followed behind. She carried a fan like those Japanese geisha used, and he wore a pith helmet. I couldn't recall actually ever seeing one in real life before, except with a little fan attached to it. This one looked authentic, but I couldn't say for sure what made a pith helmet authentic. Certainly not a trip to Palm Beach.

The big guy spoke to his clients and then launched out the door with the luggage. As we watched him stride down the stairs Ronzoni returned from the bar.

"Foreigners," he said, to no one in particular, and then he turned to Neville the desk guy. "They won't go. Say they're here for their bachelor party and it's this weekend or never. I can't make them leave until the hurricane hits category two." He shrugged as if to say they were now Neville's problem.

"Don't worry, Detective. We have everything in place. The Mornington has seen hurricanes bigger than this one and we are still here."

That sounded way too much like tempting fate to me, but I decided I'd keep that thought to myself.

"And your maid?" asked Ronzoni.

"Behind you."

We all snapped around to see a petite girl standing with her hands clasped in front of her. She was a Latina, lightly boned and dark haired. She was one of those people who could run without making any noise and move around a room as if invisible.

"You have a vehicle?" Ronzoni asked.

She nodded, although her head was already bowed to begin with.

"Yes."

Ronzoni stepped to me and was about to speak when the big guy from EvacJet pushed in through the door like he was a running back in football.

"You are?" Ronzoni asked.

"EvacJet," the guy said.

Ronzoni was processing what that meant when the elevator dinged one more time and the blond guy from the lounge stepped out, bag in hand.

"What was your name, sir?" asked Ronzoni.

"Sam, Sam Venturi."

"All right, Mr. Venturi. You're riding with me," replied Ronzoni. "Everyone else who wants off the island, we're heading to the mainland now. Follow me."

CHAPTER THREE

We followed. The EvacJet guy swept up the old lady he was chauffeuring like she was a bouquet of roses. He carried her in his arms while holding the umbrella above her. It really was a champagne service. He deposited her in the rear of his Escalade and then dashed up for Mr. Walter. The old guy was too proud to be carried but not too proud to stay under the umbrella. We watched them come down from inside my Cadillac, and then Ronzoni pulled around to lead our little convoy onto the mainland. The Escalade followed him out, and I waited until the maid joined the line in an old Civic and then took up the rear.
Ronzoni led us south along A1A. We knew Flagler Memorial Bridge was out as they constructed a new bridge alongside, and the tide surge had cut access to Royal Park Bridge, so we kept going to the southernmost of the retreats from the island into West Palm. Southern Boulevard Bridge crossed nice and high above the raging Intracoastal waters. The problem was that before it did that, it was a causeway running across Bingham Island, a low, flat sliver of land that sat in the middle of the Intracoastal Waterway. The island was a popular launching spot

for kayakers, with a sandy beach north of the road and Audubon bird sanctuaries on the islands to the south. But not this day. The birds were gone. Hell, the island was gone. As we hit the causeway the water looked like category six rapids, whirling and churning and crashing against the seawall and cascading over us like we were surfers inside a wave. The water had breached the seawall at the Mar-a-Lago club just to the north and the usually lush lawn had been reclaimed by the sea. We drove on slowly, but a sinking feeling of futility wrapped itself around me. My wipers thrashed across the windshield but barely made an impression in the sheet of water. I focused on the brake lights of the maid's car ahead. As we reached Bingham Island our convoy stopped. The water beat against the window like we were in a car wash. I knew why we had stopped. The road was cut, the water had taken Bingham Island as its own, and the bridge ahead was literally a bridge too far. That I knew. What we would do next was the question. I was pushing the selector into reverse when my phone rang. The Cadillac had a groovy hands-free system, but I couldn't make heads or tails of it so I answered the old-fashioned way. It was Ronzoni.

"No good," he said. "Lead us out."

"Gotcha," I said, wondering where he had gotten my phone number, or more importantly, why he had it stored in his phone. I pushed into reverse with the phone still to my ear and heard Ronzoni.

"Don't do it."

"What?" I said. "You said to—"

"Not you, Jones. This moron."

I leaned forward to look through the windshield as if that was going to make the view clearer and peered through the torrent.

I saw the taillights of the Escalade move left out of the convoy and pull forward.
I said, "Is he . . ."
"Don't be crazy," I head Ronzoni yell. Not at me, at the Escalade. But it was moot. There was no conversing through the sound of crashing waves. The taillights moved forward until I couldn't make out their fuzzy outline anymore.
"What's he doing?" I yelled into the phone.
"He's going for it. The idiot is going for it."
I glanced back at Ron and Cassandra, who were both leaning forward to hear my conversation with Ronzoni like they were gathered around the radio, listening to an account of the bombing of Pearl Harbor. We waited in silence for an update from Ronzoni. I was thankful he didn't work in broadcasting because he was mute. I pictured his chin dropped down into his chest with his mouth gaped open.
"Ronzoni," I yelled.
"He's in it. Damn, it's deep. Must be tire-high. No, scratch that. Maybe window-high. Jeez, I hope that thing converts into a submarine."
Those SUVs had all the latest gizmos, but I didn't think nautical controls were part of the package. We waited again, the waves crashing over us. I knew we needed to go, to turn around and get off the causeway before it disappeared too, but I was paralyzed. It was like listening to someone describe a train wreck while another train bore down on us.
"Ronzoni," I yelled again.
Nothing.
"Ronzoni."
I waited for a response and heard none, so I looked at my phone to make sure the connection hadn't been cut.
"Ronzoni, are you there?"

"He's gone."
"What do you mean, gone?"
"I can't see him. Hell, I can't see anything. But his lights are gone."
I looked at Ron and Cassandra. They looked funereal. I wondered if they knew the old folks, the Walters. Folks in Palm Beach tended to know each other like that. They frequented the same ballrooms.
"Let's get out of here," I said to Ron and Cassandra and the phone.
I backed up and swung around. I was looking toward West Palm, but it wasn't there. Just a gray wall of water. I pointed the Cadillac back toward the island and waited to see the maid do the same turn. But she didn't. She stayed put. Then I heard Ronzoni through the phone.
"I don't believe it," he said.
"What?"
"I don't believe it."
"Believe what, Ronzoni?"
"He made it. He made it."
"How do you know?"
"I see taillights. On the bridge ahead. I see them going up."
"You're kidding."
"Nope. He's off the island."
"Can we do it?" I asked.
"No chance. That water was up near his window, and he's driving an Escalade. That's a hell of a big truck. We've got a Crown Vic, a Civic, and whatever that thing is you're driving."
"It's a Cadillac."
"No way."
"Yep."

"If you say so. Still not getting through that water. We need to get off this causeway a-sap."

"Roger that."

"I'll turn round and tell the girly."

I assumed the girly was the maid, and I was glad Danielle wasn't around to hear him use that descriptor. I watched in my rearview and saw Ronzoni's brake lights flash off, and then his headlights appeared as he swung in behind me. Then I heard a honk.

"Not yet," I said to myself. "Let the girl turn around."

Then he honked again. And again. Then rapid fire. Then he must have remembered he was in a police vehicle because a siren bleep cut through the sound of wind and water.

"What the hell do you want?" I spat into the phone.

He didn't reply, but he didn't need to. I saw the answer in my rearview. The maid had come to a decision. If the Escalade could get to the bridge, so could she. It was a poor decision but I could see her point. The water was eating up all of the land around us, and our plan B was to retreat back to a thin finger of an island. But plan A was worse. The Escalade got lucky.

The water was getting higher and the flow faster. I saw the brake lights in my rearview dull as the maid slipped her foot off the brake, and she slid forward into the raging water.

"No, no, no," I said as I slipped out of my seat belt and cracked open the door. The door slammed back on me and the wind drove it closed, but I pushed myself out and was wet again before my feet hit the ground. My shoes were underwater and my eyes were on the taillights of the Civic. It wasn't a car designed for crossing large puddles, let alone hurricane storm surge. The maid eased forward and I ran.

The rain hit my skin like bullets and the breaking waves knocked me down, and then knocked me down again. My knees were grazed against the blacktop but I pushed past Ronzoni's car. I didn't stop to look at him. I knew his mouth would be open like a cave. That was his reaction to a lot of things I did. But I dashed past him. The water was pulsing at my legs as I reached the trunk of the Civic. I banged as hard as I could on the trunk. I don't know if I made the woman at the wheel reconsider her options, but the effort stole my stable footing, and a good burst of water crashed into me and knocked me off my feet again.

Only this time I didn't hit pavement. I was swept across the road, the surge of water stronger than any car. I slid right across the road and for the briefest moment wondered how things were looking in Tallahassee, and whether Danielle was even getting wet, and if she was thinking of me at that exact moment. The water washed across me and kept on going, and my feet hit a small berm of grass on the roadside. I wedged my heels in deep and ducked low as the next wave crashed across me. I dug in hard. After the berm, there was nothing. Just water, and not the Florida postcard kind. It was a washing machine torrent thrashing its way south to Lake Worth.

I felt the energy of the second wave moving onward, so before the next set could muscle its way into me I pushed up and ran. The water was knee-high and moving in the opposite direction and I was going nowhere, so I broke right and cut behind Ronzoni's car. I used the police vehicle as a break and was able to move forward until I could grab the rear door handle. I yanked it hard and flung it open as another wave crashed across the top of the car, and I dove into the back of Ronzoni's car.

"Are you crazy, Jones?"

I sucked in some deep ones as I lay across the bench seat and considered his question. I didn't think I was crazy. But I also knew I sure as hell wasn't normal. Both Ronzoni and the blond guy, Venturi, were looking at me from the front. The door to Ronzoni's car was still open, but it was on the leeward side of the surge, so I spun around and leaned out of the car.

"Where are you going?" yelled Ronzoni.

I didn't reply. I wasn't going anywhere. I was watching. I saw the taillights moving away, and I damned my boneheaded actions. She was going to make it. I nearly didn't, but the Civic was. It moved slow and steadily away, like a ship on the open water.

But it wasn't a ship. It was a car. And when I saw the taillights get closer together, I knew. The Civic rotated in its place as the water swept it up, and it spun the Civic around and across, and the taillights disappeared and I lost all vision of it in the gray water, and then the headlights shot at me like lighthouses on the New England shore. I watched the car turn slowly around, all traction lost, as the surge raged forward and swept it off the road.

CHAPTER FOUR

Two plants are ubiquitous in Florida. First are palm trees. Everyone loves them. The tourist boards, the actual tourists, even the locals. When Floridians leave the state for a time and then return, the first thing that makes them feel at home is seeing a palm tree. And not those uptight transplants they claim in California. Florida palms come in all shapes and sizes but they are universally languid and relaxed. The second plant that is more Florida than Florida is mangroves. These are not so popular. They weave a thick maze of branches that restrict views and make otherwise priceless waterfront property worth less than a bag of beans. But when the fit hits the shan, palms are like supermodels—great to look at but serving no other purpose. Mangroves are the real deal. They practically hold the state together. Most of South Florida is just a big swamp, and without the mangroves it would probably wash away and turn the Gulf of Mexico into a giant mudflat.

But this day the palms came to play. The maid's car drifted sideways off the road and I waited to lose the headlights from sight. They moved off the edge of where the blacktop would be, and then defiantly stood their ground. I wasn't sure how, but they slipped off the road and no farther. The water hit the driver's side of the Civic hard, but the little car held fast. I grabbed hold of the door on Ronzoni's car and stood up into the wind to get a better view. What I got was a saltwater cocktail in the ear. But I shook my head like a Labrador and focused on the headlights.

The Civic was wedged against two large palm trees, stopping it from dropping off the causeway and into the Intracoastal. The torrent of water was holding it against the sinewy trunks, but it wasn't going to stay there. Water has a random way about it. Call it chaos theory, call it dumb luck. But the water was already working out how to flow in such a way as to edge the car around the palms and into the tide.

I ducked back into Ronzoni's car.

"You got a rope?"

"A what?"

"A rope."

"You're crazy."

"Do you or not?"

"No."

I stuck my head back out into the weather and looked at the Civic. It seemed to have moved away from me as the palm trees lost their grip on it, but that might just have been my imagination. I ducked back in.

"You still got my phone on?"

"No."

"Call it."

Ronzoni hit the screen and we heard it connect and ring and ring. And then it answered.

"Ron," said Ron.

I said, "Tell him to back up level with us. I've got a rope in the back."

"You tell him," said Ronzoni, "you're on speaker."

"I got you, Miami," said Ron.

The call went silent but the brake lights on my Cadillac glowed as Ron took the wheel and then dulled again as he pushed backward through the water and came up alongside. I waited until he stopped beside us and I slid across the seat and out the other door of Ronzoni's car. The water was getting deeper and I wasn't sure if any of us were getting off the causeway. But I brushed the thought away and waded around to the back of my SUV. I flung the hatch up and stared at the luggage.

"Cassandra, do you think you can drive Ronzoni's police car?"

"Yes, why?"

"You need to get off this causeway now."

"I'm not leaving Ron."

"Cassandra, now!"

I think she responded to the tone of my voice rather than the words. Ron turned and nodded to her.

"Keys?" she asked.

"They're in the ignition," said Ronzoni, who had appeared behind me. He looked at me. "Let's do this," he said.

I grabbed the two suitcases and flung them into the back seat, and then I lifted the cargo floor and reached into the little cubby underneath and pulled out my rope. I tossed the coil to Ronzoni and wrapped the loose end around my waist.

"Do not let go," I told him.

He nodded and I waded past him and into the water. The maid's Civic was about two car lengths back and a few feet off the road. I stayed on the blacktop as long as I could, my hands splayed wide as if that helped with balance. I was in a crouch, trying to get my center of gravity low, but the water was stronger than me. For every step forward I took three sideways. The tide of water was slapping at the headlights of the Civic and steaming up over the hood. It was colder than Florida

water usually was, and I wondered if it had been churned up
from deep down, or if it was just that I had been wet for a
couple hours and my body temperature was dropping. People
don't think about it, but you don't have to have dropped off
the Titanic to get hypothermia. The human body liked to hang
in at around ninety-seven degrees, but even the warmest
tropical water was closer to eighty. Eventually Newton's laws
of thermodynamics worked their black magic.

Because I was low in the water it was crashing across my back
by the time I reached the grill of the Civic. For the first time
since we left the hotel I could see the maid. She was gripping
the steering wheel like folks grab the hold bar on a roller
coaster, and she had the same look of fear on her face.

The water must have risen since I had been knocked down
before because it started crashing across my back. That meant
it hit the windshield of the Civic, and the car groaned against
the palm trees as it slipped sideways. I inched my fingers under
the lip of the hood and was dragged a few inches along as the
car edged toward the Intracoastal. I felt the front of the vehicle
edge ever so slightly out toward the center of the road, and I
knew I was out of time. A few more crashes like that and the
Civic was going to spin around the palms and go trunk first
out into the water.

I gripped the fitting around the headlight with one hand and
waved to the maid to slide across to the passenger side of the
car. It was the leeward side, and as the car slid around it was
the closest side to me. She shook her head at first, but I waved
again like a madman, and she got the message. I saw her undo
her belt and slide across as I was hit by another wave. The
front of the car edged away from the first of the palms. The
second palm was acting as the fulcrum point, and the Civic was

working its way around, ready to the leave the causeway behind.

My fingers were cramping but I held fast onto the headlight and slid my body along the fender so I was closer to the door. I motion to the maid to wind her window down. At first she gave me a look that said are you crazy? It's raining out there. But the second go-round she relented.

I screamed, "You have to come through the window." I was fairly certain she wasn't going to be able to open the door against the weight of the water outside.

She shook her head. She sure was an obstinate one. I muttered a few unsavory words to myself and prepared to yell to her again. Then the car was ripped from my hand. A wave beat down hard and the Civic spun and I lost my grip on the headlight housing and the hood slipped away from me. I felt myself pushed back by the wave and for a moment all I could see was water. It was like falling off a surfboard. Not that I surf. Sharks don't come to Longboard Kelly's, so I don't bother them in their drinking hole of choice.

I flailed my hands about as the wave pushed on past me. I saw something shapeless but solid and I thrust my hand out and grabbed hold. I shook my head and got some vision in return, and I saw that I had hold of the outside rear vision mirror of the Civic. The maid was right there in front of me, she in the car, me hanging onto the outside for dear life. She wasn't screaming or flipping out. Quite the opposite. She looked scared, but calm. Like she had made her peace and was ready to meet her maker. Either that or she was a major introvert.

"You need to come out through the window," I said.

Again she shook her head.

"We don't have time," I said. "I've got you."

She leaned on the window and the water hit her face. "I don't swim."

"I swim great," I said. It was true enough. I was as good as the next guy in the water. I took regular swims out from City Beach on Singer Island and Danielle made sure I stayed in decent shape. But it was moot. Michael Phelps wasn't beating this water. He was getting washed away like everyone else. But she seemed reassured. She leaned toward me and I put my free hand in through the window and onto her arm.

"It's okay," I said.

And then it got not okay. Real fast. The wave hit the grill and spun the car past the second palm tree and suddenly we were side-on to the rush of water, headlights pointed back to West Palm and away from Ronzoni and my SUV. The water had the whole side of the car to push against so it did, and it did it hard. The car seemed to lift away from the ground and launch off the road and I saw the second palm tree come up at the rear of the car, its fronds bowed low as if bidding us farewell, and the Civic dropped off into the Intracoastal.

I'd had enough. Enough rain and enough wind and enough obstinance. I kicked hard and launched myself into the interior of the car. I got in to about my waist and I wrapped the maid up in a bear hug. She put her hands around my neck probably because there was nowhere else to put them. And we waited. There were no more waves. They were breaking on the other side of the causeway, and we were now in the flow of the Intracoastal. But my rope was only a hundred feet long. I just hoped that Ronzoni didn't let it slip through his fingers when it went taut. And then it did. It snapped tight and tugged at my guts like a punch. The wind got knocked out of me but I didn't let go of the maid. I was pulled out the window like a magic trick, and the maid came out after me. She didn't see her car

KING TIDE 31

float away on the surge. I only saw it for a couple seconds, and then it was gone.

The water ripped past us and I really didn't think Ronzoni was going to be able to pull two people against it. I was trying to think of a solution to that when I noticed that the causeway was getting closer to us, not farther away. Somehow Ronzoni was pulling us in. The man must have had more strength than I gave him credit for, which meant he worked out more than I gave him or his garlic bulb-shaped body credit for. We moved against the surge not in tugs but in a steady but slow pace. The rope felt like a guillotine to my guts but the momentum was reassuring. Then I saw the palm tree.

The second of the two palm trees on the causeway had acted like a fulcrum on the car. Now the rope was taught against it as it cut ninety degrees from the road where Ronzoni was into the water where we were. And I was being dragged back first into it. That was going to hurt, if it didn't slice me in half. So I dropped my hands down to the maid's waist like I was a teenager at a school dance, and grabbed tight. Then I leaned sideways, hard against the current and tried to kick my feet up toward the surface.

It was tough work. The water fought me all the way, but I got my shoes about a foot from the surface and pointed them at the palm tree. We edged steadily toward it, and then my foot hit the trunk of the palm. It wasn't a big target, and for a second I thought I was going to end up with one leg either side, which was the worst possible outcome. But my second foot hit home and I pushed out from my crouch and the rope came away from the trunk and I walked us sideways around the trunk.

I kicked away and then we moved toward the road, and I felt the ground beneath us. I let Ronzoni drag us across the road, which was now covered in sand and grit and pebbles. The maid rolled on top of me so my back took the brunt of it, but I didn't mind. I wasn't sure I had the energy to walk anyway. When the water got to about calf-deep we stopped moving. Maybe Ronzoni stopped pulling. Water still rushed across us in waves which made it tough to see and harder to breathe. Then Ronzoni appeared over me, like a badly dressed angel. He grabbed the maid and picked her up and carried her away. I rolled over onto my knees and took a couple more waves across the back, and then I pressed myself up and stood. Another wave hit me and I stumbled and fell, but the rope was still taut and it stopped me from going anywhere. Then Ronzoni appeared above me again, and he helped me up. I didn't care how much he had been working out, he wasn't carrying me to safety, so I threw my arm across his shoulder and he walked me out of the water.

When we were above the torrent I realized that Ronzoni wasn't as strong as I thought. But he was clever. He hadn't been pulling the rope; he had tied it to the tow bar on the Cadillac. Ron had been at the wheel, and now helped the maid into the back. Ronzoni and I wandered around the other side and I got in the back with the maid and Ronzoni in the front. Ron took the wheel again and he pointed at Cassandra in the other vehicle with two fingers like a platoon leader, that way, and I saw Ronzoni's car take the lead as we headed back from where we had come, toward The Mornington.

CHAPTER FIVE

We didn't worry about running up the stairs to the hotel the second time. We were all so wet it didn't matter, and I for one didn't have the energy. Ron pushed open the door to the lobby and we trudged inside like zombies. The English guy wasn't behind the desk. He had been replaced by a young woman who was much more pleasant to the eye, or at least to my eye. She was trim and blond and buttoned up in her dark suit. But unlike the Englishman she did come out from behind the desk when we entered. I wasn't sure if she was worried about us getting water all over the marble foyer, but I really didn't care.
"What happened? Are you all okay?" she asked.
"The bridges are flooded," said Ronzoni. "Your maid nearly drowned."
"Oh, my goodness, Rosaria," she said. "Are you all right?"
Rosaria was not all right. She didn't have anything she wouldn't recover from, but she was in shock. She had struck me as a very quiet person to begin with, but nearly drowning in a storm surge will quieten down even the chattiest Kathy. I was holding her up for fear her legs would give way.
"She needs a warm shower," said Cassandra.

The desk girl nodded. "I'll get her a room. And what about you, ma'am?"

"It looks like we might be here for the duration."

"I can get you back in your room, but it hasn't been cleaned, I'm afraid."

Cassandra waved her hand. "Any mess is our mess." She turned to Rosaria and put her arm around the silent woman. "Let's get you warm." She helped the maid toward the elevator. I heard the clinking of glasses coming from the bar and wondered if a nip of scotch might warm me up, but I didn't get the chance to follow through on the idea as the English desk guy, Neville, came out of the bar and saw us. He didn't seem surprised to see us back, but his face didn't give much away.

"I didn't expect to see you gentlemen again."

"Bridges are out," said Ronzoni. "We're stuck here."

"I see. Well, we'd best get you settled then. Mr. Bennett, your room is still available."

"Emery's taking care of it now," said Ron.

"And Mr. Venturi?"

The blond guy stood behind us, ashen-faced. He hadn't helped much on the causeway, but he was plenty wet. He didn't speak and I wondered if he too was in shock.

"Mr. Venturi?" Neville turned to the desk girl. "Miss Taylor, could you assist Mr. Venturi with a new room key?"

Venturi absently put his hand in his pocket and pulled out a key card which he held up.

"Mr. Venturi has his card. Sir, may I suggest a warm shower and a lie down. And Mr. . .?" he asked, looking at me.

"Jones," I said.

"Mr. Jones, given the circumstances I would be more than happy to extend our most generous room rate to you."

"Too kind," I said. "But I'll just hang in the bar."

"As you wish. And Detective, will you be staying or returning to the station house?"

I could see the cogs turning in Ronzoni's head. I knew where I'd prefer to bunk down during a hurricane. Ronzoni was apparently on my wavelength.

"Let's make sure you're all set here, and then I'll evaluate. Are you prepared?"

For the first time a wrinkle appeared in the fabric of the Englishman's face. "Our groundsman hasn't made it in."

"So?"

"So not all of the storm shutters are in place."

"Leaving that a bit late, aren't you?"

"The remaining guests often like to watch the weather, so we don't like to put them all in until the weather service confirms the severity of the storm."

"Well, it's going to be bad enough. What needs doing?"

"We need to put up shutters in the lounge and the north wing, and then in the gym in the south wing."

Ronzoni looked at me. "I'll take north, you take south?"

"You'll take the bar, you mean," I said.

"I need some water."

"Of course you do." It wasn't a line. Ronzoni had some kind of a thing that meant he didn't sweat, and he couldn't regulate his body temperature. He drank a lot of water. I couldn't see how he could overheat standing in a wringing-wet JC Penney suit, but I wasn't his primary care physician.

I pointed down the lobby to the south end of the hotel. "This way?"

Neville nodded and pulled a key card out of his jacket pocket. "You'll need this."

"I'll give you a hand," Ron said.

"And Detective, perhaps I can assist you," said Neville.

We wandered off in our opposite directions. Ron and I trailed wet footprints across the lobby and past the check-in desk. The marble underfoot was slippery and I wondered who would dry it. Not the maid, that was for damned sure. Past the desk we entered a corridor that was carpeted in that design style that only hotels use, the stuff that's way too busy but hides a multitude of sins. There were a couple of unmarked doors, and then another door on our right marked as the fire stairs. Beyond that on the left was a frosted glass door that didn't say it was the gym but didn't need to.

Gyms have a scent, even the ones in fancy hotels. Throughout college and my modest professional sports career I had spent more than my share of time in gyms. Some smelled like sweat and hard work and determination, and some smelled like cleaning solution. This one was the latter. I slipped the key card through the slot and pushed the glass door open. The gym wasn't large but hotel gyms rarely are. The space was lit with unappealing fluorescent tubes and had coarse gray carpet. There was a rack of fresh towels to the side of the door, and a water cooler. The equipment looked in good condition. Knowing what I did about the average guest for The Mornington I suspected it didn't suffer from overuse. There was a treadmill and a stair climber and a stationary bicycle, all vacant. Then there was an elliptical machine. There was a guy loping around on the elliptical. He was tall and lean, but not skinny. Muscular but not heavily built. His skin was the color of polished mahogany. His movements were both fluid and economical, and although his back was to me his bald head wasn't offering a drop of sweat.

On the other side of the aerobic equipment was a weight bench with an empty barbell in a contraption that looked like a steel four-poster bed. It was a large cubic frame with holes throughout it. All white-coated steel with two black bars running through either side parallel to the bench. I recalled it was called a power rack. It seemed a touch of overkill for The Mornington. A collection of weights lay on the floor nearby. Along the wall from the bench was a collection of dumbbells of various weights, backed by a mirror. Gym junkies liked to watch their muscles flex when they lifted. I never really saw the point. But I looked in the mirror as we crossed the floor. I didn't look good. My damp shirt clung to me, and my sandy blond hair sat matted across my furrowed brow.

In the corner of the room sat a machine that was designed to allow the user to lift weights attached by pulleys. Chest press, flys, lat pulls. All the standards. There was a guy working his quads on it. He didn't look right on the machine. It was like it was a couple sizes too small for him. He was stacked. He wore tight shorts and a tank top that wouldn't have passed as a napkin in a lobster restaurant in Maine. His arms had muscles on muscles. He clearly put in serious gym time. And then some more. He eyed me as I passed and I failed to see any trace of humanity in his eyes. His pupils were small and dark. I knew the look. I knew the type. I had played baseball for a lot of years, and I'd seen some guys do things to make it big that they should have left well alone. I'd done one or two of those things myself, for a time. I knew a steroid stare when I saw it.

I walked past the beefcake to the wall near the dumbbells. Neville the Englishman had said they liked to leave the hurricane shutters off as long as possible, and I could see why. Floor-to-ceiling windows ran from the wall right around in front of the treadmill, the bicycle and the elliptical. The view was a killer. Straight out the glass door from where I stood I saw a paved deck and a moderately sized resort pool. It would normally be bathed in sunshine and surrounded by lounge chairs. The loungers were packed away so the pool looked lonely and a forbidding gray rather than sparkling azure. The view out to the east looked onto the seawall and beach below. The guy on the elliptical was looking at the outer rim of a hurricane and didn't seemed disturbed by the fact that the only thing between him and the debris being flung about at ninety miles an hour was dual panes of glass.

I checked that the glass door out to the pool was open and then Ron took one end of a long storm panel and I took the other. The wind was driving the rain sideways across the paved pool deck. The air felt heavy, like swimming near the bottom of a pool. We stayed close to the glass and kept the metal panel between the window and us. Large metal panels and high winds really don't mix and I cursed the hotel's groundsman, whoever he was, for not doing his job earlier.

The windows were floor to ceiling around the gym, and held a track at the bottom and an h-header at the top to slide the panel into. It took some doing. The panel was keen to take flight, and we had to fight to keep it from doing so. Too late we realized that we needed a ladder to fix in the bolts at the top of the panel, so Ron ended up on my shoulders. We looked like a circus act at an old folks' home. I was wobbling around as if on a unicycle, the winds buffeting me into the corrugated metal hurricane panel time and again as Ron fixed the panel in place. I thanked genetics that Ron was a naturally thin guy, because with his diet and our tendency to spend a little too much time leaning on the bar at Longboard Kelly's he really shouldn't have been.

We got the first panel fixed in place and went back inside for the second. I was technically wetter than I had been five minutes earlier, but I wasn't sure how anyone could tell. Ron wiped his brow and picked up his end of the next panel and I held the door open with my foot.

"Hey, man, you're letting the rain in," said the muscle-bound guy on the weight machine. He had some kind of accent. European of some sort, but it was hard to discern against the howling of the wind and the rain beating on the windows.

I left the big jerk to his pec routine and stepped back out into the weather. It was still afternoon but the clouds were giving us a glimpse of what a nuclear winter must look like. We edged back around and repeated our circus act and got the panel in place. We got back inside and took a drink from the cooler in the water. It felt incongruous that I could be thirsty while being so wet. I was slamming down a second small cup when the big guy on the weight machine spoke.

"You gonna clean that up?" he said.

I got a bit more of the accent and landed in France. I'm not one to throw a blanket of judgment over an entire nation, but arrogance dripped from this guy's speech, and it just felt so French. I glanced down and noticed that I was dripping all over a workout bench.

"Tell you what sport, if this building is still here tomorrow, I'll be in here with a towel."

He snorted. The clichés kept coming.

"You scared of a little wind?" He said little so it rhymed with beetle, and it made me smile.

"I'm not scared of a little wind. I'm scared of a lot of wind. And if you're not, you either don't know what a hurricane can do, or you're a fool."

"What do you call me?" he said, jutting out his chin.

Ron slapped my shoulder and smiled and wandered past the French guy to grab another hurricane panel. Ron's a smart guy, so I followed his lead. The Frenchman watched us cross before him without moving his head. We picked up the next panel and headed back into the weather. We placed three more panels, and the view was gone. The gym suddenly looked like Alcatraz. The only part left open was the door we were going through. I grabbed a couple of rolled-up towels and wandered out of the gym and into the corridor, and then down to the end of the building, where there was an emergency exit. It was solid and heavy and a match for any hurricane. Except pushing it open was a real chore against the wind. I had to dig my heels into the carpet and really put my shoulder into it, and it occurred to me that the big Frenchman in the gym would have been useful for the task.

I stuck the towels in the jamb as the door slammed home and walked around to the gym door as if it were a sunny day. A person can only get so wet, and I was there. I stepped back into the gym and heard the Frenchman grunting as he did seated leg extensions. He glanced up and scowled at me for letting the rain in again.

"You know doing extensions like that is bad for your knees," I said. I wasn't trying to get him wound up. I had hated the exercise when I played ball, and a trainer at Oakland had told me about it. He said it was an unnatural position for the knee. He said regular squats with free weights on a barbell were better. Which made me wonder why such a built guy was using the machines at all. The bodybuilder types always went for the free weights over machines.

"What the hell do you know?" he said.

I shrugged. "I know real men don't bother with the play equipment. They use free weights."

Now I was trying to wind him up. Perhaps I shouldn't have because he unhooked his legs from the contraption he was in

and he stood. He wasn't tall but he was big in every other way, and he looked quick to temper like a lot of guys on steroids. "I don't use free weights because I lift heavy. Heavier than you can dream."
I wasn't sure how heavy I could dream, but I was sure that thought was going to stick around in my head for a while. Do dreams have mass?
"When you lift what I do," he continued, "you always use a spotter. You want to spot me, little man?"
"You want to help us finish out here?" I asked, nodding at the last hurricane panel.
"Do I look like I work in a hotel?"
"Do I?"
I didn't wait for his answer. Neither of us looked like we worked in a hotel. To be fair, neither of us really looked like we worked, period. He looked like he lived in a gym, and I looked like a drowned beach bum. I glanced at the guy in the elliptical as I turned. He was done, and was rolling up his earphones.
"How 'bout you, wanna do your good deed for the day?"
The guy frowned and nodded. He was a good-looking guy, strong in an athletic way. His reaction made me question if he spoke English, but then he stepped down off the elliptical and ran his towel across his bald head.
"I need a soak in the hot tub," he said in a mid-Atlantic accent.
I said nothing.
The big Frenchman said, "You do that," and gave the guy a glare, clearly his preferred facial expression.
The black guy strode out of the gym.
Ron shrugged as if to say kids, and we picked up the last panel and carried it outside. We fitted it in place, covering over the door and the last access to the gym. By the time we wandered back toward the emergency exit the sky was a shade darker and

the rain was coming in a shade harder. I pulled the door open and Ron picked up the towels that dropped and we headed back toward the lobby, leaving behind the grunting coming from the gym.

CHAPTER SIX

We met Ronzoni in the lobby. He was every bit as wet as we were. The manager, Neville, was also drenched to the bone, but somehow his suit still looked good. The benefits of bespoke tailoring. The only thing amiss was a single wet hair that had fallen across his forehead. It made him look more human.
"All locked up tight?" asked Ronzoni.
"Tighter than a drum," I said. "Now what?"
"I just called the desk sergeant. The National Weather Service has upgraded Beth to a category two hurricane. The island's officially closed. So we're all here for the duration."
The young woman who had checked Ron back into his room appeared at Neville's hip. Neville must have sensed her more than seen her because his eyes darted in her direction despite her standing slightly behind. Perhaps the guy had a great nose for perfume.
Ronzoni continued. "The weather service is saying the hurricane is likely to make landfall somewhere near Jacksonville. That means maximum winds here in the early hours of tomorrow morning."
"It's gonna hit south of Jacksonville," I said, recalling Mick's prognostication. "More likely on the Treasure Coast."
"You know better than the weather service, do you, Jones?"

"I have good sources. But it just means it will be a little earlier and a little harder."

"Well, either way I think it would be best to move the guests away from the ocean side of the hotel." Ronzoni looked at Neville. "Can we get everyone into rooms on the other side?"

Neville gave his wrinkle-less frown like he was considering the overtime implications of cleaning two sets of used rooms.

"Of course, Detective," he finally said. "Miss Taylor, please assign rooms for our guests on the leeward side of the building and create key cards as necessary."

"Yes, Mr. Neville."

"I will inform the guests in the lounge of the arrangements," Neville said, turning on his heel and striding away.

"I'll go tell Cassandra we're out again," said Ron. "Catch you in the bar shortly, I'm sure."

I was left standing in a pool of water with Ronzoni and the girl from the desk. She smiled, which was the brightest thing I'd seen that day. She looked young and alive and a little out of place in what was a pretty old-school hotel. Her immaculate suit barely contained the energy pulsing from her.

"So, Detective and Mr. Jones."

I had no idea how she had acquired my name but I figured that's what five-star hotel service was like.

"My name is Emery Taylor, and I'm the assistant general manager here at The Mornington. If you would like to follow me I'll get you both rooms so you can dry off and change." She smiled again.

"Your boss there offered me a deal on a room already, but I'm okay staying down here," I said.

She gave a stifled laugh. "Yes, I'm sure Mr. Neville offered you the best rate available. He's a bit of a stickler for that sort of

thing. But I think in the circumstances we can comp the rooms."
"Will that get you in trouble?"
She put her hand on my bicep.
"I find it easiest to ask for forgiveness rather than permission, don't you?"
"Let the girl do her work, Jones," said Ronzoni.
I did. She gave me the smile one more time and I wondered how anyone would deny her forgiveness, and then she dropped her hand and led us away.
Emery slipped in behind the front desk, created three key cards and handed one each to Ronzoni and me. She kept the third.
"I misplaced mine," she said with an embarrassed grin. "I'm keeping everyone on the second floor, as low as possible. Would that be the right idea, Detective?"
I caught Ronzoni gazing at young Emery, and it took him a moment to snap back to planet Earth.
"Yes, yes. Lower is better. Less wind speed, and easier to evacuate if we have to."
"Well, if you gentlemen would like to change, I'll fix up rooms for the other guests."
I looked at Ronzoni and he looked at me and neither of us moved. Emery clicked away on her keyboard for a moment and then looked up.
"I'm sorry. You don't have anything to change into, do you?"
We both shook our heads. Neville, the general manager, snuck up from behind us and coughed to announce his presence.
"Miss Taylor, you have assigned the rooms?"
"Just finishing that now, sir." She tapped at her computer and then passed Neville a handful of key cards in little paper jackets.
"Thank you, Miss Taylor."

"Of course. And sir, it appears that Detective Ronzoni and Mr. Jones don't have anything dry to change into."

Neville looked us up and down with what was rapidly becoming his trademark disapproval, despite the fact he was almost as wet as we were.

"Of course. The boutique is closed for the storm, but perhaps you could let them in to select some new attire?"

"Yes, sir."

Neville strode away again and Emery stepped out from behind the desk and took off across the lobby.

"Gentlemen," she said, and we followed like a couple of well-trained but mischievous puppies.

At the north end of the lobby was another corridor. On one side looked to be a series of meeting rooms, with doors the same color as the walls so as to appear not there at all. On the other side were glass-fronted retail spaces. The first room looked like a general store-type place where guests could pick up some suntan lotion or a pack of gum or a new gold-plated pen. The store was closed and dark inside. The second store had human-shaped cutouts in the window that were wearing summer dresses and tropical shirts. Emery produced a ring of keys, selected one and crouched down to unlock the glass door at its base. She pulled the door and strode into the dark space, and then with a flick of a switch canned lights illuminated the store.

There were round racks of dresses and t-shirts and swimming apparel. One wall held a collection of hats out of a Bogart movie. There was a rotating rack of sunglasses designed for movie stars. At the rear of the room was a glass cabinet holding watches that looked worth more than my car.

Ronzoni wandered over to a rack that held a range of summer suits, which made me wonder if he ever wore anything else. I scoped a rack of shirts not dissimilar from the wet one I was wearing. I selected one that had stylized blue palm fronds all over it. It was a shirt that my late, great mentor and friend Lenny Cox would have called a going out shirt. I held it up and flipped out the tag on the sleeve and checked the price. It was possible to get a return flight to Westchester County, New York, from Palm Beach out of season for about half the price of the shirt I was looking at. I had to run my hand over the fabric to feel what such an exquisite price felt like, but I found to the touch it was just like regular cotton. I glanced across at Ronzoni. He had pulled a suit from the rack and was as pale as a ghost. Clearly he had also seen the price. I wasn't quite sure what made these fabrics so costly but I suspected it had something to do with the real estate we were in. Ronzoni looked up at me, mouth agape. He looked like a boy who had made his Christmas list, behaved himself and then received nothing more than coal in his stocking as reward.

"Miss Taylor, I wonder if there is a facility to dry our clothes out? This store is perhaps a bit too boutique for a cop and a PI."

Emery glanced at Ronzoni and back at me and gave a knowing grin.

"Of course, my fault. You know, Mr. Jones, you've given me an idea. Come with me, gentlemen."

We left the store and Emery locked up and led us farther down the corridor. When we reached the end she used a key card and inserted it into the lock on an unmarked door. We walked down a bland corridor of taupe and linoleum, clearly not for guest use, and then took a left, where she unlocked another unmarked door. I knew what this room was before she opened it.

I could smell laundry. There wasn't any being done but years of detergents and softeners and hot steam had perfumed the walls. Inside was an industrial-type space, somewhat like a hybrid between a dry cleaner and a laundromat. There were carts full of discarded bedsheets and tablecloths.

Emery took us to a desk that looked like the checkout for the county lockup. There was a worn desk topped by a wire mesh grate. Emery bypassed the desk and unlocked a mesh door and led us in. She turned and waved her hand like a model on The Price Is Right, across a rack of clothing.

"Lost and forgotten property," she said. "We try to return it to our guests, of course, but they don't always claim it."

"Is it clean?" asked Ronzoni.

"Freshly laundered, Detective. If you'd both like to select something to tide you over, I can put your other clothes in a dryer." She looked Ronzoni up and down. "Detective, your suit will of course need to be dry cleaned."

"Will it?" Ronzoni replied.

The selection wasn't great. Rich people seem to have universally bad taste. I'm not sure why that is. All I know is sequins belong on a Las Vegas nightclub act, not on a swimsuit. Ronzoni found a pair of trousers and a shirt that looked like it had been left behind by the Filipino president. I wasn't so lucky. I was flicking through the rack like a bargain hunter at Kohl's, when I noticed Emery looking me over. She wasn't being shy about it. Her hands were on her hips and she was studying me hard. I stopped flicking past XXXL polo shirts and looked at her. She grinned.

"I have the thing for you." She turned and flicked her keys around and unlocked a large gunmetal gray cabinet. She opened it, rifled through for a moment, and then turned back with a flourish. She was holding a suit. It was cream-colored, and linen. It would have been perfect if I had a cruise planned down the River Nile. She stepped forward and held it against me.

"Perfect," she said.

"I'm not sure that's me," I said.

"Of course it's you." She hung it on a rack by me and then left the cage and came back with two towels. "If you're not above changing here, I'll get your wet things in the dryer now. I'll just be outside."

She stepped out of the cage but not out of the room and Ronzoni gave me a shrug. There wasn't anything for it, so we stripped off and toweled down and then got dressed. Ronzoni didn't look like Ronzoni without a suit. I could have passed him on the street without a look. I put on the trousers and the shirt, and then slipped on the linen jacket. Emery was right, they fit perfectly.

"You look like Don Johnson," said Ronzoni.

"You look like Ferdinand Marcos."

Ronzoni frowned like he had no idea who I was talking about so I grabbed my wet shorts and shirt and stepped out of the cage.

"Very nice," Emery said. "Definitely a step up." She took our wet gear and hung Ronzoni's suit and tossed the rest in a huge dryer. "Detective, I'll ask our maid to take care of your suit shortly."

"I'm not sure the maid's going to be up for much work," I said.

"Of course, I forgot. Poor Rosaria. Never mind, I'll come back and take care of it myself."

She led us out of the laundry and down the bland corridor and back into the lobby, where we ran into the manager, Neville. He had changed suits. I was guessing he didn't get his from either the boutique or lost property. But his new suit looked just as immaculate as the last one. He had even combed the errant hair.

"Miss Taylor, I have asked all the guests to convene in the lounge so we can go through procedures for the next twelve hours or so."

"Yes, sir."

"Miss Rosaria is lying down in her room. Mr. Ribaud and Mr. Zidane are the only guests I am yet to locate. Could you undertake a quick search?"

"Of course, sir." Emery dashed away and Neville gave me cursory smile and looked me over.

"Mr. Jones, excellent choice," he said, referring to my clothing. "Very dapper."

I just nodded. I was fairly certain he didn't know it had come from his lost and found. He glanced at Ronzoni.

"Detective," was all he offered. "If you gentlemen will join me in the lounge?"

He pointed the way with a slight bow and we wandered into the lounge, which I would have called a bar. It was like a tearoom, with a large chandelier and floral print wallpaper. A little too pastel for my tastes. At one end was a bar backed with colored bottles of booze and toward the ocean side were sofas and lounge chairs set around even lower coffee tables.

The sofas and lounge chairs were mostly taken by the few guests. There were three women and four men. I knew Ron and Cassandra. The athletic black guy from the gym was there. So was Sam, the guy who had attempted to get off the island with us. The fourth guy was new to me, as was a strongly built black woman and the young blond I had seen on my first visit to the lobby earlier that day. The attention of the group was on the hotel manager.

KING TIDE

"We are just waiting for two of your party," he said, seemingly to the five people I didn't know, although they weren't seated together.

Neville stood erect and quiet. He didn't look at all uncomfortable staying silent before a crowd, which I guessed was some kind of skill worthy of a hospitality professional in a five-star hotel. As we waited one of the missing guests arrived. He was tall and strong in the chest but thin in the waist, and he wore a similar look of contempt that the muscle guy in the gym had worn. His hair was wet but combed neatly.

"Mr. Ribaud," said Neville.

"What's going on?" he said, and I picked up another French accent.

"Just some routine announcements to ensure everyone's safety during the storm."

I noted that Neville was avoiding the word hurricane.

"Won't you take a seat?"

The guy called Ribaud loped by and sat next to the strong-looking woman on the sofa. Ronzoni grabbed a piece of wall to lean on, and I sat in a cluster of chairs with Ron and Cassandra and the blond woman who I had seen earlier outside the lounge. Up close she was attractive but in need of a decent feed.

"Look at you," said Ron, running his hand down the jacket I was wearing. "Very dapper."

"That's what the manager said."

"He's right," said Cassandra. "You do freshen up very nicely, Miami."

"Thanks. Ronzoni thinks I look like Don Johnson."

"Oh, pish posh." She waved the idea away. "You look very smart. Like you're going to solve one of those Agatha Christie murders."

Which was a hell of a thing to say, given the next thing we heard was the sound of a paint-peeling scream from the other end of the hotel.

CHAPTER SEVEN

I wasn't closest to the door but I was first through it, and I sprinted across the lobby. The screams had given way to cries of help, and as I reached the corridor in the north wing I saw the assistant manager, Miss Taylor, step out of the gym and look down toward me. She was panting furiously, eyes stuck on the gym door that was closed in front of her. I touched her shoulder as I reached her and then pulled out the key card I still had and opened the door.

The French muscleman was lying on his back on the weight bench, inside the power rack. The massive weights on either end of the barbell suggested he had loaded up something equivalent to a small Italian car. I couldn't image someone lifting such a weight. Perhaps it couldn't be done. The Frenchman certainly hadn't done it, because the barbell lay across his throat, his arms fallen to the side.

I thought to check his pulse but the barbell was right across where I would have put my fingers, so I stepped back as Ronzoni made it into the gym. He stopped short and took it in. He looked at the bench, and then glanced around at the twelve steel struts that made up the sides of the rack.

"We need to get this off him," he said as he stood.

"Is he alive?" I asked.
Ronzoni shrugged. It seemed unlikely. A crushed larynx is a tough one to come back from.
"You think we can lift it?" he asked.
I nodded. I had spent plenty of time in gyms. Not lately, but once upon a time. Few guys could bench what two guys couldn't deadlift. I moved to one end of the barbell and Ronzoni to the other.
"Use your knees," I said. "Not your back."
We each took an end and with a collective grunt we lifted the weight off the Frenchman and up into the rack above. Then we both leaned in. His neck was a mess. The skin was purple already, from massive hemorrhaging inside the throat. It looked like someone had smashed a chicken carcass with a sledgehammer.
The Frenchman's arms were hanging limply and one leg was off to the side of the bench, the other lay on the bench itself. Ronzoni took a wrist and felt for a pulse. He held it for longer than was necessary to confirm the obvious. Then he took out his phone and snapped pictures as the other guests opened the door. They jostled for position to see the body, so I pushed them back.
"There's been an accident," I said. "Give us a minute."
I asked Ron to get everyone back to the lounge, and then I pushed the door closed and stepped closer to the body. Ronzoni took some close-up shots for the record while I just stood back. I felt something uneasy. It wasn't guilt, but it wasn't pleasant all the same. My brief interaction with the Frenchman had not been the friendly Florida welcome that the Chamber of Commerce liked us to give tourists. I may have been wet and cold and tired, and putting up storm shutters during a storm that was someone else's responsibility, but a harsh critic

might have argued that I had taunted the guy. The question was, did I taunt him into doing something that killed him? I must have been away in my thoughts because Ronzoni asked me if I was okay. I snapped back to find him looking at me.

"Tell me what you know," he said.

"What I know?" I was sure what I knew, and I wasn't sure I wanted to share half-baked thoughts with a cop who enjoyed running me off the island so much and so frequently.

"You put the shutters up in here, right? Was this guy here?"

I nodded. "He was. He was working out on that weight machine there."

Ronzoni glanced at the machine. "So when did he move over here?"

"I don't know. Later. He was on the machine when we came in, and still there when we left."

"You talk to him?"

He asked me the question direct, so I gave him my answer the same way.

"He complained that Ron and I were letting the rain in. I told him he could help, but he wasn't crazy about that. When he complained a second time I might have suggested that real gym junkies don't mess around with the fixed weight machines, they use free weights."

"What did he say?"

"He said he did. He said he lifted heavy." We both glanced at the crushing weight in the rack. "He said that he never did that without a spotter."

"A spotter?"

Ronzoni wasn't a gym guy. He had the kind of fingers that couldn't crack a pencil in half. "A spotter. Someone who stands behind the bench to help lift the weight if it is too much, if the lift fails."

"Okay. So the guy's one of these macho gym dudes. He gets his nose out of joint about lifting the baby weights and tries for too much. Drops it on himself. Death by dumb. A Florida speciality."
"Maybe."
"Maybe? What's that mean?"
"I dunno. He just didn't seem the type."
"Dumb?"
"I can't say one way or the other. But I don't mean that. He was earnest, you know? One of those guys who takes what he does so seriously that he almost doesn't see the world around him. Like he'd brush off a remark about the heavy weights as a character flaw on my part, like I couldn't know that serious lifters use a spotter. Like a serious scuba diver might dive a reef alone but never a wreck. They always use a buddy."
"Do they?"
"I don't know. I don't dive. It's a simile, Ronzoni."
"Yeah, well, if there weren't no one else here, then this guy dove a wreck alone."
I glanced at the elliptical machine and Ronzoni saw me.
"Jones? Was there someone else here?"
"No," I said. "Not then. There was a guy working out on the elliptical, black guy, fit-looking. But he left before we did."
"So no one else here when you guys left."
"No. No one."
"So, like I said, death by dumb. I gotta call it in."
Ronzoni turned away and held his phone to his ear. I looked back down at the body, and decided to take a couple of shots of my own. Of the damaged neck, of the body on the bench, of the apparatus he lay inside, like a cube with edges but no sides.

I had done plenty of benching in my day. It was one of those exercises that guys liked to brag about. What do you bench? These days all I heard on the beach was talk about a guy's deadlift, but when I played ball, the bench was the thing.
The bench press, otherwise known as the chest press. Designed to give a guy those big pecs that everyone loved so much. As a pitcher I preferred working on my shoulder muscles, but the chest was stronger, so the number a guy could lift was bigger. It was a vanity thing. And as I looked at the body lying on the bench I got the sense that he'd been doing it all wrong. Not just alone, but wrong.
Ronzoni ended his call and turned back to me. "They're saying if he's stiff they ain't coming out until the storm passes. We should find a sheet or something to put over him."
He caught on that my attention was not with him. "What now, Jones? There's a hurricane coming—don't bust my chops."
"Do you know the bench press, Ronzoni? The idea is to lay on your back on the bench and lift the weight out of the rack, lower it down to your chest and then press back up. The barbell is held at chest level to work the chest muscles."
"Okay, Schwarzenegger, what's your point?"
"My point is, if the bar gets dropped, it would land on the chest. It would hurt like hell, maybe even do some serious damage, but it wouldn't land on the throat. Not unless he was doing it all wrong."
"So he was doing it all wrong. Like I said, death by dumb."
"There's one other thing."
"What now?"
"He was French."
Ronzoni's groan was audible. There was hierarchy when it came to bad news on the island. Death was up there. But death happened often in Palm Beach. A lot of old people lived in the

town. The grim reaper had an apartment on Worth Avenue. And the death of a tourist was worse. The tourism guys hated any tourists dying on their patch, even of natural causes. But an American tourist would get a headline in their local rag, or on some website that led with the person's detail. John Doe dies in fishing mishap. The Palm Beach connection would be in the lede, or better still buried in the article which almost no one would read. But a foreign tourist was another matter. Suddenly Jacques Doe would become a nameless national in a headline that read French athlete killed in Palm Beach. I imagined the Florida tourist geniuses had a hard enough time dragging the money away from the French Riviera without that kind of press. Ronzoni knew it too, and he answered to the guy who answered to the mayor, who answered to the tourism lobby.

"Didn't you say there were some foreigners in the bar earlier?" I reminded him. I wasn't exactly enjoying the moment—there was a dead man in the room after all—but there was a certain satisfaction in Ronzoni's squirming.

"Yeah," he said to himself more than me. "We'd better go tell them."

"Who's this we?" I asked as I flicked off the lights.

CHAPTER EIGHT

Ronzoni had the general manager, Mr. Neville, congregate all the guests in the bar. Ronzoni suggested we lock the gym down, so Neville gave me his keys and said there was a physical lock on the bottom of the door. I went via the laundry and collected a sheet to cover the body, and then I locked the gym door and returned to the bar. Neville was walking across the lobby with the blond guy, Sam Venturi. Venturi looked tired and his hair was messed up, but he didn't look like he'd been sleeping. I handed the keys back to Neville and he gave me a solemn nod.

Ronzoni took the floor. I leaned against the wall and looked at the folks in the room. Venturi took a seat in a cluster with Ron. Cassandra sat nearby with her arm around the assistant general manager, Miss Taylor, who had a balloon of brandy cupped in her hands. Rich folks always seemed to drink brandy in a crisis. Maybe there was something to it. I didn't know. Brandy was above my pay grade.

Next on a sofa was the athletic woman I had seen earlier. She had almost beaten me to the gym when we heard the scream, and given I had reacted faster, she was quick on her feet. Her face was stern, like her car had just broken down on the way to a very important meeting. Beside her sat the tall guy with the wet hair. He was athletic in a way that the dead guy in the gym wouldn't have understood. Fast, but powerful. His lip was curled as if life itself disgusted him, and his skin was pasty-looking beside the black woman.

Another cluster of chairs had been edged around to face Ronzoni. In them sat the young blond woman I had seen before, and a guy with a long face and angular nose who looked so French he could have appeared on a wine label. His mouth was turned down and I suspected he was the foreigner who knew the deceased. Next to him was the black guy who had been in the gym. He was still in workout gear, and I assumed he was one of those people who wore athletic wear all the time so you knew how athletic they really were. Behind him stood a guy dressed in a white smock and a short black cook's cap. He wore an uneven stubble and was broodingly handsome either despite or because of it. I couldn't decide which. He was sharpening a long knife with a steel, which felt like a strange thing to do, given the circumstances. Or any circumstances outside of a kitchen.

Ronzoni broke the news to the crowd. He repeated his credentials and then told them there had been an accident, and asked if anyone knew the man in the gym. Two hands went up —the black woman and as expected the guy with the long face and Gallic nose. Then the tall guy next to the black woman put his hand up half-heartedly, as if he wasn't sure of his stance on the question at hand.

"I'm sorry for your loss," Ronzoni said. "I understand that this is a shock, and Mr. Neville and his staff are here to help as much as they can. I will need to ask each of you a few questions regarding the deceased, as a matter of procedure. But as you know we also have the matter of an impending hurricane, so I'd like for you to give your attention for a moment to the hotel's manager, Mr. Neville, as he will outline the procedures for the duration of the hurricane."

Ronzoni looked back to Neville and me, and Neville stepped forward. He spoke with his hands behind his back.

"Ladies and gentlemen, we at The Mornington are devastated by today's accident, and offer our sincerest condolences to all."

I figured there would be a good amount of butt-covering going on. Hotels got sued for a lot less than death by dumb. Maybe it was the English accent, but Neville sounded genuine to me.

"My staff and I are here for you, as always. Despite these events and the storm upon us, we aim to make your stay as pleasant as possible."

He looked around the room and then continued. "However, we must insist on the following protocols to ensure your comfort and safety. We ask that you restrict yourself to this lounge and your rooms. Please do not use other areas of the hotel without letting myself or one of my staff know. This building has faced many such storms before and come through grandly, but to ensure your safety you should remain in these areas. We will be serving cocktails and dinner here in the lounge."

I'd never had cocktails in a hurricane before, but it seemed a rather Palm Beach way to go about things. The black woman on the sofa raised her hand.

"Can we still use the ballroom?" she asked.

Neville turned to Ronzoni. "Detective?"

"The ballroom?" asked Ronzoni, looking about as puzzled as I was.

"Yes. It is on the mezzanine level above us, on the leeward side, and has been shuttered completely."

Ronzoni shrugged. "I suppose. For now."

The woman dropped her hand and nodded as if that was all she needed to know.

Neville finished up by telling everyone that the lounge would be the rendezvous point in case of an emergency. Ronzoni stepped forward.

"We should also turn off the elevators."

Neville shook like he'd been hit by a small bolt of electricity. "Why on earth?"

"In case the power goes out."

"I can assure you, Detective, we have backup generators."

"Which don't always provide enough power to run the elevators. Don't need anyone trapped in there during a storm."

"That is most inconvenient."

"So's sitting in a coffin-sized box for the duration of a hurricane."

Neville nodded repeatedly. I don't think he was keen on the word hurricane. I, on the other hand, played football and baseball at the University of Miami, otherwise known as the Hurricanes. I couldn't wait to mention that.

Neville directed his attention to the guy with the knife. "Chef Dean, some hors d'oeuvres, perhaps?"

The chef nodded and moved away behind the bar, into what I assumed was the kitchen.

"Thank you, ladies and gentlemen, we will serve drinks in but a moment."

Neville moved to the door and I intercepted him. "Where's the maid?" I asked.

"Still in bed, I'm afraid. She seemed rather shaken by her ordeal. Now, if you'll excuse me, I must shut down the elevators whilst I have everyone accounted for."

CHAPTER NINE

I left the party in the lounge and went and found my room. I had a call to make. The fire stairs from the lobby were all concrete and steel and I got the impression they were rarely used by any guest except during those annoying fire drills that always happened to me at 2 a.m. but probably happened at The Mornington during midafternoon and culminated in champagne on the beach. My room was on the second floor, which was actually the third floor up, with a mezzanine having been sandwiched in between the first and second floors.

My room was smaller than I figured it would be. It was stylishly done in taupes and browns, with a king bed and a flat-screen television. The bathroom was as white as a movie star's teeth. I flicked on the television, which is something of a novelty for me. I don't own a television. The general consensus seems to be that this is an eccentric quirk, but I just never saw the point. I wasn't planning on living forever, so I had things to do, and I saw all the news I needed at Longboard's, and all the football I needed at any number of establishments designed for the purpose.

The picture was terrible, pulsing in and out and waving all over the screen. I wondered if the hotel used a satellite provider. I couldn't imagine a hurricane did much for that kind of reception. Two guys were yelling at each other about football. They were debating trading quarterbacks like they were stocks or bonds. They were fading in and out, but I got the impression that didn't harm the value of the conversation.

I flicked around until I hit the weather channel. Despite the jumping picture I got enough of the graphic on screen to know that hurricane Beth had become a category two in the Florida Straits and was aiming toward landfall around Cape Canaveral. Then the scene jumped to a guy in a slicker who appeared to be standing in rain that was hitting him from the side. He was yelling excitedly, telling how the storm had built as a confluence of unseasonably warm water and low pressure. He made it sound better than Christmas, as if thousands of homes getting blown away was like losing your cellphone during a great night out on the town. Just the price of admission.

I hit a button and killed the picture and then took out my phone. It was damp, but still ticking. I had three bars of coverage, which was two more than I usually got on a clear blue day sitting at the outdoor bar at Longboard Kelly's. I tapped to the favorites and hit the only number there.

It rang for a long time and I was about to end the call when I heard her pick up.

"MJ," Danielle said, in a voice that made me smile despite myself.

"How's school?" I said.

"We're all watching what's happening down there. Everyone's on alert. Where are you? When are you getting here?"

"Change of plan, I'm afraid."

"MJ?"

"Got stuck on the island."

"You didn't."
"Yep. Long story."
"Where are you?"
"The Mornington."
"The Mornington? They run out of room at the Y?"
"Long story."
"Can't wait to hear it. At least you shouldn't get into any trouble."
"You'd think, wouldn't you?"
"MJ?"
I told her about the bridges flooding, and about the dead body in the gym. I skipped the part about nearly getting swept away in the Intracoastal.
"Crushed larynx? Did he not know what he was doing?"
"That's the thing. He was a serious gym junkie. Seems like a bad mistake."
"My days are filled with guys making bad mistakes."
"True. If it walks like a duck."
"Right."
"But something just didn't look right, you know?"
"Like what?"
"I can't put my finger on it. Probably chasing shadows."
"Strange things happen when you chase shadows, MJ."
I said nothing to that.
"You said you took some pics? Why don't you email them to me? I can get some of the guys here to take a look."
"You mean Nixon?"
"Yes, MJ, I mean Nixon. And a few others, too. This is the headquarters for Florida's state investigators. There are a few people here who know what they're doing."
"I know that." I did know that. And I didn't quite know why Special Agent Nixon had gotten under my skin. He'd helped us

on a previous case, and had been nothing but helpful. And then he'd gone and pulled some strings that got Danielle into the investigator program in Tallahassee. She was a great deputy and she would be an even better investigator. And Nixon had never done anything but right by me or her. But the guy was just too damn good-looking to be trusted.

"Okay, I'll send you some shots."

"You stay safe down there. It looks like this thing is going to hit somewhere between Canaveral and Jacksonville."

"Mick says Fort Pierce."

"I don't know why, but Mick would know."

"He would."

"Be safe."

"Will do."

"I love you, MJ."

"And I you, ma chérie."

We ended the call and I sat on the bed wondering where the hell the ma chérie had come from. I had a whole French thing going. Before I forgot I sent Danielle a few snaps I had taken of the poor Frenchman in the gym. I wondered if he had a chérie. Which made me think such a person might be in the bar. Which made me think I should be in the bar. Which is a thought I am generally pretty comfortable with. I threw on my linen jacket and dropped my phone in my pocket and wandered out to get a drink.

CHAPTER TEN

I didn't get my drink. Not right away. With the maid in bed and the chef preparing crab-stuffed pot stickers, and the assistant manager, Miss Taylor, still suffering the effects of having discovered a dead guest, I ended up behind the bar instead of in front of it. It wasn't so bad. I think I'd make a decent bartender. I don't know boo about mixing cocktails, but I wouldn't work in that kind of a place. At Longboard Kelly's the job involved pouring beers and rums, with the occasional squeeze of fruit. It was mostly a listening business, and I was generally okay with keeping my ears open and my mouth shut. Muriel, who actually did tend bar at Longboard's, was equally good at it. Plus she had all kinds of curves I didn't, which seemed to help her in the tip department.

The general manager, Neville, waited tables and handled any beverages more complex than a straight pour, and once everyone had a drink in front of them I poured a beer, grabbed an Evian from the fridge and wandered out to where Ronzoni was sitting on a coffee table. I sat down next to him and offered him the water, which he took with a nod of thanks.

We were sitting opposite the tall pale guy. The black woman who had been beside him had disappeared while I was at the bar, and Ronzoni had chosen to sit on the table rather than next to the guy on the sofa.

"Jones, this is Anton Ribaud," said Ronzoni, cracking the seal on his water.

I offered my hand to Anton, and he took it with an effort that would best be described as less than enthusiastic. He was a strong-looking guy, but his handshake was like a dead fish. He didn't speak, so Ronzoni did.

"Mr. Ribaud is a friend of Mr. Zidane."

"Zidane?" I asked.

"Paul Zidane is the name of the deceased."

I nodded. "Zidane, like the soccer player?"

"Football, yes," said Anton. "Only now Zidane is a coach."

"I'm sorry about your friend."

Anton shrugged, like I'd given a small child a choice between cauliflower and broccoli.

"Were you close?"

"I suppose you would say that. We knew him since we were boys at school."

"We?"

"Me. And Leon." He nudged his head in the direction of the long-faced guy who had moved to the bar and was pouring himself something amber in color. "We were at school together."

"Where was that?"

"Bordeaux. The southwest of France."

I nodded. I knew Bordeaux. Or at least I had drunk something from there, once upon a time.

"What brings you to Florida?"

Anton sipped on a drink that smelled like licorice. "I live here."

I frowned. "In The Mornington?"
He looked at me like he had just walked me in on the bottom of his shoe.
"This is a hotel, no? I live in Miami."
Ronzoni chimed in. "But you're French?"
Now Anton gave Ronzoni the look. I was glad it wasn't just me. "You are quite the detective."
"What brought you to the United States?"
Anton leaned back in the sofa. "Tennis."
"Tennis?" asked Ronzoni.
Anton said nothing.
"What do you mean, tennis?"
"You don't know tennis?"
"I know tennis. What I don't know is how it brought you here."
"I play tennis. I came here when I was fourteen to practice."
"Where was that?" I asked.
"Case Academy. You know it?"
I nodded. I knew it. Case Academy was a tennis camp that became a tennis ranch that became the leading producer of wunderkind tennis talent in the world. It was the brainchild of Rodney Case, himself a decent but not extraordinary tennis player. The ranch was on a massive campus outside of Tampa, and had been sold a few years previous to an athlete management company who had added baseball, softball and football to their roster of sports. It was like a high school for gifted athletes.
"You look a little old for Case Academy," I said.
Anton grunted. "I am on the tour now."
"The ATP?"
"Of course."
"You ranked?"

"I have been top ten."

I made my impressed lip curl. Making the top ten tennis players in the world was pretty impressive. The kid could play.

"So if you live in Miami, what brings you to Palm Beach?" Ronzoni asked.

"It is what you Americans would call the bachelor party."

"You're getting married?"

"Yes."

"To who?"

"My fiancée."

I took a drink and watched Ronzoni. There's nothing a cop loves more than interviewing a guy who thinks he's the smartest guy in the room, and the cop is the dumbest. Ronzoni took a sip from his water but he didn't take his eyes off Anton.

"Does your fiancée have a name?"

"Shania." He pronounced it Shan-E-ah.

"I assume she is not here."

"No, she is not here."

We all took another sip and then I leaned in toward Anton.

"So Paul, he was into the gym pretty hard."

"Yes." Anton scrunched his nose as if he thought his friend's gym obsession was a waste of time. Either that or he had eaten a pickle that was repeating on him.

"You must do plenty of gym work yourself. Did you ever work out with him?"

"Sometimes."

"You guys compete?"

"Compete?"

"Yeah, you know. Guys in a gym. There's competition. Who can lift the most, that sort of thing."

"No."

"Never?"

"No. I am not, what do you call it? Gym monkey?"
"Junkie."
He grunted. "I am a professional athlete. I don't work out for fun." He jutted his chin at me. "You get old, you try to keep off the fat. You just waste time in the gym. Me, I don't play around. I have a program. I do what I need to do to be the best player. Not the big muscle guy. You don't get it."
I got it just fine. I wasn't any kind of gym monkey either. I used the weights to do what I had to do. I was lucky to have good trainers at Miami, guys who knew the difference between working out for beach muscle and working out to become a better pitcher. So I knew exactly what Anton was saying. I just wasn't digging the crack about getting old.
"So you never lifted against him?"
Anton shook his head. "He was stronger than me. It was not a secret, it did not need to be proven. But I did not want to lift like him. I wanted to play tennis. And we both knew who was the better tennis player."
No competition, my sweet patootie.
"So would Paul normally try to lift big all by himself? Without a spotter?"
"Normally? No. But what is normal?"
I had nothing to say to that. It was questions like that that kept me away from French cinema.
I noticed Anton's friend Leon had moved from the bar and I nodded to him that he should join us. He sat on the sofa and spoke to Anton.
"Tu vas bien?" he asked.
"Oui," said Anton.
We introduced ourselves and I watched Leon. He looked shaken by Paul's death. Shaken but not devastated. Perhaps it was a cultural thing. European stoicism or some such.

"So you guys all grew up together, huh?" I said.

Leon nodded. "Oui. Bordeaux."

I noted that Leon's English was pretty good but his accent was heavier.

"You still live in France?" I asked.

"Oui, yes. In Paris." He pronounced it Paree, as I supposed was right. He made it sound like one hell of a good time.

"And you came for the bachelor weekend?"

"Bachelor weekend?"

"L'enterrement de vie de garçon," said Anton.

"Oh, oui. Yes, I come for this party."

"And Paul?" asked Ronzoni. "Where did he live?"

"Here and there," said Leon. "Bordeaux, mostly."

I asked him, "What do you think, Leon? Paul was a serious lifter. Would he lift a dangerous weight alone like that?"

Leon thought for a moment and then sipped on his drink, which I figured was brandy. Then he frowned.

"Why do you ask me this question?"

"Just curious."

"If you think he would not do such a thing, then you think he was not alone."

"It looks like an accident to me," I said. "I just wonder how it could happen."

Leon looked at Ronzoni. "Detective, you also question this accident?"

"Mr. Lezac, I am a police investigator. I question everything."

He didn't smile but I knew Ronzoni just loved delivering that line. Normally he was the kind of guy who would come up with a witty retort three hours later and then text it to you.

"You think maybe he wasn't alone?"

"I don't have an opinion one way or the other, Mr. Lezac. What about you?"

"I think Paul was very serious about his workouts. I think he followed protocol."

Anton snorted. "He wasted his life inside a gym, and he killed himself inside a gym. Just face it, Leon." He stood and downed the last of his glass.

"I need another drink."

He trudged off to the bar and we watched him go. Then Ronzoni spoke.

"So you don't believe it was an accident?"

Leon shook his head. "I don't know. I don't know." I watched him glance toward the bar and then sit back in the sofa and put the glass to his lips. He didn't drink.

"What is it, Leon?" I asked.

He didn't look at me. He looked at Ronzoni.

"Detective, if I wanted to know if Paul was alone, I would look at the hotel security video."

Ronzoni cocked an eyebrow. Clearly he hadn't thought of that. To be fair, neither had I, but the difference between us was that Ronzoni would claim the idea as his own later on.

CHAPTER ELEVEN

Ronzoni excused himself and wandered over to Neville, who directed him to his assistant manager, Miss Taylor. She was still sitting with Cassandra and Ron, and seemed to have brightened up some, and after a couple of head nods she stood and left the bar with Ronzoni, I assumed to check the security video.

I refilled Leon's glass but not my own. I figured Leon for a guy who still had something to say, something that he might prefer to say without the presence of the police. And I figured brandy was just the social lubricant to get it out of him.

"So you live in Paris?" I pronounced it Paree, and it sounded stupid coming out of me.

"Yes, monsieur."

"What do you do there?"

"I am a sommelier. You know, wine?"

I nodded. I knew wine. Not intimately, but Mick usually had a bottle stashed somewhere under the bar for the occasional lost tourist.

"And the three of you stayed in touch after school. That's unusual."

"Is it?"

"I think so. Guys often lose touch with high school friends during college, but Anton left when he was what, fourteen?"

"Yes."

"And you went to Paris."

"Oui."

"But you kept in touch."

"We were like brothers, you understand? Our families were very close. Like brothers, we went our own ways but we always keep an eye for each other."

"Sure. So what did Paul do?"

"This and that."

"Yeah, that's what I heard. What constitutes this and that in France?"

"He stayed in Bordeaux for a time. Working in gyms mostly."

"Personal trainer?"

"What is this, personal trainer?"

"Someone who works with people in the gym one-on-one. Creates a program, motivates them, helps keep them on track."

"No, Paul did not do this."

"Okay. And then?"

"He was in Paris for a time, not doing much. Then he went away."

"Away? You mean he did time?"

"Did time?"

"Jail."

"No, monsieur. I mean he went away. From France."

"Okay. Where did he go?"

"Here and there."

"Right, doing this and that. So what did old Paul do for money? You know, euros?"

"I know money, monsieur. How to put such a thing? He lived well on the welfare of others."

I nodded. "He was a moocher."

"A moocher?"

"Someone who lives well on the welfare of others."

"D'accord. A moocher. Oui."

"He stayed with you in Paris?"

"Yes."

"Why did he leave? Did you kick him out?"

"No. Friends do not do this."

"Friends don't mooch."

He shrugged. He was good at it.

"What about Anton? Did Paul mooch off Anton?"

He nodded. The shrug came more naturally.

"Even though Anton was in the US?"

"After. When Anton got on the ATP tour. He plays a lot in Europe. He took Paul along."

"Took him along? What, to carry his bags?"

"No. For some time Paul was Anton's trainer and hitting partner."

"Hitting partner?" I asked.

"Yes. Someone to practice with."

"So Paul played tennis, too?"

"No, monsieur."

I sipped the last of my drink. The story Leon was telling was not unfamiliar to me. I'd seen plenty of guys make it big in baseball or football or basketball, suddenly flush with money, and I'd seen critters crawl out of the woodwork to claim their share of the largesse. A guy never knew how many long-lost cousins he had until he had a pro sports contract in his pocket. They could be like leeches. I'd seen it end friendships, families and careers. And even lives.

"So Anton is getting married?"

"Yes, monsieur."

"You can cut the monsieur, my name is Miami."

"Miami? This is also the capital of Florida, yes?"

"No. The capital is Tallahassee, and I'm thankful I don't have that as a nickname. Miami is just the biggest city. It's where I went to school. College. So married, then?"

"Yes, monsieur Miami."

"And this is the last hurrah, huh?"

"I think in English you say stag weekend?"

"In England you say that. We say bachelor weekend."

"For the women, also?"

"Bachelorette."

He frowned like it was a stupid word and I was inclined to agree.

"And when we are all together? Men and women?"

"Not sure we have a word for that. A recipe for disaster, would be my guess. But Anton's bride isn't here."

"She is here."

"He said she wasn't."

"She wasn't in the room."

These guys were rather precise with their language. Perhaps it was a translation thing. Perhaps they were anal. Perhaps they were hiding something.

"So where is she?"

"I do not know, monsieur Miami."

"There aren't that many women in the hotel, Leon. Which one is she?"

"Shania. The, how do you say it? African American?"

I thought of the powerfully built woman who had been on the sofa earlier. They didn't look much of a pair, but I guess couples rarely look that way except if they're in matching sweaters, and that's never a good look.

I said, "Yes, African American. What do you call that in France—someone who is African descent but French?"

"French."

I nodded.

"So what did Shania think of Paul mooching off her fiancé?"

"I don't really know. I don't think she liked it. I don't think anyone really likes it."

"So why didn't she stop it?"

"It is complicated, monsieur."

"Miami. How is it complicated? I get it, you're like brothers. But brothers have to make their own way in the world, don't they?"

"Of course. But . . ."

I said nothing. It was when thoughts trailed off into nothing that the stories always got interesting, and I had learned long ago to let them fester. People don't like silence. They like to fill it. Often with the other side of the trailing thought.

Instead Leon retreated into his brandy balloon. That was okay with me. Trailing thoughts often found momentum with help of social lubricant. I offered to recharge his drink. I was quick about it, because trailing thoughts also have half-lives considerably shorter than uranium.

"Tell me about the complications," I said, like I was the guy's priest.

He took another long slurp on his brandy. "A thing happened."

"Okay."

"You cannot tell anyone. Even the policeman."

If it was pertinent and illegal I sure as hell could tell the policeman, but I was equally easy keeping stuff to myself if it wasn't any of Ronzoni's beeswax.

I nodded.

"We were in Bordeaux for Noël—Christmas—a few years ago. We had some drinks, Anton more than most." Leon took another sip of his drink, perhaps oblivious to the story he was telling.

"Anton got quite drunk, and he told us a story of something that happened when he was at the tennis school."

"Case Academy?"

"Oui, yes. He said that there had been a big match, a final of a tournament. Their team had won well. Anton, Shania, Sam. They all won. But there was some kind of a test after—you know?"

"Drug test?"

"That's right. Anton said he had been doing something."

I thought of Paul and the steroid look in his eyes. "Performance enhancers?"

"No, no. Not that. Anton would not do that. No, this was more recreational."

"Like marijuana?"

"I think cocaine."

"Okay." Not performance-enhancing per se, but well outside the scope of acceptable pharma in the eyes of the tennis administration, whoever they were.

"So what happened? He had a positive test?"

"No. It was arranged for someone else to take the test for him."

"For him? I don't think it's that easy, Leon."

"Maybe not on the ATP, but this was high school. Anton says it was done."

"So he got away with it."

"Oui."

"And Paul decided to use this against Anton? To keep the gravy train going?"

"Gravy train?"

"The mooching."

"No, you don't understand, monsieur. Paul did not need to use it. Anton was helping him anyway."

"So what did Paul do?"

"Nothing. He said that it was something we should not speak of. To protect Anton."

"Okay."

"Unless it ever needed to be used, to protect Anton."

I sat back, but I was on a coffee table so there was only so far to go without falling backward. But I was forming a picture. Anton might have helped Paul because he was a brother, but there's nothing like a little guarantee to make sure the deal stayed sweet. And now with a marriage, perhaps the deal was going sour. Perhaps Paul was going to use what he knew. Or perhaps it was just an accident.

I leaned back toward Leon and spoke softly. "That doesn't look great for Anton, you know that, right?"

"No, monsieur. I know Anton. Look, like brothers we have grown apart. We have different lives. But you know your brothers. Inside. Anton may appear like he does not care, but he cares very much. About his tennis, and about Shania. And about Paul. And Paul felt the same way about Anton. He wouldn't use the knowledge against his brother like that."

"You ever heard of Cain and Abel?"

"Of course. But you miss the point. This is not about Anton."

"Then who is it about?"

"Someone provided the fake urine sample, for the test. Someone else was involved in the cheat. I think Paul knew who that was. I think he was doing the blackmail on them."

"Who was this other person?"

"I have no idea, monsieur."

"So this is just a wild theory."

"When I arrived at the hotel I ask Paul how he is doing. He tell me after this trip he would be doing very well indeed."

"That plan didn't work out so well, now did it?"

CHAPTER TWELVE

I left Leon staring into his brandy balloon and wandered out of the bar. Leon's comments had set me thinking, and I noticed that the bride-to-be had left her man drinking alone in the bar. Except that he wasn't alone. The young blond woman had taken a perch next to him at the bar. What her relationship to the whole thing was I had no idea. I would find out. But first, I wanted to know what was so important about the ballroom.

Shania had asked Ronzoni if they could still use the ballroom, which I found an odd request. After hearing of a death in the hotel even Fred Astaire would have taken a break from dancing for a while. For it to be the first question asked intrigued me. And once intrigued I needed answers.

I could hear the wind pounding outside as I made my way up the lobby stairs to the mezzanine level. The stairs were marble like the foyer but the mezzanine was carpeted the color of spilled cabernet. At the top I had two choices, left or right, south or north. I went south. It wasn't a subconscious choice. I wasn't a bird. But above the deep, pounding sound of the wind and rain beyond the shuttered windows I heard a rhythmic popping coming from the south side of the floor.

As I got closer the popping got louder. Pa-tank, pa-tank. It was like a chip fanatic was opening a thousand Pringles tubes one after the other. Pop, pop, pop. I found the ballroom. It was behind a door covered in taupe fabric, next to which was a brass plaque that labeled the space the Flagler Ballroom. I didn't really see how putting Henry Flagler's name on it made it any better. Surely the ballroom would have sufficed, but around the Palm Beaches when the imaginative city planning geniuses got together to name stuff, Flagler always saved them from a blank whiteboard.

I pushed the door open. It took a moment to comprehend what I was seeing. The ballroom was vast and ornate. Lots of rococo curlicues and gold leaf. The ceiling rose to a dome that wasn't really a dome, since there was another floor above it. The floor was parquet and about the size of six tennis courts.

But there was only one tennis court. It had been set up in the center of the space. A row of round dining tables clad in white tablecloths were set up as a net. White masking tape had been stuck to the floor to delineate the lines of the court. Above the makeshift net hung a large crystal chandelier. The massive lighting fixture made me think of bulls and china shops.

The pop, pop, pop was coming from the tennis racquets as a tennis ball was pummeled flat and hard from one end of the court to the other. I wandered along the sideline toward the middle of the court, where the umpire at Roland Garros might sit, or the ball boys at Wimbledon might crouch. At the near end Shania was bouncing around on her toes. She moved lightly, never touching her heels to the ground, jumping side-on to hit each shot and ending facing the dining table net each time, ready for the next. She didn't grunt or make screaming noises, but she hit the ball so hard I developed a new appreciation for the structural integrity of the Penn product. She had changed clothes, and was wearing a red sleeveless shirt and black Lycra shorts that she filled completely. Danielle's arms were well defined. She worked out plenty hard. But Shania's arms were strong. Her triceps glistened with sweat. Her forehand shot started in the shoulder and then popped in the hip like a golf swing, lots of momentum, before whipping at the wrist and catapulting the ball back to the other end.

Where Sam Venturi returned it. He was built altogether differently. He wore a white tennis shirt and baggy shorts that looked like he had stolen them from Rod Laver. He was the polar opposite of Shania. Male-female, white-black, vanilla-colorful, slight-strong. Shania wasn't overly tall but Sam was no taller, maxing out at five-nine or five-ten.

Shania glanced at me between shots but remained focused. The rally went on forever. It reminded me of hacky sack we played back in college, trying to keep the footbag in the air for as long as possible. But Shania and Sam didn't seem to be trying to rally. They just didn't miss hit. The ball never rose more than a few inches above the tables acting as the net.

Eventually Shania let one go. She just didn't swing and the ball sped by and cannoned into the wall behind her with a force that would leave a dent in drywall. She walked up close to the tables and took a new ball from her pocket and hit it to Sam, who remained at the back of the court, and he returned it with less vigor than before so Shania could practice her volleys. I didn't know a lot about tennis. I'd been once or twice to the tournament out on Key Biscayne, and I'd attempted to court a tennis player during college. I knew a volley from a groundstroke, and a lob from a smash, but that was about it.

"You play?" Shania asked, not taking her eyes off the ball.

"A little," I said. "Back in college."
She hit a few more volleys and then proceeded to catch the return ball on her racquet head. She nodded to Sam and they ambled over toward me. A table had been set up with a carafe of ice water, and they both rehydrated.
"Nice court," I said.
Shania nodded and smiled.
"They let you do this in here?"
"They let you do anything, if you got the money," said Sam, wiping his moist face with a towel.
"I'd be a bit worried about that chandelier," I said looking up.
"No lobs allowed," Shania said. "You a cop?"
She got my attention back from the ceiling. "No."
"You were helping the cop."
"I do that."
"He saved that girl, the maid," said Sam. "That was pretty awesome, dude."
I shrugged like it was nothing. My battered knees begged to differ.
"What happened to Paul?" asked Shania. She wasn't a beat-around-the-bush kind of gal.
"He dropped something heavy on himself."
Shania frowned again, and it aged her. It did the same thing to me, only worse.
"You know Paul well?" I asked.
"He's a good friend—was a good friend—of my fiancé."
"Anton."
"Yes." Her eyes narrowed. "I didn't get your name."
"Miami Jones."
"Miami Jones. Like the movie."
"But with a tropical feel."
"Were you born in Miami?"

"New Haven, Connecticut. You?"

"Lauderdale."

"So you're local."

"I guess."

"How about you, Sam?" I asked.

"Nevada, originally."

"And you play tennis, too."

He held his racquet up as an answer. It wasn't much of an answer. I hadn't recognized her before, but on the court I knew I'd seen Shania Dawson's powerful groundstrokes before. Sam Venturi I didn't know from a sinkhole.

"You play professionally?" I asked him.

"I did."

"Did?"

"Now I'm a coach."

"Not in Palm Beach."

"Why not?"

"You were pretty anxious to get off the island, as I recall."

"No more than you."

"Got that right. Hurricanes aren't my idea of fun. So where do you coach?"

"Tampa."

I nodded. "Case Academy."

"How did you know that?"

"I heard Anton went there. So that's how you knew him. You coached him?"

"No, I played with him. We all did," he said, glancing at Shania.

"You went there, too?"

Shania nodded. "Since I was ten. Still go there to practice when I'm in town."

"Ten? That's pretty young."

"Not really. In Europe they got camps for four-year-olds."

"Had to be hard. Away from family and all."
"My family was there. My dad's always been with me."
"And now you're on the tour."
"I am. You watch much women's tennis?"
"Not much. But I've seen more women's than men's."
"That's pretty sexist."
"Not at all. I just happened to have been at a couple of WTA tournaments."
"That so. Who'd you see?"
"Caroline Sandstich, as I recall."
"Caroline. She's pretty."
"Pretty good player, you mean."
Shania narrowed her eyes again like she was summing me up. I was used to it. It happened a lot. In my experience the process was easy but the final summation was usually a good few degrees off course. She kept my eye and then took another drink and wiped her brow.
"How about you, Sam? Tour life not for you?"
"Tour's not all it's cracked up to be. Listen, I've got a cramp in my calf. I'm gonna go get it worked out."
He picked up a bag of tennis racquets off a dining chair and walked out of the ballroom. His shoes squeaked like on a basketball court.
"You want to hit with me?" asked Shania.
"I'm not really dressed for it."
"Take off your jacket. You'll be fine."
"Be gentle."
She handed me a racquet with a purple grip and we each took positions midcourt. She took a ball and hit to me gently and I got the impression she was playing with me in more ways than one. I hit the ball back, and we rallied for a few shots. Then she caught one of my returns in her hand.

"No, no. You're holding the racquet all wrong."

Shania jogged around the tables onto my side of the court, grabbing a couple of balls from a wire basket as she went. She stood before me and tucked the balls into her Lycra shorts.

"You wanna hit the ball low and hard, you gotta use topspin. And to get topspin you gotta change your grip."

"I was taught to shake hands with the racquet."

"Yeah, that's the eastern grip. That's old-school. Big, strong guy like you, you could really give it some hammer, but you gotta go to the western forehand grip, like this."

She turned the racquet in my hand until it felt like I was holding it backward.

"Feels all wrong."

"You ever play golf?"

"Once or twice."

"How'd that feel first time?"

"Weird."

"Right, so trust me." Shania stepped in behind me and took each of my wrists. Her arms weren't as long as mine so she crushed up hard against my back.

"Now, you come back like this, and whip through, low to high." She dragged my arm back and ran me through the motion, like my first little league coach had done with a baseball bat a long time ago.

"Like that. Don't worry about your body or your shoulder. That comes later. That's icing. The spin comes from the wrist."

She stayed in close behind, slipped out one of the balls from her shorts and tossed it in front of me to hit. I swung through and managed to collect the ball on the frame of the racquet.

"That's all wrong," I said.

"You got that right. Do it again."

She tossed another. This time the ball hit the strings, but at such as angle that I smacked the ball directly into the parquet floor.

"Low to high, and whip the wrist, man."

She wrenched my hand back and down, and then tossed another ball. I hit through, and snapped my wrist as I made contact, and the ball rocketed over the tables, two inches above the white tablecloth.

"There you go," Shania said, matter-of-factly.

She skipped around the table net and collected her racquet, and then we hit some balls. Most of mine went in unintended directions and I started to doubt my own hand-eye coordination.

"Why don't you go back to the eastern grip? We don't want to take out this chandelier."

She was right about that. I'm not sure whose insurance would cover that, but I was pretty certain it wasn't part of any policy I had. We hit balls for a while in silence, just the pop of the ball on strings and the hum of savage winds outside. I was working up a little sweat, a combination of the atmospheric conditions and the movement, but before it became too much Shania caught the ball.

"Not enough of a challenge for you, hey?" I said.

"Every challenge worth your effort comes from within."

That one was going to keep me up nights.

Shania took a towel and poured some water, and we took a drink. I was about to sit down on one of the dining chairs when she spoke.

"Let's go take a look at this storm."

CHAPTER THIRTEEN

I had no intention of venturing out into the storm again, but that wasn't what Shania had in mind. She draped a towel around her neck and led me out of the ballroom and away from the stairs to a small area on the ocean side of the hotel. It was the kind of useless space you found somewhere in every hotel that made you wonder what the architect was thinking when he was looking at the blueprints. There was a cloth-covered table against the wall with nothing on it, but I could imagine an urn and a tray of muffins, and people in suits taking a break in a conference schedule for coffee and calls. There were large rectangular columns in the middle of the space, which made it unusable for much other than a break area, but which clearly served an important structural role in the building. Which I was glad about. Because beyond the columns were hurricane-proof windows draped in thick curtains that looked out onto one heck of a storm.

A row of palms was bent low, like they were each picking up a penny for good luck. Beyond them the Atlantic Ocean ripped and swirled and pounded the seawall that separated the lawn from the beach, neither of which was visible. The light cast from the lobby downstairs glinted off whitecaps on the water, pulsing in a myriad of directions. I knew it was raining but I couldn't actually see the drops. It was as if a single opaque screen had been dropped in front of the view, blurring the picture.

Someone had put expensive-looking benches by the windows and Shania took a seat and I followed suit.

"Odd little spot," I said.

Shania nodded. "Deshawn took Sam and me through Pilates here this morning. It's quiet. Out of the way."

We watched the wind pummel the trees and the water for a time.

"You got a good eye," Shania finally said.

"You got a good forehand."

"You played sport before. I can see it."

"Bit of baseball, bit of football."

"For fun or profit?"

I wiped my forehead with a towel. "It was always fun. Then it was for profit for a while. And then it stopped being fun, so I stopped playing."

"So you know how mean that was, what you said to Sam."

"Mean?"

"You know what you did."

I love nothing more than women who speak in riddles.

"I do?"

"About the tour. You can add it up. He played with us, but he's coaching now instead of being on the pro tour."

"Why isn't he on the tour?"

"Why do you think?"

"Either he got injured, or he's not that good a tennis player. And he doesn't look injured."

"So you know how mean that was."

"On the contrary. I know what it feels like to do something you love and not quite make it at the top level. But that doesn't make it mean to talk about it. How he deals with it is up to him, not me."

"You believe that?"

"Every challenge worth your effort comes from within."

She let out a mirthless laugh. "You're quoting me at me?"

"Folks are about as happy as they make up their minds to be."

"Who said that?"

"Abraham Lincoln. Something like that, anyway."

"You know what I think?"

"I know you're going to tell me."

"I think you're a phony."

A gust of wind hit the window with an invisible thud and it shook in its frame. We both waited for another crash but it never came.

"A phony, huh?"

"Yeah. You make out all cocky, but I don't think you're as confident as you pretend."

"I can guarantee it. But that doesn't make me a phony. That makes me human."

"You say so."

"I do. You ever beat someone at tennis that you didn't think you could beat?"

"I always think I can win. No point being there if you don't."

"Sure. But there must have been a time. Even when you were younger. Maybe you played an older girl and you really didn't think you could win."

"Maybe. I don't recall."

"Sure you do. It's etched in your brain. It's what drives you on. It's what makes you come to a bachelorette weekend and set up a tennis court in a ballroom to practice. Because you know that feeling. You know if you ever take the court again and you really don't believe you can win, you won't. So you tell yourself you can always win, and you prepare in a way that makes it so."

"What's your point?"

"My point is, you lose sometimes. No one wins every match. Can't be done. You're good, so you win most of them, but you don't win them all. But you keep telling yourself you will win, every time you take the court."

"So?"

"So you're a phony, too. You have to be. It's the only way to do what you do. Did you know that the best season ever in major league baseball is a season win ratio of seventy-six percent. Best ever. Chicago Cubs, 1906. That means the winningest team in history lost one out of every four. You think those guys believed they would win every game? You bet they did. But they didn't win every one. Not even close. They were phonies. Had to be, to get up week after week and lose every fourth game."

"You're saying fake it 'til you make it."

"Sort of. It's part of it. Like you just showed me. Hit the topspin grip, even when it goes straight into the ground. Hit it like you mean it, even when it flies out of the court every time. Hit it like you're Nadal or Williams. Hit it like you're the best. Even when you aren't. And keep hitting it until you are."

"There's more to it than that."

"Of course there is. That's my point. Let me guess. Old Sam there, he was a bright young thing. At Case Academy, right? The blond boy who chased down everything, got every ball back. Wore his opponent down. He was the next big thing."

"How do you know that?"

"It's in his face. In his attitude. I've been there. He won stuff, right?"

"He was a team captain at Case. First to win a challenger tournament. First to get an agent. He was Wimbledon boy's champion."

"Right. But then something happened. Looking at him, I'm guessing not injury. I'm guessing genetics. He was taller as a boy, but he didn't grow. His body didn't fill out. The other boys became men, strong men. Big serves that pounded him off the court."

"He was as good a counterpuncher as you've ever seen. Like Michael Chang, Lleyton Hewitt."

"Sure. But the game overtook those guys, too. Power, those topspin shots you were hitting. Hitting the ball that hard should send it into the next zip code. But you spin it so much it drops in. Fast. Too fast to counterpunch. Am I right?"

Shania nodded.

"So he's a great tennis player who isn't suited to the modern game. He went so far and no further. That's life. I get it. I know how that feels."

"You do? Really? I don't think regular people really get it."

"They probably don't. Regular people are by definition regular. Normal. Middle of the bell curve. To be great at something takes a dedication most folks aren't willing to muster."

"You're quite the expert. How so?"

I let out a deep breath. "I made it to the major leagues."

"You did? For who?"

"Oakland A's. Twenty-nine days I was a major league pitcher. Only problem was, outside of the bullpen I never got to throw a pitch. Then the off-season I got traded, and I never got back to the majors again."

"I'm sorry."

"People usually are. But that was then. I'm older than Sam, so I've learned some stuff. Maybe he will, too. Maybe not. Some

people don't. You either come to grips with the fact that you went as far as you could—you say to yourself, I did my best, left it all out there, and this was as far as I could go. Or you don't. And if you don't, it eats you up from the inside. I've seen it happen. Sam's still young, and he's bitter that he lost his shot. Hopefully he realizes that maybe he has another shot. Maybe he'll be a great coach. Maybe he'll be something else."
"You could have said that to him."
I shrugged. "What about you? Getting married."
She smiled. It was a winning smile. I bet it sold a lot of sneakers.
"Yeah."
"And you met Anton at Case Academy."
"Yeah. He was a string bean, but like you say, he filled out."
"And he's French."
"Yeah. He's got that accent going on."
"What does your dad think?"
"What's my dad think? You mean 'cause he's white?"
"No. I mean because you're his little girl. It's the dads you gotta watch out for."
"My dad's not the one getting married."
"Roger that. So how well did you know Paul?"
"I wondered when you were going to get around to that."
I shrugged.
"I knew Paul well enough. We base ourselves in Monaco when we're in Europe, and he was in Bordeaux, so not that far away."
"Word is he liked to ride Anton's coattails."
"What does that mean?"
"You know what that means."
Shania sighed. "They were close. The three of them. Anton felt a debt."
"What did you feel?"

"What do you mean?"

"How did you feel about the fact that this guy was mooching off your fiancé, and that it was likely to continue after you were married?"

"I don't think it was likely to continue."

"How do you figure that?"

"Because Anton was going to lay it out to him. Look, Paul was an okay guy, when you got to know him. But he needed direction. You're right, I didn't want him skulking around, living off us. He needed to get on with his own life."

"And Anton was okay with that."

Shania nodded, but it wasn't full of enthusiasm.

"Are you married, Miami?"

"Engaged."

She smiled again. "That so? To who?"

"Danielle Castle. She's in law enforcement."

"A cop? What is it with you and cops?"

"I know, right? She was a deputy sheriff, but she's now at the academy to become an investigator with the FDLE."

"The who?"

"The Florida Department of Law Enforcement. Kind of like the state version of the FBI."

"I'm from Florida and I've never heard of them."

"Pray it stays that way."

She nodded. "Is she pretty?"

"Danielle? Stunning."

"You have to say that."

"I don't have to, but I do. She's stunning. Period. Other folks can say what they will, but that's my take on it."

"So she's pretty."

"Not pretty. Stunning. Physically, sure. But inside, stunning."

Shania shook her head. "She sounds perfect."

"She is."

"Miami, no one is perfect. No one."

"Each of us sees the world through our own unique set of spectacles. You see what you see, and I see what I see. And in Danielle, I see perfection. Like those old Greek statues. With the arms missing and noses chipped off. Not flawless, but yet perfection."

"I hope she can balance on that pedestal you've got her on."

"Her feet are on the ground. It's me that needs to watch my balance."

I got the sense that Shania was going to say something else, but she was stopped by someone calling my name. It was coming from the direction of the ballroom.

"Hello!" I yelled.

I got up and eased around the big column and found Emery Taylor, the assistant general manager of the hotel, striding toward me. She seemed to have gotten her pep back. Or maybe she was just a phony.

"Miami, I wondered where you had gotten to."

"A spot of tennis. Now I'm looking for some cucumber sandwiches."

Emery smiled. She had one of those Florida smiles, the ones that tell you that even in a hurricane there's no place else they would rather be.

"I guess I'll just have to ask Chef Dean to rustle some up for you."

I hoped she realized I was joking. I wasn't sure what cucumber sandwiches actually tasted like, but the flavor that came to mind was water.

"I wanted to tell you that Detective Ronzoni was looking for you."

"Okay, thanks."

She smiled again. "Can I walk you down?"
"Just give me a minute. I'll see you down there."
"As you wish."
She turned and strode away. Shania Dawson stepped out from behind a column.
"You're pretty flirty for a guy who is getting married."
"You see flirty, I see friendly."
"She was flirting with you big-time."
"She's in hospitality. Friendly's what they do."
"Danielle must trust you."
"She does."
"How do you know? Maybe you haven't given her a reason not to yet."
"I've given her plenty of reason not to. But you've got it backward. You don't get trust and then try not to lose it. You start without it, and you earn it. There are always pros and cons, ups and downs. But the ledger either says you earned it, or you didn't."
Shania nodded like she was thinking about that. "Maybe you're not such a phony after all."
"Oh, I'm a big-time phony. And so is everyone else. It's how people are phony that you've got to watch out for. Now if you'll excuse me, I'm wanted by the police."

CHAPTER FOURTEEN

Ronzoni was sitting in a high-backed chair in the general manager's office, just off the check-in desk. There were three monitors on the desk in front of him but his attention was on one of them. Emery Taylor was next to him at the controls of the computer, operating the security video system.

Emery shot me the smile again and Ronzoni spun around as if he were surprised I had bothered to turn up.

"Check this out, Jones."

I stood behind Ronzoni and looked over his head. Emery clicked an onscreen button and I saw the picture come to life. It was a shot of the southern end of the lobby, looking down the corridor that led to the gym. The picture was decent without being high-definition, and the camera had some difficulty with the difference in light from the bright lobby to the dimly lit corridor. I could see down the corridor I guessed about half of the way.

Andrew Neville was behind the check-in desk. Emery fast-forwarded the video but it was hard to tell because there wasn't much movement. The few guests were in the lounge, and we were away trying not to drown on Bingham Island.

When the video reached a timestamp that Emery and Ronzoni had obviously looked at before, she clicked again and the picture resumed normal service. The athletic-looking black guy came out of the fire stairs near the elevator.

"What's that guy's name?" I asked.

"Mr. Maxwell. Deshawn Maxwell," said Emery.

"He's the guy you saw in the gym, right?" asked Ronzoni.

"Yep."

"Doesn't use the elevator," he said.

"He's a fit guy. Perhaps that's the reason."

Deshawn wandered away from the camera. He was in athletic wear, which seemed to be a thing with him, and he wandered down the corridor and disappeared from view. A quick scoot forward with the video and the elevator opened and Paul Zidane got out and followed Deshawn down the corridor.

"So the deceased and Mr. Maxwell in the gym," said Ronzoni.

Emery forwarded the video again. Neville race-walked across the lobby in fast motion toward the lounge. Emery did the same from the north end of the lobby, across to the check-in desk. Then the picture slowed and we all charged in from the rain. I was practically carrying the maid. Ronzoni was with me, and then Ron and Cassandra. Sam Venturi brought up the rear.

We spoke to Emery although there was no audio. Cassandra took the maid from under my wing and led her away into the elevator. Sam Venturi waited for the elevator car to return and then got in. Then Neville came back from the lounge. We had our chat about the storm shutters and then Neville and Ronzoni headed down and out of picture—to the north wing —and Ron and I headed up the corridor toward the gym.

Emery zoomed it forward and then stopped, and we saw Deshawn Maxwell wandering out of the corridor. He stopped for a moment in the lobby and looked back down the corridor like he had forgotten something, and then he banked around the check-in desk and spoke to Emery.
"What did he say?" I asked.
"Hello," said Emery.
Deshawn bypassed the elevator and wandered down the lobby and out of shot to the north end. Then there was a long stretch and we saw Ron and me returning to the lobby, wet as sewer rats. Ronzoni and Neville appeared from the other end of the hotel, and Emery came out from behind the desk. Then Ron got in the elevator. Emery returned behind the desk and worked at the computer, and Neville disappeared in the direction of the lounge and reappeared, and Emery handed Neville something. New key cards. Emery came out from behind the desk and led Ronzoni and me down off screen.
"Getting you some clothes," she said, glancing at my wardrobe and giving it a considered nod.
"This is the best bit," said Ronzoni.
It was a procession. First Shania and then Leon came from the direction of the lounge and took the elevator. A minute later the young blond woman did the same thing.
"Who's the blond?" I asked.
"Her name is Carly Pastinak," Emery said with a hint of disapproval in her voice.
"She with the rest of them?"
"Yes."
"How does she fit in? Is she a tennis player?"
"No idea, Jones," said Ronzoni. "Just watch the corridor."
I watched the corridor. People came and went through the lobby, mostly in a direct beeline from the elevator to the lounge

or vice versa. Eventually I saw everyone make their way back toward the lounge. Everyone except Anton Ribaud and Rosaria, the maid. Neville, Emery, Ronzoni and I joined up in the lobby. Three of us wandered away to the lounge. Emery headed for the elevator.

"Mr. Neville asked me to find Mr. Ribaud and Mr. Zidane."

As the elevator doors opened Emery stepped back to allow Anton to step out and wander limply across the picture to the lounge.

No one came or went from the corridor to the gym.

Then Emery appeared back from the elevator. She stopped for a moment next to the check-in desk, and then she wandered up the corridor toward the gym.

We didn't hear the scream, but we saw me running across the lobby, followed by Shania, and Ronzoni. Then Ron and Cassandra and Leon, and Carly and Deshawn at a gentle jog. Sam and Anton never appeared.

"So there you have it, Jones. No one went anywhere near the gym. Like I said, death by dumb."

It was a new sensation for me, but I had to admit Ronzoni was right. The idiot had gone all macho and dropped a big heavy weight on his own throat. It really was monumentally stupid.

We thanked Emery for her help and she locked the office and we wandered back into the lounge. Everyone except the maid was there. Shania had taken a shower and was sitting at the bar with Deshawn. Her fiancé was in a club chair nursing a tall glass of red. Ron was sitting with Cassandra. She was watching the room. He held up a glass of beer in salute.

Not for the first time it seemed like an excellent way to see through a hurricane.

CHAPTER FIFTEEN

Neville poured me a beer. I had to hand it to him, he was a real pro. We were in the middle of a tropical storm that had become a hurricane, and he was massively understaffed—to the point of playing bartender—but he didn't seem fazed by it. He gave me a fancy paper beer mat and a gracious nod as he delivered the beer, and I gave him the same back, without the beer mat.

"So was it foul play?" asked Shania. She had her elbows on the bar and her fingers steepled, and she was watching me across Deshawn, who sat between us.

"Nope. Looks like a silly mistake."

"I guess it doesn't matter either way," said Deshawn. "He's still dead."

"You're right about that. It sure doesn't matter to him. I'm Miami, by the way."

"Deshawn Maxwell," he said, shaking hands.

"So Deshawn, how do you fit into this crazy circus?"

He glanced across his shoulder at Shania. "Friend of the bride, I suppose."

"That right? You a tennis player?"
He chuckled. "No. Shania's dad and my dad were best friends. We grew up together."
"So you're a sort of local as well."
"Sort of. I'm in Miami now."
I sipped my beer. I was conscious it could be a long night, so I sipped slow.
"What do you do?"
"Sports medicine. Physical therapy."
"You're one of those masochists."
He didn't smile. "Yeah, I guess. Recovery can be painful."
"Yes, indeed."
Shania said, "Miami played professional baseball."
"Is that so?" said Deshawn.
I nodded. "You work with any teams?"
"Fort Lauderdale Strikers. They're a soccer team. But I've been thinking about approaching the Marlins."
"Tough gig to get, I would think. You tried minor league?"
He shook his head.
I asked, "Where'd you go to school?"
"Miami, as it happens."
"All right. Me too."
"I figured. Miami'd be quite a name to give a kid."
"I played little league with a kid who had the family name Head. His folks went and called him Richard."
"That's harsh."
"I'll say. So I know a few people up at the St. Lucie Mets. Maybe I could make an introduction?"
"Really? That'd be kind of you."
I nodded like it was a done deal and put my lip to my beer glass. Networking was really Ron's thing, but with my fancy

linen suit I was feeling like a new man. Maybe I'd start selling Amway.

"That's nice of you, Miami," Shania said, with narrowed eyes. Either she was near-sighted and hadn't been diagnosed, or she still thought I was a phony and wondered what I was up to.

I offered her a what are you gonna do? shrug.

"How's your fiancé doing?" I asked her.

That earned me a frown, just when I thought I was winning her over. She turned on her stool and looked at Anton and Leon. They weren't talking in French. They weren't talking at all.

"Perhaps I'll go see," she said, slipping off her stool. "Excuse me, guys."

Deshawn got off his stool as she left and I thought he was leaving as well, but once she walked away he sat down again.

"So you guys have been friends a long time, huh?" I asked.

He nodded to himself. "Long time."

"And you know her dad?"

"Mr. D? Sure. He's like an uncle. Do anything for the man."

"He's Shania's coach, is that right?"

"Yeah. Coach, manager, agent, all that."

"Sounds like one of those tennis dads."

"Not at all. Mr. D's a good father. He doesn't control her. She's got her life. But he'd do anything for her."

"What about you?"

He looked at me. Right in the eye. "Sure. I'd do anything for her. That's what old friends do, don't they?"

"They do if they're worth a damn."

We both sipped our drinks. I noted he wasn't drinking any faster than me, and I was going at a snail's pace. He had a level head on him, and he was a good-looking kid. I liked him.

"Did you know Paul at all?"

He shook his head softly. "Not really. Met once or twice."
"What did you think of him?"
"I thought he was an arrogant freeloader."
I nodded. "That seems to be the prevailing wisdom."
Deshawn pushed his drink away as if he'd had enough, and he turned to me.
"I think I'm going to take a shower. If you'll excuse me?"
"Sure. Say, do you always wear athletic gear?"
He smiled a half smile. "Occupational hazard."
He slipped off his stool and wandered out of the room. I watched him go and then my eye caught Ron's. He and Cassandra were watching me, so I walked over.
They were sitting comfortably with a couple glasses of red wine, and Ron offered me the open chair in their little cluster.
"Interesting times," said Ron as we clinked glasses.
"Could say that."
"What's that kid's story?"
"Deshawn? Family friend of Shania—the bride-to-be. They grew up together. Like brother and sister I guess."
"They might be close," said Cassandra, "but not like brother and sister."
"What are you saying?"
"I'm saying she might see him as a brother but the feeling isn't mutual. That young man's in love with her."
"How on earth do you know that?"
"Call it women's intuition."
I had something to say about that but I decided the best course of action was to keep it to myself. That was men's intuition.
"I've been watching him, the way he looks at her," she said. "It may be unrequited but it's there."
"Anything else your women's intuition telling you? The marriage in trouble before it even begins?"

"I wouldn't say that, necessarily."

"He seems a bit of an ass, the groom to be."

"Don't mistake cultural differences for arrogance, Miami." Now Cassandra was sounding like my mother, and it made me squirm in my seat. "She doesn't see him the same way you do." We each see the world through our own spectacles. I needed to listen to myself more often.

I said, "So what do you see, a long and fruitful union?"

"I'm not saying that either. Personally I like my man by my side." She shot Ron a smile and made the old guy blush. I swear his silver mane tinted pink. "They seem to be in each other's orbit, rather than on the same planet. But you never know."

I glanced over at the couple in question. Shania was sitting across Anton's lap, and he was talking while running his finger up and down her arm. Leon had left them alone and had turned his chair to face the blond woman, Carly.

"I wonder what her story is," I mused.

"Carly? She's Anton's agent," Ron said.

"You know that how?"

"We sat with her earlier. Nice girl. Wouldn't you say?" he asked Cassandra.

"A touch calculating for my tastes, but that's young women today. Always an angle to play."

"That's very cynical of you, Miss Cassandra," I said.

"Yes, you are probably right, Miami. There's nothing wrong with a bit of ambition."

Ron said, "Thing I don't get is why you would invite your agent to such an intimate event. A wedding reception I understand, but a bachelor weekend?"

"Agents can get pretty close to their charges," I said. "I've seen it. Some of them are like confidante, psychiatrist, bank manager and best friend, all rolled into one."

"How close would you let Carly get to him if you were his fiancée?" asked Ron.

"Office meetings and daylight hours only," said Cassandra, smiling.

We sipped our drinks in relative silence, the turbine swoosh of wind in the background a reminder of the weather. The room got quiet, and I had the sense that everyone was listening to the storm outside. The building was a hardy old thing, as solid as the day is long. Not built for hurricanes specifically—they just built them like that back in the day, when homes were constructed to pass on to future generations, not for easy knockdown to accommodate the latest fashion in kitchen countertops. I felt confident that we would get through the hurricane okay, but the foreboding sound of the wind gave the mood an edge that everyone seemed to feel.

I was restless so I stood and took a walk around the perimeter of the room. I wound up at the bar, where Andrew Neville was polishing glassware.

"What can I get you, sir?"

I shook my head. "I'm good. You been through a hurricane before?"

"The hotel has seen many, and come through relatively unscathed."

"I don't doubt it, but I meant you, personally."

"I am from Britain, Mr. Jones. We don't do hurricanes."

I took a stool, like a lonely businessman in a downtown bar. "How did you end up in Palm Beach?"

"It's a long story."

"It's a long night."

He smiled his tight smile. "I was looking for a change of scenery."
"Where were you before here?"
"Paris. George V. Before that I worked at the Savoy in London."
I gave him my impressed lip curl. I didn't stay in that caliber of hotel—hell, I rarely ventured through the front doors of that caliber of hotel—but I certainly knew the names.
"Classy joints."
"Yes, sir."
"How does The Mornington compare?"
"Well, the clientele is the same. However, I believe a smaller establishment like The Mornington can provide a more intimate service."
"Still, Palm Beach isn't quite Paris or London."
"No, sir. Quite different."
Neville glanced over my shoulder. It was the first time I had noticed him do it. He either gave you his full attention or he gave you none of it. There was no in-between with him. Not like regular people, who were always glancing around, checking their phones, worried that something better might be happening somewhere else. But I understood the glance when I saw Neville scoop some ice into a cocktail shaker and pour some vodka in it. Then he put in a splash of triple sec and a squeeze of lime and finished it with a pour of cranberry juice. He gave it a shake and then poured it into a martini glass and garnished it with a slice of lime. It was dark red like cough syrup.
"Who's that for?" I asked.
"Miss Pastinak," he said, placing the glass on a tray.
I turned to see Carly Pastinak finishing off the remains of Neville's previous effort.

"I'll take it over," I said.

Neville cocked an eyebrow at me. "As you wish, sir."

I stood and reached for the tray.

Neville said, "Sir? Be careful."

He gave me a look that suggested he wasn't talking about spilling the drink, and then he picked up another glass and began polishing it.

CHAPTER SIXTEEN

I delivered the drink with considerably less pomp than Neville would have, but it got there fully accounted for so I called it a job well done. Carly Pastinak watched me place it on the table and then gave me a thanks but not a smile. I lingered. I do that. Eventually she looked up at me and I asked if I could take the seat beside her since she was sitting alone. She shrugged.
"Whatever you like," she said.
Not a ringing endorsement but I took the seat and slipped the tray onto the table.
Carly Pastinak was an attractive woman. She was blond and thin and had Scandinavian bones. Her eyes were the color of the Mediterranean just off Monaco. Not that I had ever been to Monaco, but I had watched the Grand Prix, and it was one hell of a color. She looked like she might have been a cheerleader in college, but she had lost some of that athleticism. We all do. Some of us put weight on, some of us lose a little. Carly had lost a little. Her skin was a touch tight

across her cheeks, like the cocktail in front of her was a regular form of meal replacement.

"Miami Jones," I said. I didn't offer my hand. I wasn't concerned that I'd lose it, but it felt a bridge too far. Attractive women like Carly have a way about them. They are like Star Trek vessels, zipping about the galaxy with their shields on full power. They assume every conversation is an angle, every approach will result in them being hit on. Dr. Hook had sung about how hard it was to be in love with a beautiful woman. Actually being the beautiful woman was no picnic, either.

"Carly Pastinak," she said. She didn't reach for the cocktail. She rolled her shoulders like she was stiff in the neck. I got the sense that she was afraid of some implied contract—since I had delivered the drink, her drinking it meant she owed me something. It was way too complicated a line of thought for me. I couldn't live like that.

"Mr. Neville says he hopes you enjoy the drink," I said, trying to dismiss the idea from her head. She nodded and her hair fell across her face. She still didn't touch the drink. Maybe I was reading too much into it. It wouldn't have been the first time.

"So what brings you here?" I asked.

"Really? That's what you're going with?"

"I've never been stuck in a hurricane having to make chitchat before. Not my strong point."

"Clearly." She relaxed her face and there was almost the beginning of a smile there.

It was true. Small talk wasn't my strong suit. I was more comfortable with complete silence than most people. So I decided to play my strength and keep quiet. Most people hate silence. They feel the need to fill the void with banality. Or use an escape, which is what Carly did. She pulled out her cell phone. Frowned at it. Tapped at it a few times and then frowned again.

"No reception." She looked at me. "You have any cell phone reception?"

I didn't bother to check. "No," I said.

She gave up on the escape and silence and the implied contract and picked up the drink.

"So what is it you do, Mr. Jones, was it?"

"Miami," I said. "I'm a private investigator."

"Is that true?"

"Yep."

She put her drink down. "How exactly does a person get into that line of work? Did you go to college for that?"

"I went to college to play baseball. The PI thing happened later. What about you?"

"No, I'm not a private investigator."

"So what are you?"

"I'm a sports management consultant."

"An agent. That's what they were called when I played."

"We don't really use that term anymore. Where did you play?"

"Wherever the organization sent me."

She looked me up and down. It wasn't furtive and it wasn't seductive. It was more like a farmer checking over a prize hog. Being an athlete, even a former athlete, presented a different side to folks like Carly Pastinak. I had known a few agents in my time. To them, non-athletes were just people they had to walk around at the mall.

"And now you're a PI."

"That's right. And you're a sports management consultant. With who?"

"GSM. Global Sports Management."

"I know GSM. They're the big time."

"We are."

"Don't they run the Case Tennis Academy now?"

She stopped for a moment, just a second, as if she were reconsidering me.

"We do. It's now GSM Academy. We added baseball and softball. Football, too."

"And you manage Anton?"

This time she stopped properly. "You seem to know an awful lot."

"I usually know just enough to be dangerous."

"Is that so?" She picked up her drink and took another sip, and then she put it back down. The action seemed to be a consumption management tool.

"How did you end up at GSM?"

"Hard work."

"I don't doubt it. I'm sure they like to get their pound of flesh."

"They like to win. I like to win."

"How did you land Anton?"

Her eyes narrowed and then relaxed. "Are you playing me, Mr. Jones?"

"Moi?" I had no idea what she was talking about but I didn't want her to know that.

"I think you know more than you're letting on."

"People make that mistake about me all the time, but generally I know very little."

"I'm sure it is a mistake."

I shrugged.

"If you know the business so well, how do you think I landed Anton and GSM?"

I hadn't thought she had landed Anton and GSM. I figured she got Anton because she worked for GSM. But it got me thinking. Which was the chicken and which was the egg?

"You got the gig at GSM because you landed Anton as a client."

She nodded like I was right on the money.

"So where were you before GSM? Before Anton?"

"I joined a small firm out of college. Based in Orlando."

"And in order to land the job, you had to bring a client with you."

"Of course. That's how you prove yourself."

"But a small firm, and you fresh out of college? Hard to get a name athlete."

"Very."

"So an up-and-coming athlete."

"Could be."

"But there are rules about that. NCAA doesn't like agents, even when they call themselves sports management consultants. So you can't sign a college athlete, or a high school athlete for that matter."

"Is that so?"

"Unless they didn't plan on going to college."

"No NCAA rules if someone goes professional."

"So someone who went pro right out of high school," I said.

"Happens in basketball, from time to time."

"It does. Some guys go to Europe instead of college."

I looked around the room as I thought about it. There weren't any basketball players in the hotel. There was no link to basketball. There were professional athletes, but from only one sport.

"Tennis," I said.

"You are good, Mr. Jones."

And then I thought about the conversation I had seen in the lobby, and about what Shania had told me.

"Sam Venturi," I said.

Carly smiled. It could melt butter. Or steel.

"How did you figure that?"

"I heard he was the best of them, back then."

"He was. Wimbledon boy's champion."

"But he was at Case Academy. Surely GSM had their eye on him."

"Of course."

"But they can't sign any of their students because most of them want to play in college, and they become invalid if they have an agent."

"You know your NCAA rules."

I looked at Carly and this time she held my eye. She was a beautiful woman with one hell of a brain. A lot of men made the mistake of thinking those two things never came in the same package.

I said, "Sam was planning to go to college. Then he won Wimbledon juniors, right? And someone put it in his head that he should just turn pro."

"Did they?"

"You."

"You flatter me, Mr. Jones. But Sam made his own decisions. He saw the opportunity and he went for it."

"And you signed him up from under GSM when he did."

She smiled and went for her drink again.

"So how did that lead to Anton?"

"Anton doesn't like the rules to apply to him. He wasn't receptive to GSM's offers to manage his career."

"I bet GSM didn't agree."

"They did not. Why would they? They put a lot of effort into those kids at the academy."

"And make a lot of money from tuition fees."

"They make money off the rich kids. The ones who really aren't good enough to go pro but who might get into college on the back of a sport. Those parents pay full load to keep little Janey's dreams alive. The Antons and the Sams are there on GSM's dime."

"In the hope that they'll sign up with GSM when they go pro and GSM will get twenty percent of everything for the rest of their lives."

"Quid pro quo."

"But Anton didn't play."

She shook her head.

"Let me guess. GSM offered you a deal. Rather than be angry that you stole Sam from them, they were impressed. So they offered you a slot in their roster, on one condition. You had to sign Anton for them."

"Were you as good a baseball player as you are a detective?"

"I'm an investigator, and the climax to that story is yet to be written. So you got Anton on board. But what about Sam?"

"Sam didn't work out."

"You mean he didn't mature?"

"That's a very good way of putting it."

"So what happened? You dropped him?"

"GSM didn't want him, they wanted Anton. So they got Anton. Sam stayed with my old company."

"For how long?"

"Not long. It became obvious pretty quickly that he wasn't going to cut it on tour, and they let their agreement lapse."

"And Sam gave up a shot at a college scholarship because he had gone pro."

"Sam wasn't really college material. He's a tennis player, and now he's a coach. He'll be happier as a coach than he realizes."
She flexed her shoulders again. Perhaps discussing the shark-eat-shark world of sports management brought home the stress. Perhaps she wasn't as comfortable in the company of clients as she made out. Perhaps it was an uncomfortable chair.
"Do you come to all your clients' bachelor parties?"
"Not as a rule."
"So why here? Why now?"
She smiled again. It was disarming. I think that was the point, because she said, "Do you know if there is a masseuse in the hotel?" She rolled her shoulders again and avoided my question.
"Normally, I'm sure there is. But not in this storm."
"Shame."
"Tense?"
"Nothing I can't handle."
"I get worked on every week. You want me to do your shoulders?"
"Thanks, but no thanks."
I wasn't sure why, but I was glad she said that.
"Maybe you should take a hot tub."
"That's not a bad idea. You know where it is?"
I shook my head. "Deshawn knows. Shania's friend."
"Mmm. Perhaps I'll ask him. But first . . ."
She picked up her drink. I thought she was going to offer me a wink but she didn't.

CHAPTER SEVENTEEN

Detective Ronzoni caught my eye and I took that as my cue to leave Carly to her cocktail. I ambled over to Ronzoni who still didn't look himself without his suit. It occurred that we had swapped bodies, or at least looks. But my linen hand-me-down was probably worth a couple weeks' salary and most definitely not wrinkle-free, and he looked more like a lost tourist than a South Florida beach bum. I met him near the bar, where Sam Venturi was nursing a white wine and chatting with Andrew Neville.
"You got any cell coverage?" Ronzoni asked me.
I pulled out my phone. "One bar. But my battery's losing its will to live."
"I got nothing. Damn city and these cut-rate phones. It's no way to run a police department."
You knew the state of the world was not good when the Palm Beach police were complaining about budgets.
"You got someone you need to call?"
"I just want to get a brief on the weather."
"You try the radio?"

He looked at me like it was a crazy idea. Or maybe that was just how he usually looked at me and I hadn't noticed.

"I'm thinking we should have these folks get some shut-eye. I'd rather them have an hour or two now than have to wake everyone if something goes wrong later."

"What's to worry about? This place is built like the Titanic." I gave Ronzoni a big grin, but he didn't get the Titanic reference at all. It was like throwing fastballs at a little leaguer.

"Still. Better to be prepared," he said.

Neville appeared on the other side of the bar and asked what we wanted and Ronzoni advised that everyone get some rest.

"I could arrange for Chef Dean to prepare a late supper, for, say, 10 p.m.?"

"Très European," I said.

Ronzoni liked the plan and asked for a bottle of water. I didn't think anyone would sleep with the guttural hum of the hurricane whipping through the vents. Ronzoni made the rounds and Neville went out behind the bar to tell the chef. I took a pew next to Sam Venturi.

The kid looked like he was ready to drink himself into oblivion but didn't have the heart to do it. He was hunched over his wine like a guy in a country song hangs over a bourbon. He looked up and I gave him a nod.

"I see I'm not the only one who repulses the ice queen."

"Ice queen?"

"Carly."

I noticed that she was gone and her cocktail glass sat empty on the coffee table.

"She's no ice queen. She might feel the stress a little too much."

"That's why she drinks."

"I told her to take a hot tub. Less hangovers."

He nodded to himself and stared at his drink before he spoke. "Sorry about before."

"That's okay, it only took one lunatic."

"Huh?"

"To get the maid. Out of the water."

He frowned at me. "No, I mean about in the ballroom. Walking out."

"Oh, that. Think nothing of it."

He looked at me. "You have anything you want to say to me?"

"You okay? You looked pretty shaken up after the whole nearly getting washed away in a flood thing."

"No, I mean about what you said about me playing on the tour."

"You want an apology for that?"

"I think it's warranted."

"Kid, let me give you a nickel's worth of free advice. Grow a pair."

"Excuse me?"

"No, I won't. Normally I would, but I'm making an exception for you. 'Cause you are clearly in need of an attitude adjustment."

"Is that right?"

"You better believe it."

"You don't know a damned thing about me."

"Let's try this. You were great at sports as a kid. All sports. P.E. was probably your favorite class at elementary school. And tennis was all natural. And you were good, and you won a lot. And then you won Wimbledon juniors. And then something unexpected happened. You didn't grow. You didn't get taller, and you don't really have the body type to get much stronger. And in the blink of an eye all these kids you beat became men and started beating you. And then you found out that no one really cares a jot about winning a junior tourney, even Wimbledon. So you crawl back to Tampa to coach. How about that?"

He clenched his jaw. In another guy I might have readied myself for a sucker punch, but this kid didn't have it in him. He'd been beat down some by life and was still enjoying wallowing in it. He was yet to realize that it wasn't about him. Life wasn't vindictive. Bad things happened to everyone. But if you hung on long enough, good things happened, too. I let him stew for a minute before I spoke again.

"Don't beat yourself up, kid. But if you live your life in the memories of what you did when you were a teenager, you're gonna miss some pretty awesome stuff in the now."

"In the now? What are you, a Zen master?"

A bit of spunk. I liked it.

"Nah. I'm just a guy who was good at sports as a kid. Got a scholarship to college to play football and baseball, won a college world series, and went pro. And then I spent all but twenty-nine days of the next six years in the minor leagues learning that I was good, but there were plenty of guys who were better."

He stared hard at his drink. I had a mind to tell him that sauvignon blanc didn't grab me as the beverage of choice for a bender, but that was going well off topic, even for me.

"You did that?"

"I did."

"Don't you miss it?"

"Nope."

"I don't believe you."

"I know. And I wouldn't have either. But I know better now. I have the most amazing woman in the world who keeps me around despite everything I do, and I have great friends and I get to wake up to Florida sunshine most days."

"And the other days are hurricanes."

"You're a pretty cheery guy, you know that?"

He let out a little guffaw, and then caught himself.

"Let me ask you something. Did you play tennis to become famous?"

"No."

"To earn lots of money?"

"I'd have paid to play."

"Me too, with baseball. I loved it. So what don't you get now that you would have gotten if you were on the tour? And remember, you said money and fame weren't that important."

"Respect." He glanced over his shoulder. I wasn't sure at whom.

"I've known a few guys in the major league and the NFL. NBA, too. Guys who wanted respect. Some gave their money away to buy it. Some ended up sitting around at Thanksgiving with just their manager to crack a wishbone with."

"What's your point?"

"Why did you come this weekend?"

"My friends are getting married."

"But you weren't that keen to stay."

"Um, have you noticed the hurricane?"

"I have. I also noticed that your former agent—sorry, sports management consultant—was chatting to you before we tried to get off the island."

He shook his head. "I don't care about that."

"I think you do. I think it's deep in your craw that she took you on as a client until a better option came along, and I think you're still trying to get her respect."

"They don't care about you, man. They'll tell you anything. They love you forever when you're hot, and they forget you ever existed when you're not."

"Like baseball GMs. But you know what? You're right. They move on. It don't make it right and it don't make it nice. But it's life, kid. And the only one who gets hurt by you drowning yourself in your pretzels is you."

"Pretzels? What are you talking about? This is Marlborough sauvignon blanc."

"It's a song. Neil Diamond."

"Who?"

Now I was losing the will to live, so I took another tack.

"So you went to Case Academy?"

"Yeah."

"Did you like it?"

"If you could have gone to school and played baseball six hours a day, would you have liked it?"

"That would have been heaven, or maybe even better."

"Exactly. It was better. It was hard, don't get me wrong. We didn't just mess around. We trained hard, we played hard. But I loved it."

"What about Anton?"

"Anton? He loved it, too. He doesn't like to show it, he's Mr. Cool. Like nothing's hard work at all. But it's a front. He loves playing and he works hard. I know it's driving him crazy with his ranking right now."

"What about his ranking?"

"It's going backward. He broke into the top ten last year. Now he's at thirty-six."

"Why?"

Sam shrugged. "Who knows. I know he still works hard, and he's still got the shots. Maybe the wedding is on his mind. I don't know."

"I bet his agent isn't happy about that."

"Of course not. That's why she's here. Looking for an upgrade."

"Upgrade? To what?"

"Anton's going backward, Shania's a shot at number one. Who do you think?"

"Her dad represents her, is that right?"

He nodded.

"That gonna change?"

"No. He watches her like a hawk. Carly would need something pretty good to get in there."

"But no harm in trying."

"That depends on your point of view." He took a long swill of his wine.

I gave him a minute. I had no drink in front of me, and I found it disconcerting to be sitting at a bar without one. It would never happen at Longboard Kelly's. Muriel took her bar custodial duties very seriously. And Mick would give her the dagger stare if he ever found Ron and me with an empty glass. Product turnover was everything.

"When did you decide to go professional instead of going to college?"

Sam shrugged. "I don't know."

"I heard you guys won a big junior team tournament when you were at Case."

"Yeah. That was pretty much the end."

"The end?"

"We all went our own ways after that win."

"Good times," I said.

Sam smiled the way people do when remembering a kidney stone they had passed.

"You ever think what happens if you don't win that tournament?" I asked.

"Wouldn't have changed a thing for me. I was already into qualifying for Wimbledon."

"Maybe you go to college instead."

"Maybe. I doubt it. I just wanted to play tennis."

"What about Anton or Shania?"

"It was just one junior tournament. I don't think anyone's career revolved around it."

"What if you got disqualified?"

He frowned at me. "Why would we get disqualified?"

"Any number of reasons. Let's say for argument's sake you failed a drug test."

"Listen, mister. I don't know what you're getting at but I've never taken drugs in my life. And I don't need you spreading that kind of trash talk around. I might not play anymore, but I still have a reputation that's worth something."

"Okay, it's cool. Let's say it wasn't you, specifically. Let's assume one of your teammates."

"Who?"

"Hypothetically. Anyone."

"They'd do time, I guess."

"But they'd come back?"

"Maybe. Could do. Guys have served a couple years and come back."

"Girls?"

"You mean Shania? What do you think you know? She's clean, I guarantee it."

"I'm not saying she's not. But if one in the team went down, you'd all get disqualified, wouldn't you? Tainted with the same brush."

"Suppose. It would have hurt her."

"Why her?"

"It's harder for the women. Particularly then, with us just starting out. Expectations are higher for the women. Especially with the sponsors."

"How so?"

"You know. The sponsors expect them to be pure. Being a bad girl is cool and all, but it doesn't get you on a cereal box."

"So it would hurt Shania most of all."

"Probably. But this is hypothetical, right?"

"Of course."

"Is this something to do with Paul?"

"No. Paul just dropped something heavy on himself."

Sam looked at me like he wasn't buying it. Then Andrew Neville appeared between us.

"Gentleman, I have advised our guests that Chef will be serving late supper at 10 p.m. If you would like to take a rest in your room we will provide a wake-up call, or you may relax here in the lounge."

He didn't wait for questions, dashing away toward the kitchen. I swung around on my stool and watched the room. Ron offered me a nod as he and Cassandra headed out. Leon stood and wandered out, leaving Anton by himself with a drink. Shania had moved to sit with Deshawn, which made me think about Cassandra's summation of them.

I tossed around my options. I could stay at the bar. That wasn't going to happen without a beverage in my hand. And drinking too much in a hurricane was certainly a viable plan. I knew guys who had woken up with raging hangovers to find themselves under a mattress and the mattress under a collapsed roof, with no memory of the storm that raged through. But it really wasn't a percentage play.

I had woken that morning, sandbagged and prepped Longboard Kelly's for a battering, sandbagged my own house and then taken a dip in a raging torrent to fish a young woman out of the Intracoastal. I figured I could do with a power nap.

I made to say bye to Sam but he had resumed staring at his wine. He was in no danger of drinking too much at that pace, so I left him to his demons and headed for the fire stairs.

CHAPTER EIGHTEEN

There are few things in life as empty as an empty hotel room. Having concertina storm shutters pulled across the windows didn't help any. Neither did the howling wind that sounded like a freight train that ran on and on.
I took off my linen jacket and trousers and wandered into the bathroom to splash some water on my face. The lighting was not flattering. That was my theory and I was sticking to it. I toweled off and wandered back into the room. It was small but sumptuously appointed. The kind of place wealthy people came to escape the daily grind, the humdrum of life. To build memories, as the ads liked the say. As if the important moments, the ones that really stuck with you, only happened on a package vacation.
I flopped down on the bed. The sound of the driving wind was putting me on edge, roiling around in my soul, disturbing my chi. Or something like that. I missed Danielle. I had never had someone before that could truly be called part of me. But she was. Of that I had no doubt. And when part of you is missing it leaves one hell of a hole. Like the veteran who

scratches a leg that was lost years ago, the feeling left me restless.

I took out my phone and found I had no bars. No coverage. No one to talk to but the angels and devils in my mind. And those conversations rarely ended well. I set an alarm on my phone for a half hour. I wanted a nap, not a good night's sleep. I was a world champion napper. When you play minor league ball, you see a lot of down time. Long bus trips along boring interstates, rain delays in cold locker rooms. I learned to nap anywhere, anytime. I could probably have graduated with a degree in English literature with the time I spent napping, but I found the naps more useful.

Anything more than thirty minutes sent me into REM sleep, and coming back from that was a long, groggy process. I just needed to recharge my batteries so I could see the night through. The eye of the hurricane was just to the east, between us and the Bahamas, but the hotel was a solid structure so the whole thing was likely to be uneventful until the cleanup began. I woke up thirty minutes later to the sound of Sheryl Crow telling me something about Santa Monica Boulevard. I had been there once and traveled a mile in thirty minutes in the back of a super shuttle. Even South Dixie Highway in the middle of snowbird season moved quicker than that.

I checked my cell phone bars, still none, and washed my face again. My ears felt plugged, like a scuba diver, so I held my nose and blew and popped them. The wind still howled.

I dressed and wandered down to the bar. The check-in desk was vacant but the bar was not. Anton was perched on a stool, sitting over a brandy. He liked the hard stuff and could hold his liquor. He didn't seem to have left at all. His hair looked wet, but it always seemed to look that way so I wondered if he wore some kind of product in it. I took a stool at the other end of the bar. I had no desire for small talk with him. He didn't acknowledge my presence.

The door out to the kitchen swung open and Andrew Neville came out. He looked a little more flustered than usual. Not Black Friday shopper flustered, but he was patting down his hair and sighing. He saw me and collected himself in an instant.

"Mr. Jones, what can I offer you?"

"Coffee?"

"Just putting on a fresh pot now."

"Did everyone go for a nap?"

Neville shot a look at Anton. "Not everyone, sir."

Neville made a Bunn flask of coffee and then poured the coffee into a silver carafe, which I figured was one step too many. He brought the carafe to the bar and poured some into a delicate vessel that looked like Grandma's china. The coffee was strong and hot and tasted like the back end of a bus.

I sat and sipped my brew in the relative silence. The old building groaned. Ron and Cassandra wandered in, looking tired. They hadn't slept. They weren't world-class nappers. Not everyone plays professional baseball, or serves in the army.

"I can live without the sleep, Miami," said Cassandra, "but the sound of that infernal wind is getting under my skin."

I didn't think she was alone. Emery Taylor and Rosaria the maid came in. They both wore somber faces, as if the atmosphere were affecting their physical being. It was a deep train of thought for so late, and I made a mental note to check the research on that while simultaneously knowing I would do no such thing.

Emery gave me a smile that might have been a stunner in Manhattan but in Florida looked like a cloudy day. She told Neville that she had called all the rooms but had gotten no responses. Neville suggested a door knock. Emery took off to do that and Rosaria placed cups out for Cassandra and Ron. Ron took coffee, Cassandra hot tea.

Ronzoni wandered in. His hair was wet like he'd had a shower, or maybe just washed his head like me. He was back in his suit. Somewhere during the course of events Emery had found time to launder it. It looked new, like Ronzoni had just pulled it from the rack. He sat next to me at the bar and Neville poured him a coffee without asking, as if Ronzoni were a regular.

When Emery returned to the bar she told Neville she had gotten hold of Mr. Maxwell but no one else. Then Leon wandered in. He had wet hair but appeared to have forgotten his comb. He nodded at us but didn't approach the bar, preferring a club chair. Rosaria offered him coffee.

"I'm sure our remaining guests will be with us shortly," Neville said. "I'll ask Chef Dean to serve supper."

Ronzoni said to me, "You were with Venturi before. Did he say he was going to bed?"

"He was staring at his drink when I left," I said.

"Detective," said Emery. "I spoke to Mr. Venturi when I was at the front desk. Just after Miami went to his room. He was also going for a sleep. I suspect he's either just waking or was in the shower when I knocked."

"Who else is missing?" asked Ronzoni.

"Just Ms. Pastinak."

"She go for a sleep?"

"I didn't see her."

"Maybe she went for a hot tub," I said.

"Why would she do that?" asked Ronzoni.

"She was tense, said she wanted a massage but I didn't figure there was anyone in house to do it during a hurricane. So I suggested a hot tub."

"I don't think so," said Emery.

"Have you taken a hot tub?" asked Ronzoni.

"Not lately," I said.

"But you told her to take one?"

"She was finding solace in the bottom of a cocktail glass, and although I can advocate for that now and again, I didn't think she was going to end up in a good place. Hot tubs don't usually leave you waking up in the morning full of regrets."

Ronzoni looked at Emery. "You have a hot tub?"

"We have two," said Emery. "But I don't think she took a hot tub."

"Why?"

"Because the hot tubs are outside."

CHAPTER NINETEEN

Emery explained that there were two hot tubs. One was outside on the pool deck. The second was in a purpose-built hut on the far side of the pool. But both were accessed via the pool deck, which itself was accessed by the lobby doors, which were locked tight.

"Or the south emergency exit," I said. "That's how Ron and I got back in after putting up the shutters around the gym."

Ronzoni shrugged. "No one is going out for a hot tub in this weather."

"Not sober," I said, looking at Emery.

She got my point. "Perhaps I'll knock on her door one more time."

"Do more than knock."

Emery left and Ronzoni and I sipped our coffee. He was right. No one took a hot tub in a hurricane. Except in Florida. Between spring breakers, alcohol and humidity there was no shortage of people stupid enough to do pretty much anything. But I didn't put Carly Pastinak in that company.

Emery came back alone.

"I went into her room. She's not there."

Ronzoni shifted in his seat. I knew where his mind was headed. He'd just gotten his suit back all nice and pressed, and he didn't fancy going outside for no good reason at all.

"She might have gone for a walk," he said.

"Walk where?" I asked him. "Around the gardens?"

"Maybe she had a nap and is on her way down."

"Detective, her bed hasn't been slept in. It doesn't appear to have even been laid upon."

Ronzoni's shoulders sagged. He knew he was going to have to go have a look and he knew it was pointless, and he knew he was going to get drenched again. I should have felt sorry for him. But I didn't.

"All right," he said. "Let's go have a look." He slipped off his stool and looked at me.

"What?" I said.

"You're coming, hotshot."

"This really sounds like police business."

"You told her to take a damned hot tub, so you're coming."

I shook my head in vain and slipped off my stool. We walked out into the lobby and headed toward the south end of the building. Emery came out to the lobby with us and then walked in the opposite direction. I wanted to follow her. I was no more keen to get drenched all over again than Ronzoni was.

We walked across the lobby and down the corridor, and we both glanced at the frosted glass on the gym as we passed. We reached the end of the line at the heavy emergency exit door. We could hear the wind pounding the landscaped palms on the other side.

"Where's this hot tub?" asked Ronzoni.

"I have no idea."

"You don't even know where it is?"

"No. Deshawn mentioned it when Ron and I were putting up the shutters in the gym. I mentioned it to Carly. But I haven't seen it."

"Well, I'm not wandering around the grounds looking for it," he said.

He had my full agreement on that.

Emery strode up behind us. "Here," she said, passing each of us a small plastic packet. Disposable rain ponchos. The kind of lightweight item that one wears at a football game instead of cutting holes in a trash bag.

"Where are these hot tubs?" asked Ronzoni.

"One is on the pool deck, at the far end of the pool. Go to the right. The other is in the spa hut, around to the left. You'll need a key card to get in."

Ronzoni shook his head. "All right. You take the right, I'll take the left."

"Why do you get the indoor one?"

"You think I'm gonna stay nice and dry?"

I shrugged.

We opened the ponchos. Mine was green, Ronzoni's was pink. He took off his jacket and slipped the poncho on over the top of his shirt. I wasn't so confident in the qualities of thin plastic, so I handed my jacket to Emery, and then slipped off my trousers and shirt.

Ronzoni frowned. "Do you mind, Jones?"

"I mind a lot, but you're making me do it anyway." I shot Emery a wink and pulled the thin poncho over my head. It wasn't see-through, but it wasn't far off it, and I was glad I had worn sensible underwear.

"Sirs," said Emery, offering us each a rubber-encased flashlight. We took the flashlights and put our shoulders into the door. Ronzoni nodded and we drove forward. The door was one of those heavy items that took rhinoceros strength to open on a fine day. With a hurricane-force wind pushing it closed it took considerably more doing.

Unfortunately we got there. The door opened and we were hit by rain that stung the skin. Ronzoni broke left. He looked like a vertical puddle as his pink poncho expanded like a sail. I turned and ran the other way. The pool deck was well lit so the flashlight was superfluous, and I dashed around the thrashing water. There were practically white caps in the pool. The area was surrounded by landscaped palms that did close to zero in stopping the wind. What I really needed was those mangroves. But I pushed on around to the far end of the pool.

Beyond the deep end I could see what I assumed was a palapa-style pool bar, locked up tight. Palm fronds had been blown from it, leaving an unromantic but practical cinderblock skeleton. Between the bar and the pool was a darkened circle of water. It wasn't large, enough for maybe twenty people if they knew each other very well. I bent over against the wind and stepped to the hot tub. There was nothing hot about it. It was dark and angry. And it was empty. If we were on Daytona Beach I would have taken good odds on there being a kid or two in the hot tub, riding out the hurricane with a bottle of Captain Morgan. But this was Palm Beach, and The Mornington. These folks reconsidered a visit to the pool if a cloud drifted across the sky. But I was out in the driving rain, and I was drenched to the bone again, so I figured I might as well double-check. So I did. I stepped into the hot tub, which as expected was anything but, and I did a circuit. I couldn't see the bottom but I did a full lap to confirm there was nothing and nobody in the water.

I stepped out and looked toward the beach. Beyond the bank of light washing across the pool deck I made out the silhouette of a small hut-like building. I suspected like the bar it would have been designed to look like a palapa. Beyond the hut there was nothing. Just swirling, heaving darkness. And from the darkness I saw the light.

It was a point of light. The doorway to the hot tub hut was my guess. I took off toward it. The wind tried to dunk me in the pool but a bank of palmettos enabled me to run relatively unaffected. I ran around the pool and toward the hut. Like the pool bar, the hut had been stripped naked, its gruesome cinderblock underbelly exposed. I kept going until I got to the door, which had been blown open against the wall.

Then I stopped.

The hut wasn't anywhere near as romantic as a palapa hut on the inside. It was painted cinderblock. The hot tub bubbled away, white foam forming across the surface and the scent of chlorine heavy in the air. Posters detailing the maximum number of occupants and how to perform CPR covered the walls. Ronzoni didn't need the posters. He was trained in CPR. I knew this because he looked like he knew what he was doing as he pumped on Carly Pastinak's chest. He had clearly pulled her from the water. She was in a black one-piece bathing suit, her hair splayed across the concrete floor like spilled milk. Ronzoni was pumping with two hands on her chest. He was doing it hard, hard enough to do some damage. He was counting in shallow breaths, pumping fast like he was inflating a mattress, and then stopped and put his ear to Carly's mouth. He tilted her head back and raised her chin, and then pinched her nose and put his mouth to hers, and he blew.

Her chest rose and I waited for the coughing up of water, but it didn't happen. It was Ronzoni's air. He blew again and her wet chest rose and fell. Ronzoni pushed up onto his knees and he glanced at me in the doorway. He yelled as he began pumping on her chest again.

"911," he said.

I patted my thighs unhelpfully. My phone was in my trouser pocket and my trousers were inside the hotel.

"You got a phone?"

"No bars. Inside," he panted.

I ran. I sprinted across the pool deck like a crab, two steps forward, one step sideways. I got to the emergency door and pulled hard. At first it didn't come, and then it came fast. Emery Taylor was on the other side pushing with her back. I fell inside, a mess of water and cheap plastic.

"911," I said, gulping deep breaths.

"What happened?" she asked.

"911!" I yelled.

She got it the second time and took off along the corridor. I gathered myself some and followed. I ran down the corridor and out into the lobby. The marble floors were like an ice rink and I skidded right past the desk.

Emery held the phone in her hand and was hitting the return in frustration.

"What?" I gasped.

"No phone."

"What?"

"The phones are down." She ran into Neville's office and then reappeared. "Router's down. The Internet's down."

"I don't want to watch cat videos. We need paramedics."

"That's what I'm saying. The phone system is IP-based. It comes through our Internet provider. The whole system's down."

"How?"

She held her hands and out. "Er, hurricane?" It was more sarcasm than I was used to seeing at The Mornington, but I let it slide.

"You got a defib kit?"

"An AED? Yes, in the gym."

We ran back down the corridor and reached the frosted glass of the gym. Emery dropped to her knees and fished out a key to unlock the door. She looked up at me with a face that said she had already seen the dead man in the gym and she didn't want to go through that again.

"Where is it?"

"On the wall, just along from the water cooler."

I stepped inside. It was dark and moist. Paul Zidane lay on the bench under the sheet. I turned away from him and found the cabinet on the wall. I grabbed it and took off, leaping over Emery, who was still kneeling on the floor.

The wind buffeted me the other way as I ran back, two steps sideways and one forward. I reached the doorway and stumbled through. It was quieter. The hot tub had given up bubbling, and above the sound of the wind Ronzoni was puffing heavily, still pressing up and down on Carly's chest.

"No paramedics," I said.

Ronzoni didn't respond. I assumed he had figured there might not be any help coming in the middle of a hurricane. He kept pumping.

"But I found a defib kit."

Ronzoni looked up at that but he kept pumping steadily.

"Get it over here." He pointed to the side of the room. "Come around that way. Stay away from the hot tub."

I came around the wall and dropped down and opened the kit. It looked like a portable air compressor. I knew it packed a lot more punch than that. Ronzoni finished his round of CPR and then heaved two more deep breaths into Carly.

He took the kit from me. He turned it on and then took out two thin pads attached by wires to the unit. The unit spoke to us in a calm female voice.

"Apply pads to patient's bare chest. Apply pads to patient's bare chest."

Ronzoni put his hands on Carly's shoulders and hesitated for a moment. He looked almost apologetic. Then he grabbed the straps and pulled her swimsuit down. It peeled off her like a banana skin.

"Is there a towel?"

It was a 5-star hotel. There was a towel service. I grabbed a rolled towel from the rack and tossed it to Ronzoni. He pulled Carly's swimsuit down to her navel, and then he dried her chest and left side with the towel. He took one of the pads and removed the backing and stuck it on Carly's chest above her right breast. Then he took the second pad and stuck in on her left side below her armpit.

Then he pushed back on his knees and waited. The woman in the machine said she was analyzing and we should not touch the patient. It seemed to take forever but was only about ten seconds. Then the voice told us that she advised that shock was required, and that she was charging, and we should stand clear.

"Get back," said Ronzoni. "Out of the water."

I took a step back from the puddle surrounding Carly. So did Ronzoni. Then the woman in the machine told us she was going to shock. And she did. Carly's body jolted like she was having a bad dream. Not a huge movement, but enough to give hope. The voice told us it was analyzing and then it said that no pulse was detected and we should administer CPR. Ronzoni got back over Carly and pumped her chest again, counting to himself.

The machine recharged and we did it all over again. Nothing. Ronzoni kept going. Then a face appeared. It was Emery.

"Oh, no," she gasped. I stood and ran around the edge of the room and she grabbed me and buried her face into my chest. She had already discovered one dead body today. Another guest on the verge of death was too much. Her arms gripped me like she was hanging from a cliff, but her legs did the opposite. They simply gave way. I picked her up and held her between myself and the wall. She was wet to the bone.

"I need you to go back inside and keep trying the phones. See if anyone has cell coverage."

I might as well have been asking the cinderblock for help. Emery had checked out for the evening. She stopped sobbing but I didn't take that as a good sign.

Another body appeared in the doorway. Deshawn Maxwell stood before me. The rainwater was pouring off his bald head. He was in training gear, as usual. I wondered if that was what he used for pajamas. He took me in, and then Emery. It didn't make sense to him until he saw Ronzoni on the floor over Carly.

"Oh, man," he said, stepping into the room.

"Don't come in," I said.

"I can help. I'm trained."

"Then use your training to help her," I said, nodding toward the catatonic woman in my arms.

Deshawn hesitated, and then he swept Emery up in his arms. He was a strong guy, and Emery no kind of burden. He backed out into the rain and took off steadily across the pool deck. I watched him stride toward the hotel and was about to turn back to Ronzoni when I saw the south door open. A crowd was gathering. We didn't need more people wandering around in a hurricane, so I took off across the pool deck.

I ran into Sam Venturi. I didn't see him coming and I was bigger than he was. When I had played football at college I had been the backup quarterback. That made me one of the smallest guys on the team. But compared to regular people even quarterbacks are big. Sam and I collided like trains in the night. Only one was a freight train and the other was Thomas the Tank Engine. Sam hit me and rebounded into the pool.

He flapped around for a bit and then started yelling at me.

"Get out of the damned pool," I yelled back, and I bent down to help him. He wasn't keen on the help. He dragged himself out of the water. It didn't make much difference. The volume of water outside the pool wasn't much less. I grabbed him by the t-shirt and dragged him across the pool deck toward the emergency exit. He was wearing shorts that I assumed were now considered tennis shorts but looked like something you might wear to the beach. When I was a kid tennis gear was white. That's how you knew it was tennis gear.

I pushed Sam in through the door and he turned on me.

"What do you think you're doing?" he said.

"Shut it, Sam. I don't have time." I turned to the group. Shania had appeared. Leon was there. Ron stood at the back with Cassandra, helping Deshawn revive the spent Emery.

"It's Carly. She was in the hot tub."

"Is she all right?" asked Shania.

"Detective Ronzoni is performing CPR. What I need from you is to stay in here. We don't need people out in a hurricane getting hurt."

"We can help," she said.

"Help by staying put. Seriously. You're only putting others in danger if you go out there."

Shania didn't look convinced but she didn't say any more.

"Okay?" I said to Sam. He had redeveloped the pallor he had exhibited on Bingham Island. He nodded his bowed head but said nothing more.

"I'll be back shortly. Seriously. Stay put."

Leon said, "You aren't the cops, man. You can't tell us what to do."

"Well, let me put it this way. Anyone who's a tennis player comes through this door, I will break your damned fingers. Both hands. Man or woman, I care not. And you," I turned on Leon. "You're a sommelier? I'll just break your damned nose."

I didn't wait for further discussion. I pushed back out the door and heard it slam home as I dashed across the pool deck. I knew I had probably been a bit harsh but I was soaked to my core for the umpteenth time today and I had a bad feeling that I had suggested the very thing that had led to Carly Pastinak's death. Which put me two for two as far as people dying on my word since lunch. I pushed the thought away as I reached the hut.

Ronzoni was still going. I didn't think he had it in him. I've heard about people getting superhuman strength under intense pressure, like a mother lifting a car off her crushed son. Maybe that was just urban legend. But Ronzoni was the real deal. He was going hard, and he wasn't giving up.

I made him give up. Another forty minutes, after I had subbed in for him on the CPR, and the voice in the AED machine had become fatalistic, I called it. To his credit Ronzoni didn't want to. It took three more rounds before he sat back from Carly's body and for him to collapse to the floor. I let him lie there for a while. In his wet poncho he looked like discarded fruit from the grocery. We both stared at the hot tub for the longest time.

Neither of us wanted to look at Carly, and for reasons I couldn't fathom we didn't want to look at each other either.
Eventually we did. I got onto my hands and knees and moved to Carly. I didn't remove the electrode pads from her chest, but I felt she deserved some modesty, so I leaned over and glanced at Ronzoni. He nodded, and I pulled her bathing suit up to her shoulders.
"Two accidental deaths in one day," I said. "This group is cursed."
Ronzoni shook his head with his last ounce of energy. "No."
"No? If this isn't cursed I'd hate to see what is."
"Not an accident."
I gave him my full frontal frown. "Explain?"
He nodded to the other side of the hot tub. A champagne bottle sat on the edge, with a single glass.
"She liked a drink," I said. "Some folks do drink alone."
Ronzoni shook his head again.
"Wet footprints," he mumbled. "Too large to be the victim. And they can't be hers anyway."
"Why?"
"Because they're leaving."

CHAPTER TWENTY

I went back to tell everyone the news. I struggled across the pool deck with no sense of urgency. Something that resembled the remains of a deck chair flew past my head and barely earned a glance.

To say the mood was somber was to do the mood a disservice. Everyone had gathered in the lounge. Most were wrapped in blankets, but not the kind you get on airlines. Chef Dean stood with Neville behind the bar. There was a lot of brandy flowing. I shook my head. "She didn't make it."

There were some gasps and howls. But no one cried. Shania looked like stone. Sam looked like porcelain. Emery had left crying behind and had ventured into previously uncharted emotional territory. She stared into an alternate dimension. Cassandra came close to tears but she was one of those stoic people they don't seem to make many of anymore. The kind that live through wars without complaint. She was more focused on Emery than anything I had to say.

"What happened?" asked Neville. "What on earth was she doing out there?"

"I don't know," I said. "Having a soak. But why out there, in this weather? I can't say."

"You told her to do it," said Sam. "You told her to go out there."

"No, I didn't."

"You're a liar. You told me you told her to have a hot tub."

"I did suggest a hot tub. I certainly didn't suggest going outside in a hurricane. I had no idea where the hot tub was."

"You say that now," said Sam.

"No, I said that then. To you. And her. I suggested she ask Deshawn where it was."

"Me?" Deshawn frowned but he wasn't that wrinkly. "She didn't ask me anything."

"Then she asked someone."

"What happens now?" asked Shania.

"Now you all stay here. Detective Ronzoni has asked that everyone remain in this room for your own safety until he says otherwise."

"We paid for rooms," said Anton. He was finally sitting next to his fiancé.

I wanted to tell him he wouldn't know where his room was, since he'd barely left the bar, but I didn't.

"I'm sure the hotel will fix you up. But we've lost two people today. Let's not lose any more. Stay put. We'll be back shortly. Ron"—I looked to my right hand man—"anyone moves, shoot them."

Ron nodded like he would, despite not even owning, let alone carrying, a gun.

I asked the chef for some plastic baggies. Then I suggested to Neville that some food be brought out, and the chef recommended sandwich rounds for such an occasion. I'm not sure how he classified the occasion exactly, but I didn't think anyone looked up for a slab of porterhouse steak.

Ronzoni was down on his knees on the opposite side of the hot tub when I got back. He had placed a foldaway ruler by a wet footprint and was taking pictures of it. I wasn't sure where he kept the ruler, but maybe that explained why he preferred a suit to shorts. Lots more pockets, and less obvious than Batman's utility belt.

He asked me to shine a flashlight at a forty-five degree angle to highlight the footprint better in his shot and then he stood and pointed to the door.

"Two sets of prints come in here. One significantly smaller than the other. I'll bet they'll match the victim. We made a mess of the scene here," he said pointing to the pool of water we had created around Carly's body. "But we can assume the two sets of prints got in the tub, here." He pointed at the tub. "Then here." He turned to where he had just been kneeling, where the champagne bottle sat. "One set of footprints gets out. The larger set. And they walk out here." He pointed along the floor to the door.

"They might have been here before."

"In this humidity prints will last, that's for sure," said Ronzoni. "But she wasn't alone."

"I appreciate what you're doing, Detective. I suggested she take a hot tub, and now she's dead. Yes, she was drinking and it probably wasn't the wisest suggestion in the circumstances, but I don't see that it's my fault. Really."

"First of all, Jones, I don't care if you think it's your fault. How your brain works is beyond me. Trust me on that. And I'm not buying it anyway. You might have suggested it, but you didn't make her come out here and you ain't her daddy. But I know you're gonna beat yourself up about it anyway, regardless of what I say. So I'm not saying nothing about it. That's your problem."

"Thanks, Ronzoni, you're a peach. But people do drink in hot tubs and fall into comas and drown. It happens. This is Florida."

"I know it happens, Jones. I've seen it. Folks just fall asleep and slip right under. It's crazy but it's true."

"So how do we know that didn't happen here?"

"Because folks don't fall asleep with their eyes open."

I looked across the tub at Carly. "Hers eyes weren't open."

"They were when I pulled her out of the water."

He gave me a moment to process that and then he said, "Come with me."

We edged around the hut, I now realized in an attempt to preserve the integrity of the scene, and we kneeled by the body. Ronzoni put his hands to Carly's face and I noticed that he had put on latex gloves in my absence. He used his finger to delicately pull back Carly's eyelid.

Her eye looked like she had been on the world's biggest bender and was now dealing with the world's biggest hangover. It wasn't just red. Blood vessels had literally exploded in there. I had seen her eyes when she was alive. Mediterranean blue was what I had thought. The blue was gone. Her eye looked like an old Rand McNally roadmap, but all the roads were red.

Ronzoni dropped the eyelid. "You know what that means?"

I nodded. I hadn't been to the police academy, but I had done a postgrad program in criminology. It was generally useless to me, but I'd picked up a thing or two, mostly on field trips.

"Trauma."

"Major league," he said. "She drowned all right, but she didn't drown nice. Sure as hell not in her sleep."

"Someone held her down there."

He nodded gravely.

"You see any evidence of that on her?"

We both looked at the body. Ronzoni said, "I probably did a bit of damage to her torso during CPR, but given the blood flow had ceased there'll be minimal bruising. But I didn't do that." He pointed his gloved finger at her upper arm. Across her bicep a ribbon of bruising had developed prior to death. Ronzoni pointed to the matching ribbon on the other arm.

"Someone pinned her down," I said.

"The ME would have to confirm, but my guess is they pinned her down by kneeling on her arms."

"She's pretty fit. Was pretty fit. How does she end up under water like that without a fight?"

"Too easy," said Ronzoni, standing. His stretched out his back. He'd been on his knees for the best part of an hour. "How do two people sit in a hot tub?"

"Depends how friendly they are."

Ronzoni shook his head. "People who aren't that friendly, Jones."

"More or less opposite each other. Slightly off center. Say, twelve and five on the clock."

"Right. So if I just reach down and pull your feet"—he mocked with a yanking motion, pulling toward himself—"the person would just slide right in. Nothing to grab, no way to stop it. Then you're on the bottom, pinned down—"

"I get the picture, Ronzoni."

He nodded and sighed loudly.

"We need something to collect the evidence," he said.

I pulled out the plastic baggies from under my poncho. Ronzoni nodded like I wasn't a complete waste of oxygen. I left the evidence collection to him. It was a chain of custody thing, and I didn't look forward to wasting a day in the courthouse to be part of it, despite the county courthouse being across the parking lot from my office. He inspected a light teal-colored cloth against the wall near Carly. Some kind of light shawl or sarong to wear over her swimsuit. He left it where it was. He bagged and tagged the champagne bottle and the glass.

"Where's the second glass?" I asked.

"Maybe there isn't one."

"She's in the tub with a friend but not too close a friend, and they're not both into the champagne?"

"It's possible she didn't know the perp."

"It's possible the governor is going to send me an invite to his Christmas party, but the sun exploding is more likely."

Ronzoni shrugged.

"She knew them. We're in the middle of a hurricane. The other option is someone was just out in this weather and happened upon her here, and she was okay with them getting in the tub."

"Okay. You're right, she probably knew them."

"So where's the glass?"

"They took it. It's got their fingerprints on it."

"Maybe the bottle does, too."

"That's why we collect the evidence, Jones."

Ronzoni took a bunch more shots of the scene and then made some notes in his phone. I stood waiting, trying not to look at Carly Pastinak. Trying not to listen to the guttural howl of the wind. Like Cassandra, it was starting to get under my skin. I busied myself staring at the walls, at the CPR posters. Then I saw something interesting. I wandered over to it.

It was a timer box, the kind of dial that you turn and that then ticks back toward the off position. The exact thing you find on hot tubs all over the world. At one end of the scale was a zero, the off position. At the other end, a thirty. Thirty minutes max of bubble time. Enough time to boil a lobster, or kill a woman.

"The jets were on when I came in."

Ronzoni looked up from his phone. "Yes. They were on when I pulled her out. I had to stand right over the tub to see her in there under the bubbles."

"But it wasn't on when I came back with the defib unit."

Ronzoni thought for a second. "No, it went off."

"You know when?"

"No, I was focused elsewhere."

"Sure, of course. But I was gone what, two, three minutes max?"

"Max."

"And how long were you in here before I came across from the other hot tub?"

"Same, maybe a bit more. Three, four minutes?"

"So let's say minimum five, maximum seven minutes total. So if someone turned this dial on as they left, they only left a maximum of twenty-five and a minimum of twenty-three minutes before you came in."

Ronzoni nodded. "Not bad, Jones."

"That's assuming they turned it as they left."

"If it was on while they were in the tub, it could have been less. We could have missed them by seconds."

"Maybe. But I'm thinking. Who was unaccounted for in the twenty minutes before we came out?"

"For a period, almost everyone."

"Expect maybe Anton Ribaud," I said. "He was at the bar."

"Did his hair look wet to you?"

"His hair always looks wet to me."

"Is that a thing?"

"Not in my house. If my hair looks wet it's 'cause I went for a swim."

"Or got caught in a hurricane."

I nodded.

Ronzoni said, "Who came down to the bar before me?"

"Ron, Cassandra. Emery Taylor and Rosaria."

"And then after I came down, that Leon guy. Who also had wet hair."

"He might have taken a shower to wake up," I said.

"Not saying he didn't, just putting it out there."

"But we didn't see Shania, Deshawn or Sam. They all ran out after I went back in with Emery."

"So basically everyone but Anton?"

I shrugged. "And I didn't see the cook."

"The manager, Neville, said he would talk to the chef about supper. He didn't mention him not being in the kitchen."

"No, and he's there now."

Ronzoni collected his bagged evidence and said, "Let's get out of here."

"What about . . ." I nodded at Carly Pastinak.

"Best we leave her here. We can lock it up, and if there's any physical evidence on her it will get washed away if we try to move her inside."

"Should we cover her up?"

Ronzoni looked at her. He looked sad. I'd never seen him look sad before. Dumbfounded yes, but never sad. I knew he'd seen dead bodies before. He'd seen one with me. Another young woman, lost too young to some monster. And it hadn't seemed to faze him. I figured cops had to get desensitized to that stuff in order to function in their jobs. It had never occurred to me that he could react like a human. But I'd never seen him look more human. He wasn't on the verge of tears or anything, but often tears are like window dressing. True sadness is something much more profound. And he wore it across his face like a mask.

I didn't speak. I let the wind caterwaul and Ronzoni look. And then he came back and he shook his head.

"You covered her enough. She's beyond caring now. Better to preserve the scene. The ME's people will take care of it when they're done."

So we flicked off the light and heaved the door around and slammed it shut. We ran across the pool deck to the south exit. Someone had left a towel wedged in the door so we could open it more easily, and I thanked Ron for that. We stepped inside and shook off like ragged dogs. Ronzoni peeled off his poncho. He had jumped into the hot tub so he was drenched through despite it. My clothes were gone from the corridor so I left my poncho on. We looked at the darkened gym as we passed and I gave Ronzoni a look that he didn't return.

CHAPTER TWENTY-ONE

Ronzoni sent me in to get a set of keys from Neville. He waited by the check-in desk so he didn't show off the evidence he was carrying. I got the keys and we went back to the gym, and after some trial and error I unlocked the door and Ronzoni stashed the evidence inside. Then I locked up and handed him the keys. He looked at me in my poncho as if he were mulling something over.
"Your clothes are at the front desk, by the way."
I nodded. "You weren't going to tell me, were you?"
"You look good in a poncho, Jones."
"You look like a drowned rat."
"I'm going to change."
He left me at the check-in desk and dashed up the stairs to his room. It wasn't completely fair that everyone else was left sitting in their wet clothes in the bar, but then I figured Ronzoni wasn't a murder suspect. I collected my suit, which was hanging across the back of a chair, lest it get creased, and then I went to the lobby bathroom and toweled off. That's the thing about fancy hotels. The bathroom hand towels are actually towels, not minuscule pieces of non-absorbent paper. When I was dry I got dressed and returned to the lounge.

Deshawn Maxwell was standing near the door. He was practically dry. That was the advantage of wearing athlete gear all the time. It really wicked the moisture away.

"What the hell is going on?" he said in a half whisper.

"You tell me."

"What does that mean?"

"I had no idea where the hot tub was. I sent her to you."

"I told you, she didn't ask me."

"But you used the hot tub earlier?"

"No."

"You told us you were headed for a soak when you left the gym today."

"No. Yes. I said that, but I didn't go. I changed my mind."

"What did you do?"

"I just went to my room."

I remembered seeing him on the video. He came down the corridor from the gym, said hi to Emery at the desk and then walked north across the lobby and out of shot. Which gave me an idea. I didn't get to play it out because Ronzoni walked in. He was back in his Filipino presidential outfit. It would have looked good on some people. Ronzoni wasn't any of them.

He directed Deshawn into the lounge and looked around the room. It looked like a refugee camp for billionaires. He took his time looking at every face. I wasn't sure what he was expecting to see. Perhaps a flinch, a tell. Someone to yell I can't take it anymore, it was me, it was me! None of that happened. Shania was the first to break the silence.

"Is someone going to tell us what on earth is happening?"

Ronzoni paused. He had a flair for the dramatic that I hadn't given him credit for.

"Yes, Miss Dawson. One of your party is dead."

There was none of the shocked wails that Ronzoni might have expected. I had stolen his thunder on that count.

"One," Shania said. "Try two."

"Yes, two."

"And you're telling me that's a coincidence?"

"No, ma'am, I don't believe so."

That got a ripple of interest and some shared glances.

"What does that mean?" asked Leon.

"It means that Ms. Pastinak has drowned. It is possible that it wasn't an accident."

"Wait," said Neville. "Are you suggesting, sir, that someone killed her?"

"That would be the inference."

"Who?" he asked.

"That would be the question."

"But I mean, you think it was someone in this hotel?"

"Quite possibly."

"You mean someone in this room?"

"Yes, Mr. Neville."

Now the mood got interesting. Nothing like suggesting one among you is a murderer to shake up a bachelor party.

"Are you serious?" asked Deshawn. He had taken a seat next to Shania on a sofa. Anton sat on her other side.

I thought Ronzoni might say deadly in response, but all he said was yes.

The chef wandered out with a platter of sandwiches and placed them loudly on the counter of the bar. The slap of tray on stone turned every head. The chef gave a look like he didn't know what everyone's problem was.

"As a result I am sure you will understand when I say that I must insist that you all remain in this room for the rest of the night."

There were moans and complaints but they were half-hearted. I didn't think anyone liked the idea of a killer in the room, but they liked the idea of a killer roaming the hotel even less.

Anton said, "And if we don't want to stay in this room? You cannot make us do it."

"Actually, Mr. Ribaud, I can make you. We're in the middle of a hurricane. Don't make me arrest you. You won't be very comfortable handcuffed in the manager's office."

That quashed that little rebellion. This wasn't Ronzoni's first time at the rodeo.

"What about fresh clothes and blankets?" asked Cassandra.

"And pillows," said Sam.

"We'll sort those out shortly," said Ronzoni. "Please eat if you like." He looked at Neville. "Mr. Neville, I would ask that no further alcohol be served, as a matter of safety."

"As you wish, Detective."

"But brandy is good for the nerves," said Anton.

"So is green tea," said Ronzoni. "Drink all of that you want."

Ronzoni left Anton to mull that concept over and turned to me. I was about to tell him that we needed to go and look at the security video but he didn't let me.

"Come with me," he said.

CHAPTER TWENTY—TWO

Ronzoni led me to the general manager's office behind the check-in desk. Great minds think alike and sometimes so do Ronzoni and I. He sat in the chair and fired up the computer attached to the security system. Computers weren't Ronzoni's strong point. I was pretty sure I knew what he wanted to see because I wanted to see it too, but I stopped him before he lost his cool and tossed the computer onto the floor.
"Before you do that, just watch the damned screen, will you?"
Ronzoni turned his eyes to the bank of screens. There was nothing happening.
"What?"
"Just watch," I said, and I walked out.
I walked around the check-in desk and out into the lobby. There I turned back on myself and wandered toward the corridor that led to the gym. I walked down the corridor and stopped just before the frosted glass of the gym. And I turned away from it. It was the door on the other side of the corridor I was interested in. I pushed it open and found myself surrounded by the bare concrete of fire stairs. The concrete

hadn't been painted. The steel balustrade was painted sky blue, which gave the space a feel somewhere between a daycare and a prison. I strode up the stairs and came out on the mezzanine level, closing the door gently. Stenciled on it was the word stairs. The same word didn't appear on the door in the gym corridor. I figured most people didn't run up in case of a fire.

The stairs were directly behind the ballroom where Shania and Sam had set up their tennis facility. The walls of the ballroom were actually mostly doors that looked like walls, designed to offer maximum flexibility in the use of the space. I found one that was open and slipped inside. It was dark. Really dark. Without vision my hearing kicked into overdrive and the sound of the storm outside focused in. The only light came from a red exit sign above the nominated door on the opposite side of the room. I didn't go straight for it. I knew there were dining tables set up like mines right across the space, so I stuck to the walls and edged around the large room until I reached the door. There I stepped out into the corridor. It was bright after the dark ballroom. I slid around the outside of the ballroom, back into the little coffee break space where I had spoken to Shania earlier in the day. Then I followed the line of windows along the beach side of the building until I reached another elevator and another door.

The elevator needed a key card to operate. The door next to the elevator didn't say stairs. It didn't say anything. But I was fairly certain I knew what it was. I pushed it open and found myself in more stairs. The same concrete and sky blue steel. I wandered down until I reached the ground floor and I came out in a corridor of taupe and linoleum. This was not an area for guests. But I had been there before. I figured one way led toward the kitchen. The other way led to the laundry, where I had gotten my linen suit. I followed that path, and wound around until I came back out into the retail space in the hotel at the north end of the building. The shops were closed and dark. I walked south toward the lobby, past the bar, or the lounge as Neville would have me call it, and returned to the general manager's office.

"Okay," said Ronzoni. "Now you're gonna tell me how, right?"

"What did you see?"

"You went out toward the gym. Then you appeared in the lobby in the camera above the lounge door. In-between times I didn't see you at all. So how?"

"The security video is full of holes. It might be more accurate to say it's all holes with a couple of spots covered by video."

"What's the point?"

"I'm guessing they want to land somewhere between security and privacy. They cover the main common areas but not much else."

"Right, I get it. But how did you go from the south end to the north end? I've got video here of every elevator lobby on every floor."

I told him about the stairs near the gym and the stairs at the other end that came out near the laundry. I told him about the ballroom.

"So what are all these stairs?"

"The ones at the south end are nothing more than fire stairs. They're marked as such on the higher floors. I suppose there's no video because no one ever uses them."

"And the other ones?"

"I think they're staff stairs. You know, like the old Upstairs Downstairs thing. The help have their own hidden stairs and a service elevator so they can move around the hotel without the guests ever having to lay eyes on them."

"I don't see why they can't just use the same elevator as everyone else."

"In the kinds of hotels you and I stay in, Ronzoni, they do. But this ain't that. This is a cut above. Probably two cuts above. It harshes one's mellow to have a maid and her trolley in the elevator with you."

"So basically anyone could go down to the mezzanine floor and move around the hotel without being seen."

"They could. But remember, the elevators have a small lobby on every floor, and you said yourself those lobbies all have video surveillance."

"So someone's using the stairs."

"Right."

I told Ronzoni to get out of the driver's seat because it was too painful to watch him operate computer equipment. I was no Steve Wozniak myself, but I knew more than Ronzoni. I clicked around, following what I recalled from when Emery Taylor had operated the machine before. It worked more or less like a cable company DVR, which I didn't have but I had seen before at Longboard's. After a couple false starts I got the video to where I wanted it.

Carly Pastinak comes out of the stairs beside the lobby elevator. She is wearing a black one-piece swimsuit with a thin sarong over the top. No shoes. She walks like a ballerina—tall, head held high, light on her toes. Carly turns to the gym corridor and reaches the check-in desk, where she stops. She turns. Anton Ribaud appears from the men's lobby bathroom. He doesn't walk like a ballerina. He is unsteady, clearly feeling the effects of the absinthe and brandy and whatever else he has been drinking. He stumbles over to Carly. They talk. The picture is nowhere near high-definition, so their lips are too fuzzy to read. Then Anton shrugs. His signature move. He wanders away toward the lounge. Carly stands for moment, not watching him. Perhaps just thinking. Then she turns on her toes and floats across the lobby toward the corridor. Toward the gym, and the south exit, and the hot tub. Toward the end.

We watched the video after Carly was lost from view up the corridor, but no one else appeared. No one came out of the stairs. No one went up the corridor. But I knew Ronzoni was thinking what I was thinking. Did someone use the stairs opposite the gym? Did they meet her out there?

We watched for a while longer and saw nothing of interest. Then Ronzoni tapped the back of the chair.

"Show me how to drive this thing, Jones."

"Why?"

"Because I want to account for everyone's movements. As much as we can."

"I can work it for you."

"No. I want you to go back to the bar. I don't like the idea of so many suspects being there alone."

"Ron's there."

"Even so."

I nodded. He was right—it made sense. I was a little taken aback that he thought me capable of substituting for him in the lounge. I felt like a deputy. Except that was the sheriff, not the police. And that was Danielle's job. Except now it wasn't. It seemed everyone's position on the totem was shifting.

"Okay, Ronzoni. It works like this."

We both focused on the computer screen.

And then our entire world went pitch-black.

CHAPTER TWENTY-THREE

Most people in the world live in cities, and cities give off a lot of light. You can see it in those photos from the space shuttle, looking back at the earth at night, a million little lights all becoming one. It's a lot of light pollution. So much so that even the Milky Way gets blanketed out in our night sky. Most of us never experience true darkness.

Ronzoni and I got a good dose of it. The small office was plunged into black. The computers shut down, the lights went off, the hum of the electricity through the walls died. For a moment we had nothing but the high-pitched moan of the wind and the trees and the sound of our breathing. Then Ronzoni spoke.

"What the hell did you do?"

"Relax, Ronzoni. Power's gone out. Give it a second."

"Maybe someone cut the power. We gotta get to the bar."

"Don't be so dramatic. We're in the middle of a hurricane. It happens."

"I don't like it."

"Give it a second."

It took more than a second. It was, I thought, supposed to be instantaneous, but my information might have been bad. Eventually we heard a click and then the emergency exit lights came on in the lobby. Small halogen lamps lit the front entrance and spread a ghostly glow across the lobby.

Ronzoni and I made for the lounge. It was dark inside, but the same emergency lighting had come on. The exit signs glowed red, and a lamp near the door showed the way out.

"Is everyone okay?" asked Ronzoni.

There were murmurs of yes and complaints and questions. Ronzoni took out his flashlight and did a roll call. Everyone was accounted for. He shone his light on Andrew Neville.

"This is your generator?" asked Ronzoni.

"This is the UPS."

"The what?"

"Uninterrupted power supply. Emergency systems only."

"Wasn't that uninterrupted. We were in the dark for long enough."

"Perhaps the storm did something to the system. But the generator should have come on by now."

"Where's that?"

"On the roof."

"All right. Mr. Neville, you come with me. Ron, you hold the fort. Everyone else just stay in place until we sort something out." Ronzoni turned to me. He was lit from below so he looked haggard. "You come, too."

We strode out into the lobby. The main entrance was lit, but the emergency lights threw long shadows across the lobby to the ocean side, where it was still dark. It was as if the sun was rising inside the building.

"How do we get to the generator?" asked Ronzoni.

"Via the staff stairs. North end of the building."

I knew what was coming next. Ronzoni was going to tell me to take care of it. To send me out into the hurricane once again. I wondered why I bothered putting clothes on. I considered asking Neville for a new poncho, but I figured he'd charge me for it, and I couldn't bear to think what a cheap plastic poncho would go for at The Mornington.

"All right, Mr. Neville, let's go start this generator," Ronzoni said.

Neville didn't move.

"Mr. Neville, is there a problem?"

Neville still didn't move. His face was hard to make out in the limited light, but I saw him lift his hand and point.

"What is that?"

We followed his direction. The ocean side of the lobby was normally floor-to-ceiling windows that slid open when the weather was fair to expose the lobby to the ocean breezes. Most of the windows had been covered with storm shutters, except one bank of them. Florida building codes required that at least one exit be rated as hurricane-proof, to ensure an escape route for any occupants should it be required. We looked through the exposed window out at the hurricane. What we should have seen was nothing but darkness. What we saw was the exact opposite.

A stunning bright light blazed from outside. We all moved closer to the window to get a better look. What we saw didn't make a whole lot of sense. Outside the floor-to-ceiling window was a terrace, for sun chairs or al fresco dining. Beyond the terrace was a lawn that led down to the seawall, below which was the beach.

The bright light emanated from the beach. It shone up from the raging surf beyond and lit something on the seawall itself. That something was formless, like a cloud. It took a good minute of looking at it before I connected any dots at all.

"It's a man," I said.

"No," said Ronzoni.

"It is. In a poncho. See it flapping around. He's got his arms out."

"He looks like a crucifix," said Neville.

"Damn Florida," said Ronzoni.

The man appeared to be standing on the seawall, arms outstretched, facing the ocean and the eye of the hurricane somewhere in the distance offshore.

Ronzoni said, "You got your poncho?"

I let out a groan and retreated to the check-in desk, where I had left my poncho. I removed my jacket, shirt and trousers once more, and pulled on the cheap plastic.

"You take care of that moron," said Ronzoni. "If he doesn't cooperate, leave him out there. It's his own stupid fault. Until the power comes back I don't want to leave this group alone."

"Awesome," I said. "Let's just get this done."

Neville led us across the lobby and Ronzoni cut back into the lounge. Neville didn't run, but he walked fast. You never want to look flustered in the hospitality game. It spooks the guests. He took me in behind the lounge area and into a corridor that led out to another emergency exit—I assumed the north exit. I noticed on our right was a door with a porthole in it—the kitchen. On the other side was another door, this one solid and unmarked. That one led to the taupe corridor and on to the staff stairs and the laundry. Dead ahead I saw the red glow of an emergency exit sign.

"Through there," said Neville. "There's the oceanside promenade and you can get over to the terrace and down to the seawall."

I was about to push ahead when I noticed something. The floor below us was wet. Unlike the south exit, the floor here was concrete. There was no gym, no guest facilities. Guests would exit using the concertina windows in the lobby. But I felt the water under my shoes.

"Wait," I told Neville.

I wasn't sure what I was thinking, or why it grabbed at me like it did. But I stuck my arm out and held Neville back for a moment. Then I took out my phone and handed him my flashlight.

"Shine that at about forty-five degrees to the floor," I said.

He did as directed without question, which was a point in favor of both hospitality staff and Labradors. I took a series of photos with my phone, just random snapshots of the floor. It was too dark to compose a shot properly. I did a few more with the flash, the light bouncing off the floor, blinding me.

"Okay," I said. I swapped my phone with Neville for my flashlight, and then I hit the door.

It was windy out but much less so than the pool deck had been. I was on a walkway built under the overhang of the hotel. It ran along the ocean side of the building, cut in two by the terrace in the middle. A boxwood hedge ran along the path separating it from the lawn. The lawn was gone. A lake had formed in its place.

I ran down the walkway and out onto the terrace. Now I got hit by the wind and rain. My poncho tried to take flight and wrapped itself around my head. I pulled it down but the damage was done. I was once again wet to my core. The wind blew from the north and west, so it pushed me down the lawn lake toward the light and lunatic on the seawall.

I yelled at the guy as I got closer but my calls were whisked away on the wind, never to be heard. I reached the seawall, where he stood. He was a big unit, tall and wide. His poncho was of a much higher quality than mine. It was heavy blue material like a tarpaulin. But it was just as pointless as mine.

The guy had a bald head that shone in the glow of the light coming from below. I looked down at the light. It was bright, pure white like a spotlight. It was then I realized that the lunatic on the seawall wasn't the craziest person out there.

There was a guy attached to the light. Or more specifically the light was attached to a camera that was attached to him. He was on the beach, shooting up at the man on the seawall. Only there was no beach. The ocean had reclaimed it. The waves were breaking over the head of the guy with the light, and smashing into the seawall. I couldn't fathom how the guy wasn't getting swept away. Then I saw it. A rope, probably bright orange in the daylight, like a climbing rope, was looped around the guy's waist and then out of the water and around a palm tree on the lawn.

I left the lunatic on the seawall and grabbed the rope and pulled hard. The ocean didn't want to give up its prize, but once I got going I reeled the guy in easy enough. I looked down as he met the seawall. He wasn't fighting me. He reached his hand up and I thrust mine down and pulled him up and over the wall.

The big guy on the wall jumped down. He had a hood on his poncho but it had blown off a long time ago. His face was large and taut, and water ran like rapids along his cheekbones. He bent down to where I had collapsed into the lawn lake with the other guy.

"Are you crazy?" he screamed. I barely heard him over the wind and crashing waves.

"Are you kidding me?" I spat back. It might have been a first for the day, but I was the least crazy person out there.

"We were getting some great shots, man!"

"This guy was gonna drown."

"He was attached to a rope!"

I just shook my head. Ronzoni was right. I should have just left them there. But I looked at the guy with the light. It was a hefty spotlight, attached to a large video camera. The camera was strapped to the guy who looked like he had already drowned twice. He was spitting saltwater. He got on his haunches and vomited as waves broke over the top of us.

I gave the camera guy a second to get rid of his lunch and then I pulled at the knot to untie him. It was fixed good and proper, but the guy pulled a pocket knife out and sawed through the rope. I took that as a sign that he was done playing fish bait.

I helped him up and dragged him back toward the hotel. The big guy kept pace, yelling the whole time about what I didn't know. Now the wind was whisking his words away, and that was just fine with me.

Andrew Neville stood by the north exit. He held the door open with his back as we collapsed inside.

"Are you okay?" I asked the guy with the camera.

"Yeah," he nodded. "Thanks."

"We were getting some great shots out there," yelled the big guy, his volume not decreasing despite being inside. "What the hell do you think you were doing?"

I stood up fast. It made the guy step back against the wall, and backward steps didn't seem to suit him. Up close he looked even bigger, about my height but wider. Not flabby, but solid.

"What was I doing?" I said. "Saving your bacon, you moron. Who goes out in weather like this?"

The guy jutted his chin like he was taking up a superhero pose. I got the impression this was supposed to jog my memory or something, but I was running on fumes so I had no idea.

"What? What is that?"

He frowned. He had ripples of furrows on his forehead that rivaled my own. He had spent a lot of time in the sun.

"You don't watch the Weather Network?" he asked.
"I don't own a television."
"You what?"
"Who the hell are you, pal?"
He did the chin thing again. "Rex Bonatelli. Weather Network."
"You're a weatherman?"
"No, I'm not a weatherman. I'm a meteorological correspondent. Wherever the weather's breaking, Rex Bonatelli is there."
There's nothing I love more than people who refer to themselves in the third person. It's so endearing.
"Well, Rex. You're an idiot."
"Excuse me?"
"Nope. No chance. This guy could have drowned." I looked down at the camera guy.
"He was okay. I told you, he was on a rope."
"So it was going to be easy to pull his dead body from the ocean."
"Look, we've got a job to do. Not everyone has the balls to do it. I get it."
"You want to go back out there, you be my guest."
"The people have a right to know."
"To know what, genius? That's there's a hurricane? Trust me, everyone who needs to know already knows."
I offered a hand to the camera guy and lifted him up. "You should stay. It's dangerous out there." I didn't feel it prudent to mention that we had lost two people inside the hotel.
The camera guy looked at his big partner. "Maybe we should check the footage we got."
Bonatelli grunted. "Let's check the footage. But then we're getting back out there."

CHAPTER TWENTY—FOUR

The congregation in the bar gave our new friends some uncertain looks, and the weather guys returned the looks with interest. Neville found some more towels and the two guys dried off. The cameraman unstrapped his camera, and then removed a small backpack that looked like a parachute.

Rex Bonatelli was euphoric. "Woo!" he yelled. "It's bitchin' out there people. Hoo yeah!"

"What the hell were you lunatics doing out there?" asked Ronzoni.

"We're from the Weather Network," said Bonatelli. "Rex Bonatelli," he said offering his hand. Ronzoni didn't take it.

"How on earth did you end up out there?"

"Ha," said the big guy. "Interesting story. We were filming on the island, about to head up the coast to follow the eye, and we got stuck here."

It wasn't that interesting a story, especially given we had all lived it.

"And you're wandering around Palm Beach in a hurricane?"

"Yeah, well. We came out here to get some shots of the beach, but our Jeep got stuck in your parking lot. You know it's a lake out there, right?"
Ronzoni looked surprised. "A lake?"
"Yeah, storm surge had come in massive. It's a good three feet out there. Cars are floating around. Hope none of you are parked out there," said with a grin, as if that was actually his greatest wish. He turned to the group as if performing just for Ronzoni wasn't enough.
"See the hurricane's a freak. We got unseasonably warm water in the Florida Straits, and up the Gulf Stream. Then we got low pressure that came from across the Gulf of Mexico, surprised all the models. So a tropical storm became a cat two before anyone knew it. Now it's sweeping up the coast"—he swooshed his hand up in the air to illustrate—"and last we heard it's gonna make landfall near Canaveral."
"Fort Pierce," I said. "That's what I heard."
Bonatelli shook his head. "Nah, don't know where you're getting that from." He turned back to his audience. "But here's the thing. The wind's not the only issue. What we got here is a King Tide, or a spring tide. Due to the moon's proximity to earth, the tide is higher than normal. And now we got a hurricane spinning counterclockwise, hitting land just to the north. That means most of the wind we see from now on will be coming from the northwest. In other words, right down the Intracoastal." He smiled like this was the best news he had ever heard. The group looked at him in stunned silence.
"So the wind will be one thing, but hold your hats for the flooding. Oh, yeah. It's gonna be something awesome."
Literally speaking he was right. It would be awesome, as in we would be in awe of it. But the way he said it, he made it sound like a kid who just got tickets to Disney World. I thought about

my little rancher, and wondered if my house would still be there when I got home.

"Good news is, this hotel is on a high point. It might make it." Bonatelli and the camera guy took off their ponchos. Bonatelli was dressed in khaki shorts and shirt, and he was wet through. He didn't seem to mind.

Neville offered them coffee, which they gladly accepted. I wasn't sure the big guy needed the caffeine.

"We'll just recharge our batteries a bit," said Bonatelli. "Then we got to get back out there."

"I'm afraid not," said Ronzoni.

"Sorry, chief," said Bonatelli. "Duty calls."

"I know," said Ronzoni. He pulled out his ID and flipped it open for Bonatelli to see. "Palm Beach PD. I'm gonna have to insist you stay here for the duration."

"You can't do that. This is freedom of the press."

"No, it's not. And I will arrest you if you make me."

"For what?"

"Public nuisance, reckless endangerment, having eyebrows that look like caterpillars. I'll find something."

"Outrageous," said Bonatelli. "You are infringing on my civil rights."

"Try me," Ronzoni said, turning away and shaking his head at me.

"Let's just check the footage, Rex," said the camera guy. "We might have enough."

Bonatelli didn't look convinced but he didn't argue. The camera guy looked relieved to be inside and not be playing the part of live bait. Bonatelli wiped down his bald dome and sat at the bar, where he sipped some coffee. He nodded to the chef.

"So what's going on here?" he asked.

Chef Dean shrugged. "Two guests are dead. How about you?"
Ronzoni turned to me. "Since you're already wet."
"You want me to figure out the generator."
Ronzoni raised his eyebrows. Ron appeared at my side.
"Need some help?"
"Let's see how we go."
Neville came from behind the bar. "I'll show you where."
"Excellent. It's such a nice evening to be out and about in Florida."

CHAPTER TWENTY—FIVE

Neville led us back around toward the north exit, and then in through the unmarked door into the taupe hallway. We climbed the stairs all the way to the top. Fortunately the hotel was low-rise, like downtown Palm Beach in general. We paused at the door to the roof.

"It's the large unit directly in front of you when you get out there," said Neville, who had clearly decided he was staying in the stairwell. "Check the control panel. The generator should have come on automatically."

"A lot of things should happen during a hurricane." I replied. "You know anything about generators?" I asked Ron.

"Enough to be dangerous," he said.

"Well, keep low—the wind is something else."

I was about to put my back into the door when I heard an electronic bling. Neville reached into his jacket pocket. "It's your phone, Mr. Jones. Seems you have a message."

"Hold that for me, will you?"

Perhaps being up higher up had given my phone a signal. Perhaps the wind blew my way. I didn't really care. I pushed into the door. It exploded open and almost tore from its hinges. If anything the wind was harder on the roof, and my poncho felt like a kite, destined to pick me up and deposit me in the Bahamas.

I dropped to my knees and crawled across the rooftop toward the large machine ahead. It was rectangular and the size of a car. As I crawled I checked on Ron. I think the wind took him by surprise. It's one thing to know it's a hurricane, it's another thing to feel it. Out to the west it was black. A few spots of light, hotels and apartment complexes with their own generators, the kind that actually come on when the power goes out. But mostly Palm Beach and the mainland beyond were blanketed in darkness. There was nothing familiar about it. No party lights, no boats floating by on the Intracoastal. Just a black hole. It felt primal, as if this was how Florida had been for eons, and would be again, given half a chance.

I reached the generator and turned back and offered a hand to Ron. I pulled him in hard against the side of the big machine.

"Now what?" I yelled.

"Controls," screamed Ron. "Hold me."

We stood using the side of the generator and I held Ron's waist. It was purely ceremonial. If a gust came that was big enough to blow him off the roof it was going to take me along for the ride too. Ron edged to a box attached to the side of the generator and opened it. Inside were all sorts of displays and readouts and buttons. Most notable was a big green button and a big red button. They seemed self-explanatory. Ron thought so too, because he punched the green button with the side of his fist.

The generator hiccuped deep within but gave no more. Ron tried the button again but got nothing. He hit the red and then the green again. Nothing. Then he shone his flashlight on a dial. He looked at me and shook his head, and then nodded toward the door.

We crawled back to the door. It was open, the door pressed hard against the wall of the entry hutch. Neville had retreated half a level down to keep out of the rain pouring in.

Ron ran his hands through his wet hair. He was soaked.

"There's no fuel," huffed Ron. "Dial's on empty."

"Oh," said Neville.

"What's the fuel?" I asked.

"Diesel."

"Where is it?"

"In a tank," said Neville.

"Where?"

"In the maintenance compound."

"Which side?" I asked, looking up at the rain driving in through the open door.

"Not on the roof. It's on the ground level."

I wasn't sure what genius came up with that plan but I let it slide. "Show us," I said.

Neville led Ron and I down to the ground level and the along the taupe corridor. He grabbed a towel from the laundry and then headed to a utility door at the far north end of the building.

"There's a fenced compound just across the lawn. Inside the fence you'll find the diesel tanks."

"Why on earth are the tanks down here but the generator is on the roof?"

"The generator is up there to keep it above the flood line. I guess they decided that having tanks of flammable diesel fuel on the roof of a hotel wasn't very safe. But they're just tanks. The water shouldn't affect them."

"We'll see." I nodded to Ron and we pushed out into the hurricane. There was definitely less wind on the ground than on the roof, but that was balanced against the water. The ocean was pounding in from the east and expanding across the lawn. It was sweeping through the streets of Palm Beach to the west of us, pooling in the low points, like the hotel's parking lot. And the maintenance compound.

Rex Bonatelli had been right about the hotel being on higher ground. But only just. Florida was as flat an expanse of swamp and sand as there ever was. Roads were long and straight and the highest points in most parts of the southern half of the state were the trash dumps. The Mornington sat on a slight rise, probably by design to improve the views. The maintenance compound sat below the grade of the hotel, away from ocean.

It was underwater now. Ron and I waded in. There was a real current ebbing and flowing, pulling us one way and then the other as if it just couldn't make up its mind whether it was coming or going. We reached the maintenance compound at knee-deep. I pulled open the gate and stepped in. And I dropped another foot down.

The diesel tanks were in a concrete bunker, a further foot below the ground. Ron joined me a little more than waist-deep in the thrashing water that spun around the tank bunker like a whirlpool. It was as close as I'd ever come to being in a blender. Ron directed us to a pump system attached to the end of one of the tanks. He opened a cabinet to inspect the pump motor.

He shook his head. "It's water-logged. Shorted out," he yelled.

"Can we prime it?"

He shook his head again. "Saltwater. Bad news for the components."

I was considering our options when I felt something grab at my left leg. I glanced at Ron, thinking it might have been him despite being on my right. A second later Ron shot me a look.

"What was that?"

I shrugged. I had no idea. The water kept swirling around the tanks like a wet carousel, and I decided there and then I wanted to get off the ride.

Then something grabbed me again. I felt it wrap around my leg. At first I thought it might be seaweed or kelp, driven onto land by the storm surge.

Then the kelp moved from my left leg to my right to get a better grip.

"What the hell is that?" I yelled.

Ron looked down as a thick arm pulsed up from the thrashing water and grabbed his arm. Ron reflexed backward and in one fluid motion a large octopus launched up out of the water. It wasn't massive, but it was way stronger than I expected an octopus to be. From tip to tip it was probably four feet, but its arms wrapped around my leg and Ron's arm like a python. The cephalopod pulled Ron and me closer together and almost off our feet, and its dark, bulbous head rose up out of the water like something out of an alien movie.

I didn't know what to do. The tentacle around my leg was flexing like a bodybuilder and was getting far too friendly with parts of me I had no intention of sharing with a creature of the deep. I was fairly certain that an octopus wasn't going to eat me, although my recall on such matters wasn't all it could be. I remember being told that most animals are more scared of us than we are of them, but I wondered if the octopus had gotten the memo. He reached out toward the tank with another two arms. I had no idea what he thought he was doing. But Ron did. Ron was better schooled on all aspects of the sea than me. He spent a lot of time sailing. Perhaps he'd read up on what lay beneath him when he did. Ron grabbed the tank with his free arm and reached in under the tank with his other.

The octopus went with him. The two arms that were reaching out grabbed onto the framework that held the tanks in place. When he had a good grip, he let go of Ron and then let go of me, and coiled himself around the frame. Within a blink I lost sight of him.

"Where'd it go?"

Ron yelled, "Nowhere. He's still hanging on."

"I don't see it."

Ron smiled. "He changed color."

"No kidding."

"Let's get inside."

We pushed our way across the bunker. Getting out of it was another matter. It was only a foot or so below ground level, but at that point ground level was two feet below the water. My poncho was dragging me down so I ripped it down the chest and threw it away, and then climbed up the steps to the lawn. I helped Ron up and we waded back into the hotel.

"Oh, Mr. Jones," was all Neville had to say as we burst back in through the utility door. Granted, I was wearing nothing but my underwear, and I was covered mud and debris, but he didn't say it like he was disappointed.

"Do we need to restart the generator?" asked Neville.

I shook my head. "It might have been to code putting the tanks on the ground, but the pump starter is another thing."

"Really?"

Ron said, "the saltwater has fried the circuit. The only way to get diesel to the generator is to carry it up there in a bucket."

Neville seemed to take the news pretty well. Better than me. I wanted to track down the moron who put the tanks at sea level right next to the ocean and rip him a new one. But Neville was British so maybe that explained it. They were a take it on the chin kind of folk. We Americans preferred the talk quietly and carry a big stick method. I wasn't able to say which was a better methodology.

"I need a shower," I said.

"Perhaps we should check in with Detective Ronzoni first," said Neville. "He didn't want people wandering around the hotel."

"When Ronzoni gets attacked by an amorous cephalopod, then he can dictate when I can and cannot have a shower."

I stopped at the check-in desk to grab my suit and then I went straight to my room. I did not stop in the bar, I did not pass go and I did not collect two hundred dollars. I launched into the darkness of the shower. I felt slimy, as if the octopus had left some kind of secretion on me, but that might have been my imagination. The shower cubicle was completely black, as if I was totally blind. I washed off in cold water with fancy hotel body wash and then did it all again. Then I toweled off and got dressed. My undies were trashed so I threw them away and went commando. It was a risk. If I ended up having to go back out into the storm, things were going to get dicey. Or I would have to upgrade my quality of poncho.

CHAPTER TWENTY—SIX

"So no power then," said Ronzoni.
"That's about the sum of it," I said. "Unless someone wants to carry bucketloads of diesel fuel up to the roof."
"I'll do it," said Rex Bonatelli.
"I don't think it's a great idea," I said. "In the middle of a hurricane."
"Doesn't bother me. Plus we might get some great footage up there."
"I'm not sure, Rex," said the camera guy, clearly not keen to go back out into the hurricane.
"There's nothing to see up there anyway. It's pitch-black all around. Power's down in West Palm too, by the looks of it."
"I say we get this place fired up," said Bonatelli. I wasn't sure what this guy was on, but he was certainly gung-ho.
"Let's wait until daylight," said Ronzoni. "Hopefully the worst will have passed by then. Mr. Neville, what do you think?"
"An excellent suggestion, Detective. We have battery-powered candles and camp lights we can bring in, and the emergency system will provide basic lighting for about ten hours."
"And the food?"

We all looked at the chef behind the bar. He looked indifferent to everything.

"The cool room will be good for twelve hours or more. We might lose some desserts and some seafood. Any longer than that'll be a problem."

"Can you prepare any food?"

"Kitchen's gas so we're good. Who wants to eat?"

"Sounds good to me!" said Bonatelli.

I noted that the sandwiches hadn't been touched. The chef passed a bar menu to Bonatelli, who looked at it.

"Who's up for nachos?" He canvased the group, who looked at him with the collective enthusiasm of high school kids looking over a math test. Bonatelli shrugged his solid shoulders. "Just me then. How about you Ken?" he asked the camera guy. It was obviously a rhetorical question because he handed the menu back to Chef Dean and said, "He'll have some."

With the focus on the hulking weatherman I took the opportunity to drag Ronzoni to the side.

"I need to show you something." I patted my pockets and realized I didn't have my phone, so I got it from Neville, who had stashed it safely in his breast pocket.

"When we—hell, I mean when I went out to save this idiot weather guy, the corridor was wet."

"What corridor?" asked Ronzoni.

"There's one that runs behind the kitchen back here. It links with the area near the laundry."

"Okay. So a spill?"

"Don't think so. There's another emergency exit there. Goes outside to a walkway along the front of the building. Or is it the back?"

"Whatever. So you're saying the water was from outside?"

"I don't know." I opened the photos on my phone. "I haven't looked at these yet."

I held the phone so Ronzoni could see, and I flicked between shots. The first few were blurred gray. They could have been of anything.

"Don't give up your day job there, Jones."

"I was taking random shots in near darkness, smart guy."

I kept flicking. Most were garbage. Then I hit on one that made sense. The flashlight and the flash on the camera had combined to capture a perfect image of a wet footprint.

"Interesting," said Ronzoni. "Make it bigger."

I pulled the picture out until the footprint took up the entire screen. Ronzoni took out his own phone and pulled up a shot he had taken in the hot tub hut. A wet footprint with a ruler measure next to it. We held the phones together to compare.

"They both look like footprints to me," I said.

"Both bare feet, both high arches, similar size. Would be better if you had used a scale. Can we go take some more?"

I shook my head. "It all got pretty messed when we brought these bozos in from outside." I motioned at the weather guys.

"Still, it looks like the same print. And this door goes outside on the north end, you say?"

"North end, but onto the ocean side," I said. "And the walkway runs all the way along to the south end of the building."

"So a perp could run across the pool deck and down the back of the building without being seen?"

"It's possible."

"So they wouldn't have had to use the gym corridor to get out there."

"Or more importantly back in. Remember the hot tub timer? We might have come close to interrupting them."

Ronzoni looked around the room. Neville had placed fake candles on the tables, and the space glowed romantically.

"Not close enough," said Ronzoni, sighing.

I left him to his thoughts and made for the bar. I needed a drink. But not of the alcoholic kind. I found it strange that in the middle of a hurricane, having been so thoroughly drenched so many times, I could be dehydrated. But my mouth was dry in a way it felt like Palm Beach never would be again. I wandered behind the bar and took a water from the fridge. I could see the chef in the kitchen, slipping some corn chips under the broiler. I took a couple of the little sandwiches off the platter and wandered over to a free club chair. It was in a set of three, one of which was occupied by Sam Venturi. He was wrapped up in a blanket like he was a human burrito.

I didn't say anything to him. I nibbled at a sandwich. I felt like my body was shutting down, and I needed the fuel. It tasted like watercress and Swiss cheese. It was decent enough, but I would have killed for pastrami on rye.

"I can't believe you can eat," said Sam. "I feel so terrible."

"It's fuel, kid. Not Thanksgiving."

"Still." He sipped some coffee from a china cup. Apparently drinking fell into a different category. He leaned toward me.

"Who did it?"

"Did what?"

"You know. Carly. The detective said it wasn't an accident."

"Who do you think did it?"

"I really couldn't say."

"Couldn't or shouldn't?"

"What's the difference?"

"You have an opinion. I'd like to hear it."

Sam glanced around the room as if everyone was listening. No one was.

"If it were me, I'd look at Anton."
"I thought you guys were friends."
"We are. But this is different."
"What makes you say that? She was his agent. Didn't they get along?"
"Oh, they got along."
"Meaning?"
He whispered, "They were having an affair."
"You know this how?"
"It's just like her."
"To have an affair."
He nodded and sipped his coffee.
"She have an affair with you?"
"Why do you say that?"
I shrugged and nibbled on another sandwich. It was smoked ham and pretty good. "You said it was just like her."
"I was just a kid when she recruited me."
"You were sixteen."
"Exactly."
I thought back to when I was sixteen. It must have been a different sixteen from the one Sam Venturi lived through.
"So if what you say is true, why would Anton do anything to Carly?"
"Er, he's getting married."
"But he's not yet."
"You think Shania should be okay with that?"
I shrugged. I had plenty of opinions on it but I wasn't going to share with this kid.
"Seems like a pretty drastic step all the same. Seems Carly had just as much to lose."
"Maybe. Or maybe Carly had her eye on a bigger prize."
"You mean Shania?"

"Wouldn't have been the first time she'd dumped someone to move up."
I said nothing. I didn't see it.
"Two birds, two stones," said Sam.
"What do you mean?"
"Come on. It's got to make you wonder about Paul, right?"
"What about Paul?"
"He was a freeloader. Everyone knew it. He was taking Anton for a ride. And Shania didn't like it, nor should she. She wanted a clean slate. No freeloaders, no affairs."
"You think Anton killed his friend and his manager to placate his fiancé?"
"I don't know. I'm not the detective."
I wasn't a detective either, but I didn't feel like making the point. I didn't buy the Anton-Carly thing, but add in Paul and it got whole lot murkier.
"And there's this manager guy. Mr. Neville." He said Mr. Neville in a fake English accent.
"What about him?"
"There's something funny about him."
"Funny how?"
Sam looked at his drink for a moment. "I heard him arguing."
"With who?"
"The chef."
"Chef Dean?"
"Aha."
"Where?"
"In the kitchen."
"Arguing about what?"
"The chef smoking weed on the job."
"He said that?"

"In not so many words. But I think the chef was smoking weed and Mr. Neville smelled it on him."

"What happened?"

"The chef guy said to remember his little French secret."

"What secret?"

Sam shrugged. "No idea. But maybe Mr. Neville has killed before. Maybe that's why he's in the US. You thought about that? It's always the quiet ones."

"It's not a hundred percent certain Carly didn't drown," I said.

"It's not?"

"She was drinking a fair bit before."

"She always did."

"Don't we all."

"No."

I looked at him. He wasn't being righteous, he was just that naive.

"You don't drink?" I asked.

"Not often, and never to excess. You can't be a professional athlete and do that to your body. Athletes have more self-control."

He must have hung around a lot of different athletes than I did during my career. Or maybe it was a generational thing.

"What about Anton? He drinks."

Sam nodded. "Yeah. He does."

CHAPTER TWENTY—SEVEN

I noticed Ronzoni at the bar and I was still parched so I drifted in behind the counter and grabbed two more waters and handed one to Ronzoni.
"Thanks," he said.
Anton sat down with a flop on the stool next to Ronzoni.
"The manager will not serve me because you said it was not okay."
"I don't think drinking any more during a hurricane is very smart, Mr. Ribaud," said Ronzoni.
"Is this America or Russia?"
"It's America. Where if you get drunk and do something stupid in the middle of a hurricane people will disregard their own safety to come to your rescue. I don't think they should be put in that position."
"I will not do anything stupid. I just want a drink. It's my bachelor party." He sang the last line, and I wasn't sure if he was mocking himself or the whole concept.
"It's a free country, as you point out," said Ronzoni. "But if you appear intoxicated it is unlawful for the hotel to serve you."
"Do I appear intoxicated?"

Ronzoni looked him up and down. "No, sir. You do not."
"D'accord." He got my eye. "Can you pass me that brandy?"
I looked at Ronzoni, who shrugged, and I passed Anton the bottle. He poured himself a shot. I thought he would gulp it down in some sort of show of defiance, showing us who was boss. But he didn't. He sipped it.
"What do you think about Carly?" I asked him.
He made a face that suggested he didn't care one way or the other. "I guess I must find a new agent."
"You don't feel sad?"
"Sure. She was okay. I don't think she should be dead."
"You spoke to her just before she went to the hot tub," said Ronzoni.
"I did?"
"Yes, you did."
He looked from Ronzoni to me and back. "Okay."
"In the lobby."
"Yes."
"What did you talk about?"
He swirled his drink as if he were recalling the conversation. "She said she had a plan."
"A plan? A plan for what?" Ronzoni sipped his water.
"She did not say."
"What did you think she meant by that?"
"I did not know."
"You had no idea and you didn't think to clarify? To ask her what she meant?"
He shrugged again. "No."
"I find that hard to believe, Mr. Ribaud," said Ronzoni.
I said, "Perhaps we should ask Shania?"
"Okay."

"Perhaps we should ask her about the possibility of you having an affair with your former agent."

Anton laughed. Not like he'd heard a great joke. More like he thought I was ridiculous.

"Look, Carly was ambitious, yes? She worked for a big agency that expected her to grow their business. It was natural that she looked at Shania as a client."

"So you think she was interested?"

"Of course. But there was nothing to do. I told her that there was no point. Shania's papa looks after her affairs and that was not going to change."

"But you think the plan she referred to might have been in relation to getting Shania as a client?" asked Ronzoni.

"It's possible."

We each sipped our drink. Anton got the best deal on that count.

"So, Anton. Who do you think killed Carly?"

"Honestly, I don't see how anyone could do it."

"Really? No motives among the group?"

He shrugged once more. "Of course Sam had reasons."

"What reasons?"

"She recruited him, she used him to get to me, and when he didn't make it she dumped him. And he doesn't get that."

"Why should he get it?"

"It's not personal. It's business. But Sam, he is a boy in a man's body. A small man's body. He thinks she did this to him. But she did not make him fail to grow. She didn't make him not be able to compete on the tour. That just happened. But he doesn't get this. He takes everything too personally. She was his agent. He thought she was his lover."

"His lover?" asked Ronzoni. "They had an affair?"

"No, Detective. But she was a beautiful woman. I think Sam wanted that to be true."

"What about you?" I asked. "Not tempted by beautiful women?"

"Monsieur, it is French to appreciate the beauty of a woman. And I am many things. But unfaithful is not one of them."

I leaned back against the rear of the bar and looked at the guy. He wasn't a fun guy. He had the personality of an electric eel. But on the faithful thing, he sold me. I believed him. I had nothing to base it on. He and Shania had spent more time sitting apart than together in my presence, and for a bachelor weekend there was a distinct lack of public displays of affection. But it takes all kinds of people. Maybe Cassandra was right. Maybe they would find a way. Or maybe they would crash and burn. But at that moment, I believed in his fidelity.

And then, as if on cue, Shania appeared at the bar. She put her arm around Anton. It was a strong arm, well defined and powerful. She looked at the drink but said nothing.

"Join us," Anton said, and Shania took the stool next to him. "A drink?"

"Is that okay?" she asked Ronzoni.

He shrugged like the whole thing was out of his hands.

Shania looked at me. "Can I have a vodka?"

I was behind the bar so I played the part. "With tonic?"

"Neat. So what are you guys talking about?"

"You, ma chérie," said Anton.

It was the same phrase I had used to Danielle earlier on the phone, but delivered in a French accent it was a whole other thing.

"Me? What about me?"

I took it up. "You're from Miami, right?"

"Aha."

"And you went to Case Academy, which is in Tampa."
"Yeah."
"So why have your party in Palm Beach?"
"Why not?"
"The Mornington seems a bit stuffy for a young couple like yourselves."
"Well, Leon is the best man. He arranged it."
"Interesting choice."
Shania looked at Anton. "I think he knew someone here, didn't he? From Paris?"
Anton nodded a solid maybe.
"Not too many friends made it," I said.
Shania said, "A hurricane will do that."
"So you were expecting more?"
"Yes." She smiled at Anton. "A few more of my friends."
I believed her. I figured Anton had two friends in the world, and one of them had been crushed under a barbell.
"What did you think of Carly?"
Shania looked taken aback by the question. "What did I think? She was Anton's agent. I didn't really think much more than that."
Ronzoni said, "The assistant manager, Miss Taylor, said she couldn't find you before we found Miss Pastinak. Where were you?"
"I went up to the ballroom to hit some balls. I was in the lobby when I saw Miss Taylor run back in, saying something had happened to Carly."
"Did she want you as a client?" I asked.
Shania took a deep breath. "I suppose so. That's what agents do. But my dad looks after me. Always has."
"And that works? With your dad?"

"Of course. I told you, Miami, he's not some stereotype crazy tennis dad. I love him as my dad, but I love him as my mentor and manager, too."

"Did you think Carly drank a lot?" I asked, glancing at Anton's brandy.

"No, I didn't. She had a drink here and there, I suppose. But that was part of the job. She spent a lot of time doing hospitality."

"Does your dad do that?"

"No. You don't know my dad. You wouldn't ask if you did."

"So what do you think of the idea that Carly took a bottle of champagne to the hot tub and slipped into a coma?" I asked.

"Is that what happened? I thought someone . . ."

"Just asking."

"I don't see it. She was a social drinker. Not over the top. She was too focused for that. Never unprofessional."

"What about what she did to Sam?"

Shania glanced around at Sam, I figured to see if he was within earshot. "Look, I love Sam. He's like a brother to me. But Carly did nothing to him. He's a coach at a tennis ranch. He'll be a great one, too. But he didn't need an agent anymore."

"Did you use the hot tub, either of you?" Ronzoni asked.

They both shook their heads.

Shania said, "It's not really spa weather, is it?"

I had to wholeheartedly agree with that.

CHAPTER TWENTY—EIGHT

I was standing behind the bar when Andrew Neville came back around to join me. Well, not exactly join me. He didn't say as much but I got the feeling it offended his sense of duty to have a guest, even a comped guest like me, behind the bar. I made to slip out and as I did I glanced through the porthole in the door to the kitchen. The chef was in there, working with something on a chopping board by camp light. I hadn't spoken to him but I knew one thing. There are always people who get to float about unseen, hiding in plain sight.

I backed in through the door and turned into the kitchen. It was one of those spaces that certain folks had dreams about. Lots of stainless steel counters and prep space, large fridges and gas burners and deep fryers, all top-of-the-line stuff. The chef noticed me but didn't stop slicing open the fish he was working on.

"Help you, mate?" I hadn't noticed before but he sounded Scottish.

"Bored. What are you making there? Fish dip?"

"Nae, bouillabaisse. Fish stew."

"Someone order that?"

"Nae. But if the fridge is gonnae be down, the fish'll go bad. Might as well make something of it while I can."

"Thrifty thinking."

"Oh, yeah, mate. This place is all about thrifty thinking." He shot me a wink. "So this fish dip, it's big here, aye?"

"Yeah, pretty big."

"Aye, we get it in from some place. New England Seafood or some such."

"Nice."

"Aye. Do you know what they make that from? Back home we use salmon."

"Guy I know uses whatever he catches. But the big meaty fish is best. Marlin, tuna, swordfish."

"Aye, nice. Got some swordfish. Might have to give it a go."

I nodded. It sounded like a plan. "You work here long?" I am nothing if not a master at the segue.

"Few months."

"Right. And before that?"

"Why do you ask?"

"Noticed the accent, that's all."

"Aye, Scottish. But I trained in London. Worked last few years in Paris."

"Paris. Not bad."

"Two Michelin stars. More than not bad."

I didn't know a lot about Michelin stars except they went to expensive restaurants I never ate at, and Longboard Kelly's didn't have one despite Mick's smoked fish dip.

"So what brings you to Florida?"

"Not the sun."

"Not today."

"Just the job."

I stepped over to a second counter and leaned against. I noticed a walk-in climate-controlled wine fridge. It had a keypad entry but the door lay ajar.

"What do you think about this business with the woman?"

The chef stopped slicing. The knife in his hand was long and thin.

"I been in here the whole time."

"Not saying different. Just talking."

"Aye, talking."

"So you didn't see anything?"

"Not a thing."

"What about when you were out for a smoke?"

He frowned. "What makes you say that?"

"You do smoke."

"How do you know that? What are you, Sherlock flippin' Holmes?"

I wasn't Sherlock Holmes. I wasn't a drug user, for a start. Unless you counted beer, which I did not. But I did know a few chefs. Although most of the ones I knew called themselves cooks rather than chefs. But most of them smoked. I never got it myself. I always figured that taste was a fairly central sense when it came to cooking, and a pack a day had to kill any sense of taste stone-cold dead. But plenty of them did it. Plus this guy had nicotine-yellow teeth. He'd been smoking since he was a boy.

"Aye, I take a quick ciggie break e'ry now and then."

"Where do you go?"

"Just nip outside the door here." He nodded at the door that led to the corridor near the north exit. "You can stand just outside there and no get wet, even in a hurricane."

"You ever get locked out?"

"Locked out? Nah. The outside door is no locked, and the kitchen door, well, I just prop it open. You don't get any guests coming back here unless they're lost."

I wandered over to the door in question and pushed it open. The corridor was still dark and the floor was still wet.

"Floor's wet," I said.

"Aye, I thought that was you, when you brought that big yin in from the seawall."

"Yeah, you're right. Wasn't wet before?"

"Not last time I was out."

I stepped back into the kitchen and let the door close. Just inside the kitchen were trays of glassware. I pulled one out. It was a champagne glass. I slipped it back in its slot and wandered back toward the door to the bar.

"Thanks for sandwiches by the way."

"No problem. Hope you enjoyed."

I got to the door and the chef picked up slicing the fish before him. I stopped before the door and turned back.

"So why did they fire you?"

"Who? What?"

"In Paris. Why did they fire you?"

"Who says I got fired?"

"You didn't leave one of the culinary capitals of the world to take up making fish dip in Palm Beach. So what was the reason?"

"Listen, pal, I don't know you, but I don't owe you an explanation for anything."

"You're right. You don't. I'll just make up my own conclusions and discuss them with the police detective outside."

"No, listen. No cops."

"Okay."

"I'm serious. No cops. I'll lose my work permit."

"No reason for that to happen."
This time he put the knife down. "There was an incident. It was a substance abuse issue. Can we leave it at that?"
"Not alcohol, I take it," I said, glancing at the open wine fridge.
"No. Not alcohol."
I knew plenty of cooks who snorted all manner of stuff up their noses. I didn't get that either. After taste, I had to nominate smell as important sense number two for cooks.
"Who hired you?"
"Mr. Neville. And no, I dinnae lie to him. He knows about the whole thing. But he also knows I'm a good cook."
It was the last bit that sold me on it. He had no pretension about himself. He didn't refer to himself as a chef. He called himself a cook. Most of the good ones did.
"I know that," I said. "Thanks again for the sandwiches."

CHAPTER TWENTY—NINE

The bar was quiet. Shania and Deshawn were talking in whispers at the bar. Anton was standing at the back of the room. Rex Bonatelli and Ken the camera guy were hunched over an iPad in the corner, looking at stuff they had filmed. Emery Taylor had laid out on one of the sofas. She was asleep with her head in Rosaria's lap. Cassandra and Ron were on another sofa. They weren't talking but they watched me walk over.

"Hell of a night," I said quietly as I sat.

"Indeed," said Cassandra.

Ron said, "That poor girl." He waited a moment, and then he added, "Are you all right?"

I nodded. It was a lie and he knew it. But I didn't feel like giving voice to what I was feeling because I didn't know what words to use. I had watched Ronzoni work on Carly for over half an hour. I had worked on her for another fifteen minutes myself. Nothing about that felt right. And nothing about this group felt right. There were lots of people in the world who weren't my crowd. I didn't get them and they didn't get me. We all have our own tribes. But the thing was, with this tribe, no one seemed to get anyone else. It was like they spent time together because tennis threw them together, rather than choosing to remain together after tennis brought them to the same starting place.

"Do you have any leads?" Ron asked.

"Not much. Fragments."

"But definitely not an accident."

I shook my head.

Ron waited a bit, and then said, "Thoughts on who?"

"Everyone? They all seemed to have a reason. Take him." I nodded in the direction of Anton. "He claims to be faithful but exhibits no signs of being so."

"Do you believe him?"

"Does it matter?"

Cassandra sighed. "Maybe it's the wrong question, Miami. Maybe it isn't whether he has shown signs of being faithful but rather has he shown evidence of being unfaithful."

"The difference being?"

"The difference being that he is he, he is not you. I know you're mister tough guy, but I also know you dote on Danielle. That's how you see these things working. He's different. He doesn't feel the need to prove anything to anyone."

"I don't feel the need to prove anything to anyone," I said.

"If you say so, Miami. But think about what you did for a living before, and what you do now, and why."

I didn't want to think about that. Not now. Maybe not ever. But Cassandra had gone and put it in my head. I was a baseball player. Had been since elementary school. Everything else was secondary, even my fleeting college football career. And then I met Lenny Cox. Lenny changed everything. I hadn't spoken to Cassandra much about Lenny. She hadn't been on the scene when we lost Lenny, but I had no doubt Ron had told her plenty. Lenny was the kind of person who left an imprint. He never suggested I become a private investigator, but I did. He never directly suggested I join his firm, but I did. He did leave me the firm in his will, but he gave no directions on how I should manage it, or the people who worked for me. Maybe because he knew. He'd left an imprint. I hadn't always worn palm tree print shirts. Or linen suits, for that matter.

"I know he's not the most personable fellow," said Cassandra, "but that doesn't mean he isn't faithful." She smiled softly. "We don't choose our character flaws. They choose us."

"Well, try this. Word is he cheated on a drug test at a team tournament they were in—he, Sam and Shania. And somehow covered it up."

"And on the other hand he could be exactly what he appears to be," she said.

"Maybe he cheated the test to save her. There seems to be a few people around trying to look after her interests. Good or bad."

"Anyone other than Anton?" asked Ron.

"Deshawn. He's like a brother to her. And her dad saw him like a son, apparently."

"As I said before, Deshawn certainly has her interests at heart," said Cassandra, "but his eyes say there's more to it than brotherly love."

"Maybe. Sam cares for her, too. Then there's her dad. Everyone says he's not one of those crazy tennis dads, but in the same breath everyone suggests he watches over her like a hawk. Carly didn't have Shania as a client because she had her dad doing the agent thing."

"Families can be tight," said Ron.

Ronzoni moved across the room. I noticed he had been talking with Leon, and he angled toward us. He sat on the coffee table.

"Shania said Leon chose the hotel," he said.

"Yeah."

"Turns out he knows the chef. They worked in the same restaurant in Paris."

"I spoke to the chef earlier. He neglected to mention that. But he did say he got the job here through a connection to the general manager."

"Neville?"

"Aha."

"So Leon knows Chef Dean and Chef Dean knows Neville."

"And what completes that circle?"

Ronzoni shrugged.

"Does Leon know Neville? And if he does, why isn't anyone saying so?"

"Maybe they have something to hide?"

"Everyone has something to hide," I said. "But is it relevant? Maybe they have a secret. Maybe Paul Zidane found out that secret. Leon mentioned that Paul said all his problems were going to be sorted out this weekend. That he'd be in a good place."

"That might be relevant if Mr. Zidane's death wasn't an accident, but it was."

"Or maybe they don't even know each other."

Ronzoni slouched. "That isn't helping."

"I suppose you need to know all our whereabouts, Detective," said Cassandra.

Ronzoni squirmed in his seat. There was nothing he hated more than bothering Palm Beach society folks about police matters, because there was nothing his boss hated more than getting calls of displeasure from Palm Beach society folks.

"I don't think that's necessary, ma'am."

"Really, Ronzoni?" I tried not to smile. "A woman is deceased and you don't think a full investigation is warranted."

"I don't think Lady Cassandra is involved, Jones."
"Based on what facts?"
"Based on . . ." He clenched his jaw at me. "All right. Lady Cassandra, where were you between the time you left the lounge this evening and the time you returned?"
She smiled. "In my room, resting."
"Thank you. Happy, Jones?"
"What's her alibi?"
Ronzoni said nothing. He just stared at me and then glanced with abject sorrow at Cassandra.
"I was with Ron."
"See," Ronzoni said to me.
"They could've have been in it together."
"Jones—"
He stopped mid-insult as Rosaria appeared beside him, laden with blankets. We already had enough blankets to cover the Red Army, and it wasn't like we were in a New England winter. There might have been a hurricane outside but it was still balmy. Since the power had gone out and AC with it, the room had actually warmed up a tad. But I figured she was bored and was trying to be useful. Cassandra took a blanket. Ron didn't. Ronzoni didn't. I had no plan to. I looked up at her to say no thanks. The expression on her face was weird.
She was grimacing and frowning at the same time, and jutted her head to the side like she had developed some kind of spasm. I thought for a second it was some kind of posttraumatic tick, but for the fact that her eyes were locked on mine. Then I got it. I stood.
"Let me help you." I took the blankets from her. Clearly she wanted a private word, but she could have just asked. I couldn't imagine Ron, Cassandra and even Ronzoni not picking up on her attempts to signal me.

We walked in the general direction of the bar. Neville was down the end near the kitchen door. I angled to the other end but stayed off the bar itself so Neville didn't get the idea I wanted something from him.

"Rosaria," I said.

"Sir, Miami, thank you."

"For what?"

She looked confused. "For saving me."

"Oh, that. No problem. De nada."

Then she stood there looking at me like that was all she had to say but she couldn't think of the words to end the conversation.

"Is there something else, Rosaria?"

"Sir, there is something. I know what has happened to the lady. It is terrible."

"Yes, it is."

"I don't know if this is important."

"Everything is important, Rosaria. No matter how small."

"I heard something."

I nodded but said nothing.

"The lady was talking with the man."

"Which man?"

"The blond man."

"Mr. Venturi?"

"Yes."

"And what did they say?"

"They have an argument."

"What did they say?"

"The lady, the lady who died. She said that it was over. They were done. She said that yes, maybe he should leave."

"Leave? When did you hear this?"

"Before. This morning. Before we all try to go to West Palm."

Sam did want to leave. I knew that already. Now Rosaria confirmed why. But it didn't change anything. The fact he tried to leave and got stuck here like me didn't mean a thing. Necessarily.

"Did she say anything else?"

"No, not her. Not then."

"Not then? When?"

"This evening. I was helping to bus the lounge. I did not mean to hear."

"I understand. We don't get to close our ears. What did you hear?"

"I was coming from the kitchen. The man, Mr. Venturi, he step in behind the bar and use the house phone."

"Do you know who he called?"

"I think it was the lady."

"You think? But you don't know?"

"No."

"Okay. What did Mr. Venturi say?"

"He say to not hang up. He say I need to speak to you. I know how you can get her on board. Slam dunk, he say."

"Anything else?"

"Yes. He say okay. I meet you there. He say he knows where it is. Meet me at the south exit."

"He knows where what is?"

Rosaria shook her head. "I do not know. But now I think, maybe the hot tub room?"

"Then what?"

"Then nothing."

"Nothing? Did he go in the kitchen?"

"No. I was in the kitchen. He walk out of the bar area and sit down in the lounge."

"Okay. Thank you, Rosaria."

"No, sir. Thank you. I should not be on this earth anymore, but for you."

"No, Rosaria. You should be on this earth. That's why I did what I did."

CHAPTER THIRTY

Rosaria left me standing at the bar so I did what I do and I took a stool. Ronzoni was helping himself to some sliders that the chef had knocked up. No one loves free food more than cops. If sourcing free chow was a sport, cops would win the gold, silver and bronze. The chef had also put out some crudités—raw carrots, broccoli and snow peas—but Ronzoni left that stuff the hell alone. He sat next to me.
I gave him an update on what Rosaria had told me.
"He did try to leave," said Ronzoni. "That wasn't for show. He was in my car, remember?"
"Yeah, I remember. But what if it wasn't planned. What if it was more like a crime of passion? We know the kid had a thing for her. We know she dumped him—in a professional sense, if not a personal one—and we know he didn't take that so well. Maybe he meets her in the hot tub and tries to win her over with champagne."
"Why would she meet him?" asked Ronzoni. "She's just given him the brush-off, big-time."
"Like Rosaria said, he's got a plan for her, a slam dunk."
"For what?"
"Maybe to win Shania as a client? That seemed to be why she was here."

"It's thin."

"But plausible. So let's walk it through. The timer's going. He's got the bubbles, both in the hot tub and in the bottle. He meets her at the south door, he takes her there, he gets her in the hot tub. Then he gives her the plan."

"But she's not impressed," Ronzoni said, chomping into a slider.

"Right. Maybe she disses him. He loses it." I paused. "He does what he does."

"Okay. So how's he get away?"

"We come out looking for Carly. Maybe interrupt or maybe not. But the timer is still ticking. He doesn't go out the south exit or we'd have seen him on the video. So he doesn't go back in that way either. He goes down the walkway along the back of the hotel. To the north exit. He goes in that way. But then he comes out again."

"Out again? How do you figure?"

"He's wet. From the hot tub and the storm. But the water in the corridor doesn't go anywhere. No footprints up the stairs, not into the kitchen."

"So now he's outside again? I don't know, Jones."

"I don't either."

"And what about the champagne? One glass?"

"Maybe he takes his glass, to make it look like she's drinking alone."

"Now it sounds premeditated."

"Maybe it was."

"So let's say he took the glass. Where is it?" he asked.

"There's a rack of champagne glasses in the kitchen. Maybe he took it from there. Maybe he tried to replace it."

"Tried?"

"Like I said, the wet footprints don't go into the kitchen."

"So now he's outside with a champagne glass? You've got a hell of an imagination there, Jones."

"That might be true, but that doesn't make me wrong."

Ronzoni said nothing. His mouth was full. At least his mother had taught him well.

"I got an idea," I said.

"Another one."

"Let's go take a look."

Ronzoni took another slider half-wrapped in foil to go. We walked past Rex Bonatelli, who was tapping his feet and starting to look like a caged lion. We slipped in through the kitchen. Chef Dean looked up, stirring his fish stew, but we didn't stop to chat. Ronzoni paused at the door and glanced at the crate of glasses, and then at the floor. Not wet. He pushed through.

The corridor was eerie. Emergency lighting is like that. Perhaps it makes people get out faster if it looks creepy. But the floor was wet. Ronzoni used Emery's card and opened the door opposite, into the taupe service corridor. The floor wasn't wet. Ronzoni stepped back out and made for the exit. He pushed the door open.

The eye of the hurricane was probably somewhere to the north of us, hammering down on Fort Pierce if Mick was right. But it made no difference to us. The rain was still pounding but the walkway was under the cover of the hotel. The ocean was crashing over the seawall and pulsing in toward the boxwood hedge that lined the walkway. We were getting sprayed, but compared to what we'd been through we didn't even notice.

"Okay, now what, Jones?" Ronzoni said over the wind.

"You've got a glass in your hand," I said. "Do you keep it, hide it for later or throw it?"

I looked out at the pounding ocean. That was my choice. Toss something in there and it would probably wash up in Freeport, or maybe Cape Hatteras.

Ronzoni didn't agree. He didn't have to. That's what made rock, paper, scissors work. Different folks looked at the same exact scenario in their own way. Ronzoni reached into his pocket and pulled out a latex glove. He stretched it onto his fingers and pulled it down with a snap. Then he stepped forward to the hedge and reached inside it. Then he pulled out a long thin champagne glass.

"You really were born with a rainbow up your butt, Jones."

I had absolutely no idea what that meant so I just grinned like an idiot. A lucky idiot.

Ronzoni stood and directed me inside. Once in the corridor he held up the glass with his gloved hand.

"Go to the kitchen," he said. "Find the biggest plastic baggie you can find. A garbage bag if you have to. And ask Neville for some super glue. You got a Mr. Coffee machine in your room?"

"I don't think this is a Mr. Coffee kind of hotel. But it doesn't matter. Power's out, remember?"

"See what you can find. Then come to Neville's office."

I didn't ask him what he was up to. I had a fair idea. I had never done it, but I'd seen it, so I nodded and Ronzoni slipped Emery's card through the slot on the pad on the kitchen door and I pushed through. Ronzoni took off down the corridor.

I asked Chef Dean for the largest baggie he had, and he handed me a bag large enough to brine a turkey. I asked him if he had some kind of portable coffee warmer. He went to a cupboard and pulled out a silver carafe, and then he pulled the base away from the carafe. The base was a round disk with an electrical cord, except where the plug should have been there was an adapter for a twelve volt plug, the kind that sticks into the cigarette lighter of a car.

"Not sure I'm going to get near a car," I said.

Chef Dean grunted, or it might have been a word in a dialect I didn't know. But he strode into a small storeroom off the kitchen, and returned with a portable battery pack, like the sort of thing someone might use to jump start the dead battery in their car. It had a slot just right for the adapter on the heating pad.

"You moonlight for the AAA?"

"We sometimes do breakfasts on the beach. Easier to use a portable battery than to run cables everywhere."

"Clever."

He nodded at me. "Fingerprints, eh?" he said.

I gave him a nod in return. He had hidden depths.

I walked out into the bar and asked Neville for some superglue. He suggested I look in the drawer in his office. I strode out to his office and found Ronzoni at the check-in desk. He was fanning the glass from the hedge with a yellow notepad. He had collected the champagne bottle and the other glass from the gym where he had housed the evidence. I rifled through the drawers in Neville's office and found some superglue. Neville knew where his office supplies were.

The light was better out at the desk, but it wasn't good. Ronzoni had a camp light going. The emergency lighting near the front door of the hotel added ambience but not much more. Ronzoni made a small tray out of the foil from his slider. He put the foil on the heating pad of the carafe and then squeezed the tube of glue into the foil.

Ronzoni placed the glass from the hedge next to the heating pad, took a Post-it and wrote the word hedge on it and stuck it on the desk in front of the glass. Then he took the champagne bottle and the glass we found by the hot tub out of their baggies and placed them on the other side of the heating pad. He took two more Post-its and wrote hot tub on both and stuck them in front of the bottle and the second glass. He took photos of his work. I figured he was concerned with the chain of the custody for the evidence. He had to worry about things like that.

He plugged the heating pad into the battery pack and then pulled the marinating bag over the whole lot. He asked if I had any tape and I found some in Neville's office, so Ronzoni taped the bag to the desk to make it air tight. Then he sat back and waited.

"You seen this before?" he asked. He was looking for his moment in the spotlight. I had seen it, and ninety-nine times out of a hundred I wouldn't spare the time to give Ronzoni's ego a boost. He didn't need it. He might start thinking and that could only mean trouble for me in the long run. But I must have been tired, or going soft, because I said no.

"Superglue contains an ingredient called cyanoacrylate. When heated it creates fumes that adhere to the moisture in the latent print. Watch, it's like magic."

I watched. The glue warmed up on the heating pad's element and started fuming, and within a couple minutes it was done.

Ronzoni said, "Stand back, these fumes can be a bit nasty."

I was already back. I had smelled superglue fumes before. Like I say, I learned a lot of stuff on field trips.

He unplugged the heating pad and pulled the baggie off the machine carefully, and then picked up the bottle. It was covered in white powdery smudges.

"Looks like this has been wiped." He then picked up the glass from the hot tub. He carefully turned it around in his gloved fingers. I saw nothing on it.

"Hard to see anything," I said.

"That's the downside of fuming. The latent prints come up white. We could dust them, but . . ." He looked toward the front door. "There's no prints on here anyway. It's been wiped as well. Ronzoni put the glass down and picked up the one on the other side of the coffee machine. He rotated it around.

"Huh," he said, smiling. "See."

"Is that something? It's hard to see."

Ronzoni looked around the desk and found an advertising leaflet for the hotel. The back was black. He rolled it into a tube and slipped the tube inside the champagne glass. Then he held up the glass to show me the big fat white fingerprint against the black background. It was a nice full print.

"Not bad, Ronzoni."

"Look, there's two. Like it was picked up with two fingers and the side of a thumb."

"Was that glass wet? Why didn't the glue fumes stick all over?"

"They did really. But I fanned it dry enough, and the prints don't come from water but oil in the skin, which won't evaporate from a little fanning."

"So we can connect someone with Carly's death."

"Not really," said Ronzoni. "Circumstantial at best. This glass wasn't at the scene. Defense would argue whoever owns the print dropped the glass in the hedge while enjoying the view."

"As opposed to the weather. So what now? Can you print the suspects?"

Ronzoni shook his head. "Not right now. Tomorrow when the storm is done, and I can get some backup in. We don't want to spook the horses."

CHAPTER THIRTY-ONE

Ronzoni photographed everything and then he rebagged the evidence and we took it back to the gym to lock up. Ronzoni told me to put my thinking cap on about things but I had no ideas left. I was confident in my theory of what happened and how, but the who was what needed proving. And on that count I had nothing but theory.
We went back to the lounge. Most everyone was asleep. Shania was napping against Anton's shoulder. Anton was sitting up, but I couldn't tell if he was sleeping. Leon had made a bed on the floor at the rear of the room, cushions from a sofa and a blanket. Deshawn was in a club chair, his head resting against the side. Rosaria was in another club chair, curled up in a ball, feet tucked in, breathing softly. Neville was standing behind the bar, as still as a statue, eyes open but unmoving, a semi-awake state. I wondered if he'd ever done time in the military, maybe on sentry duty. Cassandra was asleep across a sofa, her head resting on Ron's lap. Ron was sitting up but his head had fallen back and his mouth was open like a cave. It wasn't glamorous but it was real. The wind hummed and the waves crashed

outside. I wanted to sleep but didn't think I could. The idea of a hotel blanket filled me with an unusual melancholy.

Inevitably it made me think of Danielle, tucked up in a dorm room bed somewhere in Tallahassee. I felt the compulsion to call her despite the late hour. She wouldn't mind. She was like that. But I knew there was no coverage to be had. Except on the roof. Where I recalled the bleep of a message coming in. I sighed and pulled out my phone.

The message was from Danielle. That made me smile. Shania wouldn't have understood if I told her that everything Danielle did made me smile, because Shania didn't understand that even the things that Danielle did that drove me crazy still made me smile. I looked at her name on the screen and a picture formed in my head of a white t-shirt and denim jeans, her walking across the courtyard at Longboard Kelly's, which morphed into her running in Lycra along City Beach, which became her in nothing but a Modesto Nuts t-shirt, lying on a lounger on the back patio of our home on Singer Island.

I touched her name and the message came up. I read it. Then I read it again. And a third time. My mind flew back in time, trying to recall what I had seen and what I had not seen.

I jumped up and turned to Ronzoni, who had taken the chair beside me.

"Come on," I said.

He frowned but I didn't wait. I turned and walked out of the lounge. I strode out to the lobby and turned back. Ronzoni wandered out to me.

"What the hell?"

I held the phone up to his face. He recoiled some from the bright screen and then he read the message.

"Where are the safety bars?"

"We need to go to the gym."

I turned and walked down the corridor, snatching up a camp light off the check-in desk as I strode by.
"What does that mean? Where are the safety bars?"
"I'll show you."
We reached the gym door and Ronzoni dropped and unlocked it.
"Who sent that?" he asked as he stood and pushed open the door.
"Danielle."
"Deputy Castle?"
"She's not a deputy anymore, Ronzoni."
"Right, I heard. FDLE."
"Yep."
I held the camp light up over Paul Zidane's body. He was covered in a sheet, and the light bounced off it.
"Why is she sending you texts about this?"
"I sent her some photos of the scene earlier."
"You had no right to do that."
"Ronzoni, you're missing the point."
"No, I'm not. This is not an FDLE case. This is a Palm Beach matter."
"For crying out loud, Ronzoni, the FDLE don't want to steal your damned collar. Something didn't feel right so I played a hunch. Got a second opinion."
"You are the second opinion."
"Third opinion, then."
"Don't do it again."
"Ronzoni, I will call or text or email or flipping FaceTime whoever I please whenever I please, whether you like it or not. Now do you want to know what this message means?"
Ronzoni sulked for moment, and then he said, "Go on."
"Look at this structure."

"The white thing?"

"Yes, the white thing. It's like a frame for a cage, right? Like the edges of a box without any sides."

"I've got eyes, Jones. What's your point?"

"You see how the steel edges at the top and bottom end of the bench have holes in them."

"I do."

"The barbell there, sits on racks, like big hooks, perpendicular to the person on the bench."

"Yes."

"But these holes are for something else. Something without which this whole rig is pointless."

"Safety bars."

"Right."

"Pretend I'm not an athlete, Jones. What are safety bars?"

I pretended Ronzoni wasn't an athlete. It wasn't hard.

"Safety bars are steel bars that slip into these holes. They go across here, parallel to the bench, on either side. You put them in at a height where if you are lying on the bench they are at chest level if your back is arched and your chest is high. So they don't get in the way when you bring the barbell down."

"All right, so now I'm a world-class weight lifter. I still don't see a point, Jones."

"If you drop the weight on yourself with the safety bars in place the barbell lands on the safety bars, not your chest, and sure as hell not your throat."

"But there are no bars."

"Exactly. If you're not going to have safety bars then there's no point having this power rack at all. Those safety bars are the reason for this rig. It's expensive and it takes up a lot of space. Without safety bars you might as well just have a regular lifting bench."

"So they've got a whatever this thing is called but no safety bars. Sue them."

"Exactly, Ronzoni! That's what would happen. Hotels are always so conscious of liability. If they only had a bench, no power rack, and someone gets hurt the hotel could claim the guest used the equipment improperly—user error, not hotel liability. But if they have the rack and no safety bars, then the court would ask why the hotel didn't have the correct equipment for the rack—now it's hotel liability not user error."

"You're saying the hotel would have everything in place or nothing. No in-between."

"Right. It's stupid, but in my experience liability law has very little to do with common sense."

Ronzoni looked at the power rack and at Paul Zidane's body under the sheet.

"Were they here before?"

"I think so."

"You think so?"

"I looked at the rig when I came in but I didn't take an inventory. But I've worked out in plenty of gyms and seen plenty of these rigs, and I didn't notice the bars missing."

"That's not going to wash in court."

"It doesn't have to. It doesn't matter if I saw them. The question Danielle sent wasn't are there safety bars? She wrote where are the safety bars? So . . .where are they?"

Ronzoni shrugged. And then he set about looking. It wasn't a big gym. There were only so many places a person could put long steel bars. That they were matte black made it harder work, using a camp light and a flashlight.

But it didn't take long.

"Ronzoni," I said, looking down behind a rack of dumbbells near the wall. I could see something that looked like black bars, but could have been shadows.

Ronzoni took a look and then tried to move the rack of barbells. There must have been four hundred pounds on there so he didn't get far. I took the dumbbells off the rack two by two, and then dragged the rack away from the wall enough so that Ronzoni could squeeze in.

Ronzoni pulled on another pair of latex gloves. I wondered if he had a box of them in his pockets, or maybe he moonlighted as a magician. Then he bent down and pulled.

"It's heavy."

"Come on, Arnie, you can do it."

He did it. He dragged a steel bar up and out. It was colored in a black paint that didn't reflect the camp light.

"This what you're looking for?"

"That would be it."

"What do we do with it?" he asked. "I don't want to disturb any prints.

"Let's put it in the rack."

Ronzoni took one end near Paul Zidane's head and I took the other end near his feet and we slipped the bar into the holes on the port side of the rack at about waist height. Then Ronzoni dragged the second bar out and we repeated the effort on the starboard side. Ronzoni was huffing when we were done. He really needed to get out for a walk once in a while.

"So, can you do your superglue thing again?" I asked him.

He shook his head and breathed deeply. "No. We'd need a big enough chamber and a bucket of glue. But there is another way."

"Which is?"

"The print kit in my car."

"You have a print kit in your car? Why didn't you use that before?"

"You seen the weather outside?"

I had. I'd been out in it too many times already. But I had a horrible feeling that I was going to experience it one more time.

CHAPTER THIRTY-TWO

I was starting to develop the opinion that Detective Ronzoni couldn't swim. It never occurred to me that there were people in Florida who couldn't swim, and it amazed me when I met one. I would probably be less startled to run into Elvis on Worth Avenue. But I guessed it was a skill that some people just never picked up, despite the sun and the fact the state was a peninsula surrounded by water.

He didn't out-and-out say he wasn't going to go out and get the print kit, but he more or less assumed it would be me who ventured out again.

There were two problems with Ronzoni's plan. The first was that after he unlocked the storm door on the front of the lobby we couldn't find his car. The forecourt lights on the hotel were out, so we searched with flashlights. It shouldn't have been difficult because he had parked at the base of the front stairs. But his Crown Victoria wasn't there.

It's a hell of thing to see a cop looking for his missing car. Losing a car is no picnic for anybody, and it can be an out-of-body experience to think that someone has stolen your vehicle.

But it's all magnified by an order of ten for a cop. It just doesn't happen. People don't steal cop cars. Maybe on television, but not in real life. Ronzoni looked positively dumbfounded. But his car wasn't stolen.

The parking lot was a lake, or perhaps an estuary, a brackish extension of the ocean on the other side of the hotel. The hotel itself had become an island, and the vehicles in the lot had been lifted by the storm surge. Cars were bobbing around like rubber duckies in a tub.

My Caddy had gotten off light. It was a first. I don't have good luck with cars. My insurance company had a special category of risk with my name on it. But my SUV had somehow gotten wedged with the tailgate up on the south end of the front steps, and was half out of the water. It didn't look like it was going anywhere.

We scanned the lot for Ronzoni's car. I found a vehicle with a remotely similar shape to a Crown Vic doing pirouettes on the north end of the front lawn. The flashlight was struggling at the distance, but it looked about right.

"Maybe," said Ronzoni. "But what is that? Looks like a mast?"

"Might be behind. Hard to say."

"How you gonna get out there?"

I shook my head. "Not this way."

I walked back inside. Ronzoni's car looked like it was at the north end of the building, closer to the utility exit near the diesel tanks than it was to the main entrance. So I headed that way.

But then there was the second problem with Ronzoni's plan. I was in a borrowed linen suit that was the only dry thing I had, and I was traveling commando, so stripping to my underwear wasn't an option. I had trashed my cheap poncho in the diesel bunker so even if I did strip down to my birthday suit I had nothing to cover up. And I had already had an octopus get friendly with my manhood so there was no way in hell I was going out there in the buff.

I made Ronzoni stop and unlock the door to the boutique so I could find something suitable. I think he assumed I was going to grab another disposable poncho, but then I saw something a lot more stylish. It was a trench coat, tan in color, with the buttons and the belt and the whole nine yards. The tag said Burberry. I thought it made me look like Columbo, or Inspector Gadget.

"Are you stealing that?" Ronzoni asked.

"No. I'm borrowing it."

"If you wear it out in the flood you'll ruin it."

"You didn't seem so concerned about the poncho," I said.

"The poncho was worth a nickel. This thing looks like a month's salary."

"So at what cost does something become stealing?"

"When it becomes material goods. And that coat is definitely material goods."

"So I'll put it back and you can go out in the storm and get your damned kit."

Ronzoni huffed. "Try not to get it dirty."

"Yes, dad."

I led Ronzoni through the service corridors to the utility exit that led out to the diesel tanks. I wrapped the coat tight around myself and pulled the belt in hard. The wind gushed up underneath the coat. So this was what it was like to roam around the highlands of Scotland in a kilt. A touch more drafty than I'm used to.

I didn't head out toward the tanks. I edged around the hotel building, staying on the high ground as long as I could. The wind helped with that goal because it was driving me back into the wall. I got to the northwest corner of the hotel and peeked around.

A dark lake lay out before me. Random spots of light twinkled off the surface, scattered here and there in the darkness. I scanned the water with the flashlight, back and forth. There was a surprising amount of debris floating around, random edges and shapes that were impossible to decipher in the wind and rain and darkness.

I spotted more than one vehicle. But I focused in on the one slowly rotating in an eddy that had formed just down from where I stood. From my closer vantage point it definitely looked like a Crown Victoria except for one unexplained shape that threw all the lines of the car off kilter.

Ronzoni said the fingerprint kit was in a case inside a waterproof bag in the trunk, so I waited until I saw what I thought was the trunk end of the car slowly ebb around toward me. Then I waded in.

To say I felt foolish was an understatement. I was sneaking around in the dead of night, in the middle of a hurricane, wearing boat shoes and a trench coat and not a stitch more. I felt like some kind of weirdo pervert. The water crept up my legs as I got in deeper, and then it got uncomfortable as everything started to float.

I reached the car at the rear door. The vehicle was slowly rotating like one of those tea cups on the kiddies' ride at Disney World. I put my hand on the rear fender and made my way around. As I did I shone the flashlight all over the car and I figured out what was so out of place.

Ronzoni had thought he had seen some kind of mast, and in a Robinson Crusoe kind of way he had. The windshield of his police-issue vehicle had been punctuated by a wayward palm tree. It had been uprooted and tossed like a spear right through the middle of the windshield. It stuck up into the night, leaning away from the prevailing wind, and I realized it was acting as a sail of sorts, moving the car around dependent on the movement of wind.

It spun the trunk toward me, so I edged around and pulled Ronzoni's keyring from the top pocket of the coat and opened the trunk. I leaned on the bumper to reach in and it dipped down, nearly sending me head first into the trunk. I had visions of me falling into the trunk and it closing behind me. That would have been the perfect end to a less than perfect day, but I kicked my feet and used them like a keel to keep my balance. I reached in and grabbed the bag. It was heavy plastic and orange in color, as if Ronzoni expected to find himself lost at sea in his Crown Victoria. It was a ridiculous notion until I reassessed my current circumstances.

I didn't close the trunk. I didn't see the point. The wind would do it, or not, but the Crown Vic wasn't likely to be worse off either way. The bag more or less floated, so I dragged it across the surface until I reached the upslope to the hotel and then I threw it over my shoulder and trudged up out of the water.

I made it back to the utility door and banged on it, and then again. I got no response and wondered if Ronzoni had fallen asleep. So I banged again. The door cracked open, Ronzoni pushing it against the wind with his back.

I barged my way past Ronzoni into the corridor and he eased up his weight against the door and it slammed home, nearly knocking him off his feet.

"You didn't hear me banging?" I asked.

"All I hear is banging. You got the coat dirty."

I snarled. I almost told him about the palm tree planted in his car, but I figured he would enjoy it so much more if he got to see it for himself with the coming of the sun.

CHAPTER THIRTY—THREE

Ronzoni let the bag drip-dry and carried it back to the gym. I quickly got toweled off in the lobby bathroom and changed back into my suit. I would have gone to my room for a shower but I didn't want to miss what Ronzoni was up to. I left the trench coat on a hook in one of the bathroom stalls. I figured a cleaner would find it and would send it to lost property, or someone would do a stocktake and find it missing and write it off. There was insurance for those sorts of things.

Ronzoni had taken the bag to the far end of the gym, near the treadmill that should have been overlooking a stunning ocean view but was instead looking at the inside of a storm shutter. The wind was still banging the shutters a touch every time the direction of impact varied slightly.

I watched Ronzoni take out a small toolbox and open it. It looked like a makeup case. He had a selection of plastic jars and he chose one along with a long-bristled brush, like the kind of thing a lady might use to apply rouge. He opened the jar. Inside was powder.

"I'm using orange powder. It will show up better on the black bar."

I nodded and smiled. I didn't need the running commentary. I knew exactly what he was doing and why. It was the results I wanted to see, so I didn't see the point in getting into a whole pissing contest about who knew what.

He used only his forefinger and thumb to hold the brush and he spun it around lightly over the surface of the safety bar. His touch was light. He would have been a good makeup artist, in another life. He spun the brush back and forth, leaving a light dusting of print powder on the bar. The orange powder showed up all the smudges and marks and traces of oil left on the black bar. But when he was finished, what it didn't show was a clean print.

"They've been wiped," he said. "See these smudges here and here? They were latent prints. But whose is anyone's guess."

"The fact the safety bars were hidden tells us something. Paul Zidane didn't crush himself and then get up and hide the bars."

"You can't say for sure that he didn't remove them before he lifted. Defense would argue he got all macho after talking to you and took the bars off himself to prove a point."

"Usually you prove a point to someone, not when there's no one in the room."

"Maybe he was going to tell you about it later. Maybe he was proving the point to himself."

"That doesn't make sense with what everyone says about him. He's a lifter, he's into the whole scene. I guarantee the ME will find some kind of steroid in his bloodstream. When you do something as often as he lifted weights it becomes habit. There's a process. The challenge isn't in bucking the process—

it's in doing the process and winning anyway. It wouldn't be his process to take the safety bars off, quite the opposite."

"Except he did take them off, Jones. They were off when he lifted because he doesn't get crushed if they are in place. Even if someone else was here, even if someone else let the weight drop on him. Hell, even if they pushed it down on him—"

"The point is someone else was here."

Ronzoni stuck the palm of his hand up at me to demand my silence. I didn't think much of that, and was about to tell him so when I noticed he was thinking. It was such an unusual occurrence that I let the palm thing slide and watched him go about it. He turned his head one way, and then the other, and then he stepped behind the bench above Paul Zindane's head and looked down over the bar at the sheet below. Then he stepped back to his print kit. He switched to a new brush and selected a different jar of powder.

"What?" I asked him.

He moved back to the head of the bench and opened his jar and swished around his brush with his forefinger and thumb.

"If someone else was here, if it was not an accident, then someone made sure the bar stayed on his throat. You said before that if he was doing it right it should land on his chest."

"It's called a chest press, not a neck press."

"So maybe someone helped it roll down to his neck."

I nodded. "And maybe their prints are on the bar."

Ronzoni said nothing. He focused on the weight bar. He twirled his brush and left a light dusting of powder again. This time I noted the powder was black not orange. But the barbell that had crushed Paul Zidane's throat was shining chrome. The black showed up nicely. I stepped over and watched Ronzoni do his thing. The bar had areas where it was smooth chrome and other areas where the metal had been crosshatched to make a rough surface that helped the lifter grip the bar better. No one wanted a few hundred pounds to slip from their grasp.

"Can you get prints from the crosshatched areas?" I asked.

"No," said Ronzoni. "Not a flat surface so there's no prints to be had there. But logic says if Mr. Zidane was lifting the bar he would have gripped it there, right? So anyone pushing down against him would probably have their hands on the smooth bits."

I nodded. Ronzoni was on a roll.

He dusted the full length of the bar. There were some prints at either end of the bar, outside of the weights.

"Those are ours," he said. "From when we lifted the thing off him."

But the rest of the bar was more long smudges. Like someone had wiped down this bar as well.

"Makes sense, I suppose," I said. "If you wipe down the safety bars, you're gonna wipe down the murder weapon."

Ronzoni nodded but kept looking at the lost prints on the bar.

"Worth a shot," I said.

Ronzoni said nothing. He didn't look like he was thinking now. He looked like he had zoned out, like his brain was fried. That was the Ronzoni look I knew.

"Tell me how you would do this," he said. "Would you stand here?"

"Makes most sense. If he doesn't have the safety bars on, then he has a spotter. That's the process. He might have both but he would never have neither." I moved closer to Ronzoni and pictured the scene in my head. "So the spotter might help him lift the weight out of the rack, or not. Some guys don't like the help. So no, the spotter doesn't help. Paul was one of those guys. He's lying there, and he brings the weight down to his chest, and then extends his arms fully to raise the weight up."

"How many times?"

I looked at the weight plates at either end of the barbell, which hadn't been touched.

"Once. He's going for max rep. The most he can lift in one go."

"So does the spotter help him put the bar back into the rack?"

I thought about Paul again. "No. Same rule applies. Some guys don't want anyone to touch the bar except in emergency. It's a pride thing. He's that guy."

"So the spotter doesn't touch the bar."

"Not then."

"When?"

"If all goes well, never."

"So then the spotter could be a woman?" Ronzoni asked. It sounded like he was asking a rhetorical question, but it really required an answer.

"Shania could out-lift you."

Ronzoni shrugged. "Just saying'. It widens the field. Does the lifter do the weight again?"

"Sure, maybe. Maybe he starts a touch light and goes up in weight. Then he does it again. Just one rep. But the second time the spotter knows the process. Paul gets it from the rack, holds it high and then lowers it down to his chest. That's when the spotter makes their move."

"How?"

"While it's down, or maybe on the way down. Already got gravity helping you. Push right down on the bar." I pretended I was pushing down on a bar, my hands wrapped around and my palms facing down. Ronzoni nodded.

"Help me," he said. He moved to the end of the barbell and motioned for me to take the other end.

"Just rotate it, one-eighty degrees."

We twisted the bar around so the black powdered smudges were facing down, and fresh gleaming chrome was facing up. Then Ronzoni got his brush and his powder and started dusting again.

He said, "If they're pressing down with their palms . . ."

He dusted the smooth chrome section of the bar. And he started grinning like the Cheshire cat as he did. I saw big fat finger prints appear from nowhere on the chrome bar.

"They're wrapping their hands around the bar and touching their fingertips on the underside. But they didn't think to wipe there because they didn't realize they'd touched it."

Ronzoni powdered the length of the bar. Eight clean prints came up. A hand wrapped around the bar, pushing down. Not lifting. All the fingers. They wouldn't have looked cleaner if they had been taken during a booking at the police department. I stood back and let Ronzoni take his pictures and then use his collection tape to stick and peel each latent print off the bar and onto a card. He labeled each card with its position relative to the other fingers. When he was done he laid them out in a row, and he picked up the champagne glass with the print on it and compared the prints.

They didn't match.

CHAPTER THIRTY—FOUR

"How can they not match?" asked Ronzoni.

"Is that a serious question?" I chuckled. I had dragged Ronzoni into believing my hypothesis that the two deaths were not only both murders but also possibly even linked. That there was a two-time killer among us. Now that he had gotten there, to have the theory blown out of the water rendered his brain frazzled.

"But what are the odds? Two murders within a few hours, in a small group of people, but not linked?"

"Who says they aren't linked?"

"The evidence?"

"No, Ronzoni. You're the one always thinking about how defense will say this and defense will say that. The evidence says there are two different people involved. It doesn't say the two events aren't connected."

"How are they?"

"I don't know. But it's possible that one begat the other. Like the second might not have happened if the first didn't happen.

But I think we need to get prints from everyone. Pronto. You've got the kit."

"I don't have enough to do everyone. And if I can't do them all at the same time it creates an issue with evidential continuity. Better to do them all at one time. Plus, whether it's one killer or two, I don't want to tip them off that we're on to them. Not at night and in the middle of a hurricane."

"You might not get backup for ages. Your boys are going to be super busy tomorrow. What if you can't get word to them? What if the killer slips away?"

"How will they slip away? By boat?"

"Stranger things," I said.

"No, we need to do it the right way. We don't have to tip anyone off just yet. Let's get this evidence secured and get back to the bar."

"All right, you're the detective, Detective. But let's do one thing on the way."

Which he let me do. I wandered back via the north corridor and slipped into the kitchen with Emery's card. I used one of Ronzoni's collection of latex gloves and took a champagne glass from the crate, which I slipped into the boxwood hedge outside the emergency exit.

We got back in the bar as folks were stirring. Despite the lack of sleep there was something in the group's circadian rhythms that had them restless. There was rubbing of eyes and confusion as brains processed exactly where they were and why. Ron waved me over. Cassandra was awake but still laying her head on Ron's lap.

She said, "Miami, could you ask the detective about the bathroom situation? I'm sure he doesn't mean for us to stay in the room quite literally."

It was a good point, and it gave me an idea. I told Ronzoni what Cassandra had said. Her being Palm Beach royalty gave it extra credibility, and then I added my own thoughts to it. He decided it was fine, certainly better than fingerprinting everyone.

Ronzoni cleared his throat and spoke clearly but not loudly. He told them all that they would be free to use the bathroom. Each person who needed to go would be allowed a few minutes to do so. He told them to use the lobby bathroom only, don't wander, come straight back to the bar. Andrew Neville reminded him that it was called a lounge, and then suggested that someone stand sentry at the lounge door to watch the people as they crossed the lobby. Ronzoni suggested in the circumstances, given the hurricane and all, that such a precaution wasn't necessary.

Rex Bonatelli bounded over to Ronzoni like he was incontinent and desperately needed to be first cab off the rank.

"Detective, this is ridiculous. I'm going nuts here. There's this great storm going on outside, and I, a meteorological correspondent, am stuck in here hiding from it rather than reporting on it. It's an outrage, sir!"

I wasn't sure where the outrage bit had come from but it was a nice touch.

"Mr. Bona—"

"I know what you're going to say, Detective. But we have to be reasonable. You're letting people wander around the hotel."

"We're letting people go to the bathroom, Mr. Bona—"

"Whatever, Detective. But the point is, this is a free country." He was pacing back and forth in front of Ronzoni, and I could smell the animal scent radiating from him. He looked like a beast about to explode.

Ron appeared beside me. "He's been like this for some time. He is literally driving everyone else crazy, and I'm not sure given one of these people has killed someone tonight that we want to be aggravating them like that."

I nodded and glanced at the cameraman, Ken, who was sitting back in a club chair with a look of horror on his face. He didn't share Bonatelli's enthusiasm for standing outside in a hurricane. I'm sure he would have preferred filming the whole thing with a green screen in the Weather Network studios. I stepped over to Ronzoni.

"Ronzoni. Let's remember we have a killer in the room and this guy is like a live electrical wire. We don't want to set anyone off. Perhaps if you let him shoot something from where we just were on the front steps. It's not too dangerous, and they can get some good footage."

Ronzoni took it in and said to Bonatelli, "Okay. You can shoot some footage from the hotel entrance."

"Hotel entrance?" Bonatelli exclaimed. "A shot of the parking lot? Are you kidding?"

"It could be all right," said cameraman Ken.

"All right? I don't do all right. CNN does all right. WPEC does all right. We are the Weather Network, Ken. The Weather Network."

"It's that or nothing," said Ronzoni.

I said, "There are cars floating around out there like a demolition derby on water."

Bonatelli cocked an eye. "Demolition derby?"

I nodded. "There's even one with a palm tree right through the windshield. Be great footage."

"A palm tree. Like a little potted palm or what?"

"No, a big one. Pulled from the earth and slammed through the windshield like an Exocet missile."

"That could be something. All right, Detective, you're on. Let's go."

Bonatelli nodded at Ken to lug their stuff and he took off at pace toward the door. Ken the cameraman strapped on his backpack and his camera equipment and headed after. He stopped next to me.

"Thanks, man," he said.

"You're welcome. But I need a favor."

"Name it."

"You got any other cameras in that pack?"

"Of course. Got a couple of GoPros."

"They waterproof?"

"We're the weather channel," he smiled.

I told him what I wanted and where I wanted it and he said no problem, he'd take care of it.

"When you get out to the front, stay by the storm door," I said. "Send him down into the lot. You won't even have to get wet."

Ken smiled again.

"But it's still pretty dark out there. Not sure how much you'll actually get on film."

Ken tapped the spotlight mounted to his camera. "My spot's pretty good. It lit up the back of the damned hotel from the beach. I reckon it'll get a car anywhere in that parking lot."

He nodded and strode after his so-called talent. Ronzoni made to follow them to let them out the locked hurricane-proof door. He hesitated.

"There's a car out there with a palm tree through the windshield?"

"Yeah," I said. "I'm sure they'll get a shot of it. Ask them about it later."

He frowned, nodded and then marched away.

I waited. Ronzoni was gone a few minutes and then came back. He assigned people one at a time to use the facilities. Cassandra went first. She came back looking tired but relieved. Then Ron deferred to Shania, but she found his deferment sexist and refused to go. The detente occurred only after Ronzoni told Shania she would go next or she wouldn't go again that day. I got the feeling Ronzoni needed some sleep. But Shania went next, returning looking like she had enjoyed a shower and eight hours sleep. She was followed by Ron, who wet his hair but dried his face, Sam, who also wet down his face and hair, and Deshawn, whose bald head made it hard to know if he'd done anything at all. The staff all waited until the guests went, and then Rosaria, Emery and Neville all went. Anton, Leon and Chef Dean all declined. Ronzoni prompted me but I told him to go first because I didn't need the bathroom. I wanted to do something else, and I wanted to do it last.

When Ronzoni got back he nodded to me and I wandered out. I angled toward the bathroom but then banked away and moved north into the corridor behind the kitchen. I pushed open the north emergency exit and stepped outside. The rain was abating. Or perhaps it was the wind, because it was still raining but it was coming down vertically now. In the distance across the heavy gray ocean I saw the first faint glimpse of daybreak. Not so much light as a line of less dark along the horizon.

I pulled the glove from my pocket and stretched it onto my hand. It was limp at the tips of my fingers but it would do the job. I shoved my hand into the hedge right where I had placed the champagne glass. And I found exactly what I was looking for.

Nothing. The glass was gone. It confirmed what I thought, that it had not gotten there by accident. That it had been in the hot tub hut with its twin that we found there. Someone in the group had used their bathroom leave to retrieve it. I didn't expect to burst back into the bar and find it on their person. Whoever it was had more than enough time to think through what to do about it. They had stuffed it in there in panic. But they had collected it with a plan. I suspected that plan was to throw it into the ocean. That felt like the best play given the circumstances.

As I stood there sheltered from the rain and the wind the conversations played back in my mind, like an audiobook on high speed. Before, I thought I knew who had killed Carly Pastinak. Now I knew I knew. But more importantly, I now knew why. And the why was the important bit. Because the why told me everything I needed to know about Paul Zidane's death.

I looked out at the pounding ocean to where a glass might have been swallowed. Then I looked at the seawall, waves crashing over where Ken the cameraman had been standing, strapped to a rope. On top of which a lunatic weatherman had been standing lit up like Christ the Redeemer. And I glanced along the hotel, at the walkway I stood on, along the concourse to the south end of the hotel, in the darkness beyond which lay the pool deck and hot tub hut and Carly Pastinak's body.

And then I looked again at the angry sky and I decided I needed a weatherman.

CHAPTER THIRTY—FIVE

Ken the camera guy was standing on the front steps of the hotel. He was staying close to the hurricane-proof door and under the overhang of the building. The rain was coming down nice and straight, which kept Ken nice and dry. Rex Bonatelli was another matter altogether. Not that Bonatelli wanted to keep dry. Keeping dry was not on his bucket list. He had donned his heavy blue poncho and had waded down into the water. He was down there getting nice and wet, the rain cascading off his bald head. His poncho had a hood, and it was collecting fresh rainwater behind his head in case the whole thing turned to drought before our eyes. He was talking into a microphone but I couldn't hear what he was saying. And the guy was loud. But he was pointing at the parking lot and the motor vehicles doing a steel and aluminum version of Swan Lake. I didn't see Ronzoni's car with the palm tree in it, but my SUV was still stuck high on the berm up to the hotel as if it were waiting for me to make a fast getaway.

There were cars slowly spinning and floating around as they had before, but with Ken's spotlight I saw more of them at once. It was a lot brighter than my flashlight had been. Six or seven vehicles were doing a slow-motion waltz. I knew from my limited music lessons with sax player Buzz Weeks that a waltz was in fact defined not by the steps but by the three-four time of the music. I was pretty confident some segment editor down at the Weather Network would have a library of Mozart or Beethoven to drop in over the visuals Ken was taking. At least in the places Bonatelli wasn't bellowing his prognostications about the hurricane.

Ken saw me coming and nodded. His camera was attached to him with a rig that put the weight into his hips, which was good for his back and meant he didn't have to stare through a viewfinder to keep his eye on Bonatelli.

I nodded. I wasn't sure if I could talk or if that would get caught on the mic. Ken confirmed the status on that by speaking.

"Thanks," he said. "Good shots."

"That's a bright light you got there."

"Told ya. Haven't seen that palm tree car yet."

I pointed to the north end of the hotel where I had encountered Ronzoni's car. Ken turned his camera in that direction and I heard Bonatelli for the first time yelling through the headphones on Ken's head. He had been plunged into darkness and apparently wasn't all that impressed by the notion that someone other than him should be under the watchful gaze of the camera.

"Hold your water, Rex," said Ken. "I've got the car with the palm tree."

Ken listened and then asked me, "How does he get over there?"

"He doesn't. Not right now. Tell him the sun's breaking. Tell him he'll get his shot in a half hour. But right now, I need you."

Ken repeated what I said, more or less, to Bonatelli. "He says he needs you now."

Bonatelli trudged in from the pond in the parking lot and up the steps. He looked like a whale in a slicker. He didn't brush the water off his head, preferring to allow the excess to run down around his eyes and ears.

"What do you need from me?" Bonatelli asked me.

"You? Nothing." I looked at Ken. "I need you."

"Him? Why do you need him?"

"Because I don't need anyone to tell me the weather. It's usually pretty self-evident."

"You think you're taking my cameraman?"

"I am."

"What am I supposed to do?"

I thought on it. "The sun's about to break, and you're all wet. You could go out and get some diesel and get that generator going on the roof."

I was surprised to see his face light up. He really was an interesting piece of work. Perhaps he saw power as the key to filing some of that footage Ken had taken. I think it was killing him that the hurricane was passing us by and he hadn't had a second of screen time.

Bonatelli strode off in the direction of the utility exit at the north end of the hotel. Ken the camera guy and I went to the manager's office.

"I saw you looking at an iPad earlier."

"Uh-huh."

"Can you connect that to a TV?"

"Uh-huh."

"And you were viewing the footage you took?"

"Uh-huh."

"Okay," I said. "Show me."

CHAPTER THIRTY—SIX

I gathered everyone in the bar. It wasn't a big job, since everyone except me, Bonatelli and Ken the camera guy were there already. I left Bonatelli to his diesel run. I didn't need him, and his rampant energy would be a distraction. Ronzoni gave me the floor and a short leash. He wasn't sure where I was going but he sure didn't want me to solve his case. He liked getting the credit.

Everyone but Ronzoni was seated. Chef Dean was sitting on a stool at the end of the bar. Neville was in a club chair for the first time all night. He didn't look comfortable. I don't think he liked to relax among the guests, and the act of sitting was surely an act of relaxation. He was perched next to his assistant general manager, Emery, and Rosaria in a cluster of chairs. Leon Lezac sat on the love seat next along, beside Sam Venturi. Then in another cluster of chairs Deshawn Maxwell sat alone. The sofa beside and forward of him saw Anton and Shania, the wedding couple, sitting side by side. Toward the right side as I faced them were Cassandra and Ron. I paced slowly before the room. Detective Ronzoni stood at the back of the room. Ken the camera guy was on the floor at the front, connecting iPads to cameras and the silent flat-screen television on the wall.

I didn't look like me, and I didn't feel like me. I generally favor the direct approach, and this didn't feel like it. It felt like a roundabout way to the end. But I couldn't figure the direct route. Ronzoni's route was to wait for the storm to abate and to call in backup. Not only did I have no idea when that backup might actually appear through the flooded streets, but I also wasn't confident that the evidence that backup confirmed would solve the case. It was possible, as it had been every time so far, that the evidence came to another dead end. I needed to set a cat among the pigeons. But first the pigeons needed a little agitating.

My linen suit looked the part even if I didn't feel it. I put my hands behind my back and paced back and forth. I looked each person in the eye. They all looked tired or wary or annoyed or all three, except Cassandra, who wore a grin. She was old-school. She liked linen suits. I stopped and turned to the room. I couldn't think of how to begin so I said, "I'm sure you're wondering why you're here."

I got some frowns.

"No, not really."

"We've been here all night."

"You're going to tell us who killed Carly."

I nodded. "Okay, so maybe you do know. One of us has been taken, and I for one would like to know who. And why."

I didn't get the great nods of agreement that I expected. They were tired and aloof, not a cooperative combination.

"Do you know who did it?" asked Shania, finally.

"It could have been anyone," I said.

"That's not exactly genius, is it?" She was right. It wasn't. But I too was tired. I had gotten thirty minutes sleep in twenty-four hours and four hours in forty-eight. I had sandbagged two properties, dived into a raging Intracoastal after a woman in a car that had delusions of being a submarine, waded out to a police-issue vehicle that had become a palm tree habitat, and wandered out into a hurricane more times than a person really ought to do. I decided to hit the ball straight back from where it came.

"How did you feel about Carly Pastinak, Shania?"

"Feel? She was okay. She did her job."

"The rumor was that she was having an affair with your husband-to-be. How do you feel about that?"

"Like you say, rumors. Not fact."

"You'd be surprised how often rumors that are not fact end up with someone dead."

"Mr. Jones, are you saying I killed Carly? Because I didn't think you were that crazy."

"That's because you don't know me that well. I'm plenty crazy. And the number one suspect in the death of a person involved in an affair is the third party to the affair."

"There was no affair."

"You know who police look at after the third party to the affair?"

"Dazzle me."

"One of the people involved in the affair."

I moved my eyes just a touch, just enough to lay them on Anton.

Shania said, "So now it's Anton?"

"Maybe. Anton was involved in the alleged affair. But he's also a proud man. A man whose tennis career has hit a speed bump. And we all know what Carly Pastinak does when her charges start dropping down the rankings, don't we? It happened to Sam. He got dumped, didn't he? Maybe Carly was planning on dumping you, Anton."

Anton shrugged.

"Maybe you figured she was going to dump you for someone better." I looked at Shania. "Maybe that was too much for such a proud man."

Anton said nothing. He was unflappable. Lots of people pretend that they don't care. They act cool, dispassionate. But Anton was the real deal. He genuinely didn't give two figs about anything. But Shania did.

"He wasn't going backward. His ranking's going to bounce back. Every player goes through a tough patch. And the way the rankings get calculated, if you don't do well at a tournament where you've done well before, you get slugged. Doesn't mean anything."

"It meant something to Sam. He didn't bounce back. He got dropped by Carly."

I noted that Shania said nothing. She said nothing because she knew what I had said was true, in a fashion, and anything she said in reply would be hollow or a lie. There was no doubt in my mind that she cared about Sam Venturi. She cared about Deshawn Maxwell. She loved Anton Ribaud. She was the kind of person you wanted on your side.

Sam sunk into the side of his seat. Leon Lezac was sitting next to him and Leon suddenly looked like he was twice Sam's size.

"Isn't that right, Sam? She dumped you when your career went into free fall."

"I wouldn't call it free fall." His voice wavered and even he didn't buy it. But it was harsh. My career had stalled just short of the brass ring. I knew exactly where Sam was coming from. He had become a coach because the game was still in his

blood, like a cancer. Maybe it was because I played a little longer, or maybe that had nothing to do with it, but when I hung up my cleats at the end of my second year in Port St. Lucie, I knew I was done. I didn't want to coach, even though I thought I might be okay at it. I wanted to move on.
"Carly was a painful memory for you, wasn't she, Sam?"
"What?"
"You didn't know she was coming this weekend, did you?"
"No, but . . ."
"And when you saw her, spoke with her, you tried to leave the island. With Detective Ronzoni."
"Yes. She wasn't a nice person."
"She wasn't a nice memory."
Sam frowned and stared off into the distance.
Deshawn Maxwell was sitting in a group of chairs beyond Sam's left shoulder. I glanced at him.
"What about you, Deshawn? Friend of the bride. How did you feel about Carly?"
"I didn't know her at all."
"But you know Shania. The general consensus is that you're like a guardian to her. And you grew up together. You knew her father, you told me."
"I did."
"You were like a son to him."
"You'd have to ask him about that."
"The feeling among the group was that Carly wanted to get Shania as a client. I wondered if maybe she knew something—perhaps something that could hurt Shania—and was going to use it as leverage against her."
Deshawn shifted in his seat but he said nothing. I left him thinking and turned my eye to the other side of Sam.
"Or you, Leon."

Leon raised an eyebrow, which was as close to a who me? expression as these French boys got.

"You and Anton are like brothers. That was the word you used, wasn't it? If Carly wanted to hurt him in some way, wouldn't you stand up for your brother? Or maybe you had your own reasons."

Leon grunted. It may have been a French expletive, but I didn't think so.

"You organized this little sojourn, didn't you? You chose this hotel. Was it because you knew you could do things here that you couldn't do anywhere else?"

"No," he said.

"You mentioned before that you knew Chef Dean. That was part of the reason you came here. Old friends from Paris, wasn't that it?"

Leon shrugged. He didn't look toward Chef Dean, sitting at the bar.

"But here's a funny thing. We've been stuck in this hotel for the better part of a day and night, and I haven't seen you chat to your old friend once. Not once. He's been a max of fifty feet away in the kitchen the whole time. Almost everyone else has spoken to him. But not you."

Leon said nothing.

"Mr. Neville told me he had hired Chef Dean because of a past working relationship, and Chef Dean told me Mr. Neville had worked with him in Paris." I glanced at the chef. He was looking right at me. Chefs are often like that. They can be very direct. They are often not what you would call people people. Hiding away in kitchens creating food was a reflection of their personality. Chef Dean had skeletons in his closet. He hadn't been keen to share them, but that's why they were called skeletons. And I didn't feel it relevant to lay his past out for all to see.

"So it occurred to me. Chef Dean knows you, and he knows Mr. Neville, and you know Chef Dean, but you don't speak to him. Is it possible you know Mr. Neville?"

"What is your point, monsieur?" asked Leon.

"My point? Sam here overhead Mr. Neville and Chef Dean arguing. Not long before we found Carly Pastinak's body." I glanced at Sam. "Isn't that right, Sam?"

Sam nodded slowly. "Yes."

I looked back at Leon. "Yes. Chef Dean told Mr. Neville that he needed to do the right thing, or his dirty French secret might get out." I turned to Chef Dean. "Was that it, Chef? His dirty French secret?"

Chef Dean shrugged. There was a lot of that going on. Perhaps it was a mannerism they all picked up in France.

"I saw Mr. Neville directly after that, coming out of the kitchen. He looked shaken. And Mr. Neville is not a man who looks easily shaken."

Neville lifted his head and jutted out his chin. He looked stoic and defiant.

"So I wondered, what is this thing that Chef holds over Mr. Neville, this French secret? So I wonder, does Carly Pastinak know this secret somehow? Does she plan to use it? Perhaps use Leon to get to his 'brother'?"

"No," said Andrew Neville. And then I knew. I had suspected for some time, but then I knew. Neville's mask dropped and I saw his face. The human beneath. He didn't look at Chef Dean, his tormentor. He looked at Leon Lezac, for the briefest of moments. And the faces on both of them told me. I didn't know the particulars. I didn't want to. They weren't relevant, not to this, not to me. They had known each other in Paris, in a more than professional context. Perhaps there were other parties involved—wives, husbands, whoever—that had led to Andrew Neville leaving Paris and coming to Palm Beach. Leaving behind Leon Lezac. But Chef Dean knew their secret. When his own fortunes took a turn for the worse he used his knowledge to garner himself new employment in faraway Palm Beach, Florida. If Chef Dean had turned up dead, I would be very much looking at Mr. Neville and Leon. But he was alive and tormenting them. And I didn't feel the need to dig any further into their story. I had what I wanted.

"No," I said. "There was no reason why Carly Pastinak would know such a thing. But it did raise an interesting question. How it was that Sam Venturi came to know about it all."

Sam looked up at me, confused. "I told you. I heard them."

"You did. And I believed you. You were in the north exit corridor, just outside the kitchen, when you heard Mr. Neville and Chef Dean argue. But my question is, what were you doing there?"

"I was—what?" he said.

"Everyone here knows that you were dumped by Carly Pastinak, just before she took on Anton as a client. The rumor was that she had dropped you so she could snatch up Anton and get a gig with Global Sports Management, who also just happened to own Case Academy, where you all played tennis. But that still isn't completely accurate, is it Sam? Shania, Anton, they know how this works, but they consider you a friend so they did nothing to dispel the rumor you started. That she dumped you for Anton. One or the other. But I played pro sports, Sam. I knew plenty of agents, here and there. Never signed one up, never felt the need. But I knew plenty of guys who did. And guess what. It's not a one-for-one deal. One agent, one client. Big companies like GSM have hundreds of agents, but they have thousands of clients. They push their agents to sign up as many clients as they can, often more than they can handle. The big ones, the stars, get all the time and attention, but an agent never dumps a client. Unless the client costs more than he earns them."

Sam frowned and wiggled on the love seat.

"Carly didn't drop you because she wanted Anton. GSM would happily take you both. Except your career was done. Before it even began. You were good, but the other boys grew into men and became better. You were going to cost GSM money, not earn it. So they cut you loose. And you act all hurt by that, but you get it. You've been around tennis a long time. You know how that works. You weren't upset that you got dropped as a client. You didn't try to escape the island because an agent no longer wanted to represent you."

"What do you mean? I wanted to leave. You were there. We tried to get away."

"I don't dispute that you wanted to leave. I'm talking about why. Not because Carly dropped you as a client. You wanted to leave because you were in love with her, and she had repeatedly, and once again yesterday, told you she wasn't interested."

"That's crazy."

"Really? You suggested to me the idea that Anton was having an affair with her. You planted the idea of that being her M.O. Like that was what she did to you. As if you had been lovers, as if that was how she got clients. She was a beautiful-looking woman. She slept her way into clients. That's the story you were spreading. You implied that was why she couldn't get Shania. But it was all a lie. You were never lovers. Carly never worked like that. Did she, Anton?"

Anton and Shania's sofa was forward of Sam so Anton looked back over his shoulder at his old playing partner.

"No," he said.

"Anton, that's not true. I never said that. I wasn't in love with Carly."

"I didn't think so," I said. "Until Lady Cassandra pointed it out. And I might think woman's intuition is bunk, but I trust Cassandra's intuition one hundred percent. You were in love with her, and you were shocked to find her here. So you tried to leave. But we missed our chance and you got stuck here with her."

"I really don't know where you're going with this."

"I'm going here: I was thinking about the big high school tournament final that you won. You, Shania and Anton. The end of the road for your time at Case, but the beginning of your careers. From that final, agents were circling. You got into Wimbledon juniors and won, and then got talked into going pro. It was all happening. And it all seemed to go back to that tournament."

I paused and ambled to the right of the room, gave a wink to Ron and then wandered back.

"But that final held an ugly secret. I found out that someone had faked a drug test after the final. I wondered how that might affect all your careers if that came out, so I asked you about it. You put two and two together, didn't you? You knew it wasn't you, and you couldn't believe it of Shania. So it had to be Anton who faked the test."

Anton shrugged.

"But you saw an opportunity. You figured that Carly could use that information to blackmail Shania into becoming her client. You thought that would ingratiate you with Carly, get into her good books, maybe more. Maybe she'd fall for you the way you had for her."

"That's ridiculous."

"It is. But the mind is often a ridiculous tool. I had also told you that Deshawn had mentioned that he was going to take a hot tub earlier, so I told Carly about it because she was feeling stressed. But I had no idea where the hot tub was. Neither did she."

"Neither did I," said Sam.

"But you found out. And you told Carly."

"Says you."

"Says you. As heard by Miss Rosaria here. She heard you call Carly from the house phone here behind the bar. You told her you knew something that was going to get her Shania as a client. You told her you knew where the hot tub was and you would take her there and share your plan. You told her to meet you at the south exit near the gym."

Sam had developed some color to his face for the first time.

"So she went to the south exit. I saw her do it on the security video. But I didn't see you."

"Because I wasn't there."

"At the south exit, that's true. You took a different route. You didn't want to be seen, maybe because you didn't want any of your friends trying to stop you from making a fool of yourself. Maybe for other reasons. But you played tennis and did Pilates yesterday morning, up at the ballroom. So you knew that there were staff stairs that could get you down to the north exit without being seen. On a normal day those corridors would be full of staff, but during a hurricane? No one was around."

"You're way off the mark. I didn't hurt Carly."

"I don't know that you necessarily planned for it to go the way it did. But I know you went down the concourse walkway along the ocean side of the hotel and met Carly at the north exit. You took her across to the hot tub hut. You brought champagne to lighten the mood, maybe create a little. I've been in that hut, that lighting has the ambience of a prison cafeteria. So you were trying every trick in the book. But there was a problem. A flaw in your plan. She already knew about Anton. Am I right, Anton?"

Anton shrugged. "What is there to know?"

"Exactly. Agents always know. That's their job. I've known a lot of sports agents, and the good ones don't just do the deals. They don't just know folks at Nike and Under Armour. They look after their clients, keep their secrets hidden. The stuff that Nike and Under Armour don't want the fans to know. So I'm betting Carly asked a lot of uncomfortable questions of Anton when she signed him, and I'm equally confident that Anton shared nothing. But Carly knew what she was doing. She went digging. And found out."

I looked at Sam. He wasn't looking at me.

"And that was the problem, wasn't it, Sam? Carly didn't go to the hot tub to learn something she could use against Shania or Anton, she went to find out what you knew and how you knew it, so she could shut it down."

Sam shook his head. More and more, side to side.

"No, no, no!" he said to his feet.

"So she's not only not into your romantic scene, she's on a completely different page. And if I had a Hong Kong dollar I'd bet that she didn't just deflect your bombshell news, she turned it around. She told you that if you used it, she'd turn it back on you. Spread the word that it was you who faked the test and that's why she dumped you as a client."

"No, you're wrong!"

"Am I? Then I must be wrong about her telling you to keep your mouth shut. I must be wrong about how she told you she was leaving the hot tub and you should leave her the hell alone. Forever."

Now Sam looked at me. It wasn't a friendly look. Through gritted teeth he repeated, "No."

"But you lost it, didn't you, Sam? That was too much, too mean. You're at opposite sides of the hot tub and you just leaned down and grabbed her feet and pulled her under."

He shook his head again, harder and harder.

"Then you jumped on top of her, your knees on her arms and pinned her down. You were angry, weren't you, Sam?"

He was shaking his head side to side so hard I thought he might give himself a concussion.

"So you held her there until she stopped thrashing. Until she was dead."

The head shaking slowed and he looked in my direction.

"It was an accident," he said to someone who lay in the ether between us.

"But then you covered it up. You realized that she was dead. Did you fish her out to see, or did you just leave her there? Either way, you get out of there. You wipe down the champagne bottle and her glass and grab yours and run away. You run back across the pool deck and down the concourse, right? Back to the north exit. You plan to put the champagne glass back in the crate where you took it from and then sneak up the staff stairs. But you get into the corridor and you can't go into the kitchen. Chef Dean and Mr. Neville are in there, arguing. That's how you hear about the dirty French secret. And you try the staff corridor but there's a key card lock on it, for staff only. You're stuck in the corridor, leaving wet footprints that we can trace back to you."

I didn't know that last bit for sure, but I was confident it would be the case, and it made for good theater.

"And then you hear us. All of us. Now we've found Carly and the news is spreading and you panic again. You go back out the only open door. You're on the walkway outside. And you hide the glass in the hedge."

"That's baloney, I was never there." said Sam.

"Sure you were. You ran back along the concourse to the southeast corner of the hotel, and you see people running out from the south exit toward the hut. Emery had spread the word in the hotel—that's what you heard inside. But after her, Deshawn was first on the scene. I have to admit that made me suspicious of him. But you were second. I'm always more suspicious of the second guy. You saw Deshawn run across and you saw your chance. You ran over too, like you had been just behind him. Everyone was soaked through. The perfect cover. And then you made your run so you bumped into me and got knocked in the water. So now you're really wet. Not someone who had been running around outside, but a guy who had been knocked into the pool."

"You're out of your mind. You can't prove any of this."

And then the room burst into light. It was like blazing sun, or dropping into hyperspace, or maybe being born. Darkness and then complete and consuming light. Bonetti had obviously gotten the generator fired up because the walls began to hum like hotel walls do, as AC and electrical and goodness knows what else came back to life.

The light was harsh. It didn't do any favors for anyone. But Sam was who everyone was looking at. They didn't stop looking at him when I spoke.

"Actually, Sam. I can prove all of it."

I turned to Ken the camera guy. He was on the floor playing with his tablet computer and his cameras.

"Ken?" I asked.

He winked. "You wanna look on the iPad? Now we got power I can connect to the flat-screen TV."

"Do that. I'm sure we'd all like to see."

Ken pulled a cable out of his backpack and attached it to the side of the big dark television on the wall. Then he fired up the screen and hit a button on his camera.

It took a minute to decipher what we were looking at, just as it had when I saw it live. Rex Bonetti was standing in a hurricane, arms outstretched, lit up bright on the seawall behind the hotel. There was no sound. Ken had saved us that by not bothering to attach the sound connection to the television. But we got the general idea. Bonetti was in his element. His enthusiasm was in his face. He was standing in a deadly hurricane and loving every minute of it.

"There," said Ken. "In the background."

The rear of the hotel was lit by Ken's harsh spotlight. In the corner of the picture, on Bonetti's left side, the north exit opened and someone stepped out onto the walkway.

"Hello, Sam," I said.

"Are you kidding? That could be anyone."

He was right. It could have been. The distance was great and rain was heavy and there were long shadows from the spotlight. But then Ken pinched his fingers on his iPad and the picture on the television zoomed in, and we got a nice full-frame shot of Sam Venturi, walking along the concourse with a bottle of champagne in his hand.

"Going somewhere, Sam?"

Sam said nothing.

Ken zoomed the picture back out and we saw Sam disappear from frame toward the south and the pool deck and the hot tub hut beyond. We got more of Rex Bonetti. He wasn't much less annoying on mute. He was clearly talking about how awesome the hurricane was, and how it was moving and what it needed to do in order to grow and become something even more spectacular. Like he was talking about the Cubbies making a run in the play-offs rather than a natural phenomenon that was going to destroy homes and businesses and kill people.

Ken zoomed forward a little in time, and then we saw more of Bonetti, and the waves crashing over the top of Ken, who was down on the beach and tied to a tree for a lifeline. Then Ken pinched his fingers again and the picture zoomed away from Bonetti and onto the concourse behind, where Sam Venturi was running along the concourse. He looked in a hurry. He pulled open the emergency exit and stepped inside. We all sat and watched the closed door on screen. It felt like he had gone into a bank branch to make a transaction it took so long. But eventually Sam stepped back out.

He looked around, bent down behind the low hedge that ran along the walkway, and did something there. Then he stood up and ran back down toward the south end of the hotel and out of shot. Then Ken pulled the cable out of his iPad and the television went blank.

"That's it?" said Sam.

"What were you doing in the hedge, Sam?"

"Nothing."

"Discarding a glass, perhaps? A glass you had been using in the hot tub?"

Sam lifted his head. The shock in his eyes was replaced with something else. Perhaps the notion that he had me.

"What glass?" said Sam. "There's no glass."

"Are you sure, Sam? You didn't hide your glass in the hedge there?"

"Why don't we go out and take a look?" he said, challenge written all over his face.

I shrugged. I figured it was my turn.

"No need to get all wet, Sam. Right, Ken?"

Ken nodded. He had connected one of his GoPro cameras to the television. It was a small thing, designed to attach to a helmet or a surfboard to catch those action shots that those lunatic adventure sports folks like to get in lieu of nice sunsets and shots on the beach.

The television popped to life. Again it took a moment to figure out what we were looking at, because this time the angle was strange. The image was all gray at the bottom, like frost-bitten grass. Except not grass. It was the top of hedge. Ken had placed the camera in the hedge by the first pylon along from the north exit. Right where I had asked him to put it.

In the corner of the shot there was movement as we saw a dark shadow move—the emergency door opening. And a body stepped out of the shadow and crouched down by the hedge. And it was then that I realized that Ken had outdone himself. It was dark out—no power, little light, heavy clouds. Too dark to see anything on camera.

But Ken's camera was infrared. A night camera. I supposed those lunatic adventure sports folks liked to skate where they shouldn't after hours, or scream down a half-pipe by nothing but moonlight. I supposed there was a market for an action sports camera with night vision. Perhaps it was just the weather camera market. But either way it showed a gray but well-focused shot of Sam Venturi's face. He reached around inside the hedge for a moment. Then he pulled something out. He held it up to look at it. A long, thin glass, perfect for champagne. Then he stood and threw it away, into the ocean that was crashing across the lawn of the hotel. Then he turned and stepped back inside. The television went dark and all eyes turned to Sam.

Sam was focused on his feet. His eyes dropped and slowly closed.

"I thought your whole angle, the reason you wanted away from the island was because of your career. The fact that it hadn't happened the way you planned. I get that. The realization that the other guy is faster, stronger, better. No matter what you do. I thought that was consuming you. But I was wrong. It wasn't that feeling that ate you up inside. It was the oldest heartache in the world. Unrequited love."

We all looked at Sam. He was done. The color that had appeared was gone and his face was pale again. Even his blond hair seemed to have the color sucked from it. I glanced around the room. Everyone was looking at Sam. But despite the fact that he had killed someone, I didn't see anger or fear in their eyes. I saw pity. I saw it in them all, even Anton. Everyone except Leon. He wasn't looking at Sam. He was looking at me, looking at him. He lifted his chin and spoke to me.

"Did he kill Paul, too?"

CHAPTER THIRTY-SEVEN

"**It's a good** question," I said. "When two deaths happen in such close proximity they are often linked in some way. Right, Sam?"

Sam didn't open his eyes.

He said, "I didn't even really know Paul."

"But did you kill him?" asked Leon. I saw a flash of something —anger? grief?—across his face.

"The signs suggested it was an accident," I said. "But I didn't buy it. Because linked doesn't just mean the same perpetrator. It could be linked in some other way. Linked in time, or circumstance. Or linked by a secret. Linked by poor judgment from otherwise smart people. And then I thought about the secret that everyone seemed to be dancing around the edges of. The same secret that had seen Carly Pastinak killed. The high school tennis tournament. Case Academy. The faked drug test."

"Paul was, by consensus, a moocher. He lived his life on the goodness of others. Particularly his 'brothers'—Anton and Leon. Anton has been overly generous. Done more than any real brother could be expected to do. He gave Paul money, lodging, even a job at times. But Anton was entering a new phase in his life. Marriage. And marriage changes everything. The feelings and thoughts of another person must be considered, possibly for the first time ever. Whether you look at it as a religious thing, or a civil union, or just a pledge, marriage is a step above all other commitments. Even the nonchalant Anton knew this. Perhaps he didn't want the moocher on his coattails anymore."

I looked at Anton and got nothing. So I looked to his left.

"Certainly his wife didn't. You told me yourself. You wanted a clean slate."

"That doesn't mean I killed Paul. That's crazy," Shania said.

"It's not crazy. People who get into relationships, marriages, often want their partner's past forgotten, or even erased. It happens." I put my hands behind my back and stepped away. "But it isn't what happened here. Paul knew things about his so-called brothers. Maybe, like Sam, he knew Leon's secret from France."

"You don't understand fraternité, you Americans," said Leon. "I would never hurt my brother."

"Oh, we understand better than you think. Maybe too well. Your national motto is liberté, égalité, fraternité. Liberty, equality, fraternity. All concepts encapsulated in our constitution, our bill of rights. We've fought wars for those ideals. Sometimes in the right, sometimes not. Sometimes protecting your brother leads you to do the wrong thing."

Leon shook his head.

"I did nothing wrong."

"Maybe. But you weren't the only one affected." I wandered back across the room toward the bar and stopped short of it. Between Chef Dean and Mr. Neville.

Neville said, "I feel no compulsion to defend myself, Mr. Jones. There has been no wrongdoing on my part."

I nodded. "I agree. But Paul did know something about his brother. He knew about Anton and the fake test. But Leon, your argument was persuasive. You convinced me that he would never use that against Anton. That he didn't need to. You guys weren't really brothers, but you stick together like you are. I know real brothers who aren't that loyal."

I took a couple paces back and glanced at Leon.

"But Leon gave me another idea. The notion that someone else was involved in that test. Someone substituted for Anton in the urine sample. But that presented me with a problem. Who would do that? Let's face it, he might be loyal, but Anton's not an easy guy to love. But someone did it."

I looked at Leon, and Sam next to him.

"Sam," I said.

He shook his head. "I didn't."

"You explained how it might affect you and your teammates if Anton failed that test. It would result in some kind of a ban for Anton. But he wasn't pro yet, so how bad could it be? And it might taint you, but you could offer a test to refute it. But you told me the one person it would affect most of all. It's an uneven playing field out there. Men earn way more than women. Hell, the US women won the soccer world cup and earned a tenth of what the last place men's team got in their world cup. No one's arguing it's fair. Expectations for the women are different. They have to be great athletes, but feminine. Be strong, but look great in a skirt. And they have to be fierce competitors, but pure. And a failed drug test, even if it wasn't actually hers, was going to hurt Shania most of all."

Shania's mouth dropped open. "Are you going back there again? You can't honestly believe that I killed Paul."

"I don't. Not you. But someone who would do anything for you. Someone who felt that fraternité."

"If you say Anton, you've lost me," she said.

"No. Anton can't substitute in a test for himself. And I couldn't think of anyone who was in Florida for the tournament in question who would do it for him. But for you? Would someone do it for you? Who would come up with an idea like that? Who would protect their charge like that? An agent, that's who."

"But Carly wasn't Anton's agent back then," Shania said.

"I'm not talking about his agent. I'm talking about yours."

Shania laughed. There was no joy in it. "I didn't have an agent. I still don't. My dad—"

She stopped and stared at me, or perhaps through me. Then she came back.

"You are certifiable," she said.

"A claim often made."

"You're saying my dad took the test for Anton?"

"No. I'm not saying that. I'm saying he arranged it. He saw the big picture. He knew the damage that it would do. A girl at the beginning of a great career, tainted by a positive test of a teammate. A teammate she was also in love with. Your dad knew that the public, the fans, wouldn't make the distinction. You would be guilty by association. And if the fans thought that, so would the sponsors.

"So he arranged it. He knew that Anton had no one in the country who would do this thing for him. Leon and Paul were in France. But your dad knew someone who would do it for you. Someone he saw as a son. Deshawn."

Deshawn was sitting at the back of the room. Every head turned to him. Every head except one. All those eyes on him and he didn't flinch. Didn't move. Didn't sweat. And then the one head that didn't turn got stupid. Sam broke from his seat next to Leon and made a break for the door.

He was fast. They said he was a great counterpuncher on the court, and I could see why. He would chase down a lot of balls with that burst of speed. I wasn't going to stop him. I was only a couple steps away, but he was past me before I realized he had moved. I wasn't sure where he was going. Out of the lounge, yes. But beyond that? There were hurricane shutters everywhere and the only glass was hurricane-proof and locked. And if he did get past that, the hotel was a little island surrounded by a moat of floodwater that was itself on a bigger island surrounded by ocean and the Intracoastal. Perhaps Sam hadn't gotten that far in his thinking. Sometimes you can't plan beyond the next pitch. You just need to focus on what you are going to throw, and what the batter doesn't want to see. And sometimes you get it right, and you get to throw another one.

And sometimes you get hit into the stands.

Sam launched across the room and was at the doorway before most of us had moved a muscle. The doorway was the first objective. The doorway that had been vacant and open when Sam drove up and out of his seat. The doorway that got filled by the massive wet frame of Rex Bonetti. His poncho flapped and served to fill the void around him. Sam used that court agility to step around Bonetti. I don't know what Bonetti heard, or what he knew. But he stuck out his arm. Like a coat hanger. Like a chin-up bar.

Sam Venturi ran right into it. His head stayed behind but his legs kept going. He spun around Bonetti's thick arm, his chin as the fulcrum, his feet flying up, and then his head down, and he crashed into the floor, unconscious.

Bonetti didn't even look down.

"Got the power on," he said.

CHAPTER THIRTY—EIGHT

I looked back at Deshawn. No one was looking at him now. It was the perfect time for him to make a break for it if he planned to. But he hadn't moved. He was sitting quietly. I figured he must have thought he was too clever, that he had every base covered. Then I noticed Detective Ronzoni. He had slipped in behind Deshawn's chair and had placed his hands on Deshawn's shoulders.
"Not going anywhere, Deshawn?"
He slowly shook his head. "No reason to," he said.
"You are cool, I'll give you that. But that's why Shania's father came to you. You and Shania grew up together. He knew how you felt about her. That you loved her. That's true, isn't it, Deshawn?"
"What if it is?"
"Like Sam, it's the worst kind. Unrequited love. But harder for you, I think. The woman you love is marrying the very guy you are linked to forever. Because Shania's dad asked you to provide a clean urine sample. But Paul found out. Anton got drunk with his 'brothers' one night and told all. Leon told me he didn't know who provided the sample but he suspected they were here because of something Paul said. Because Paul knew.

Anton didn't just tell about his end of the test. He told them who provided the sample."

"I did not know," said Leon.

"No, I don't think you did. I think you might have been too drunk to remember. But Paul remembered. And with the Anton gravy train coming to an end, he decided to make a new plan. To blackmail Deshawn. To threaten him. I suspect not with exposure to the authorities. Hell, it was a high school event. The samples were probably discarded long ago. But he could threaten to tell Shania. Tell her that her knight in shining armor, the man she had grown up with and looked up to as a brother, the man who had been in love with her for years, was a part of a cheat."

Deshawn didn't move. Ronzoni wasn't allowing that.

He said, "That's a great story. But even if it were true, it doesn't translate to murder."

"Oh, but it does. You see, Paul knew that this was the weekend that he was going to get the bad news from Anton. So it was the weekend to put you in play. He followed you to the gym. I saw him do it on the security video. He broke it to you there, didn't he? I think Ron and I might have interrupted you when we arrived to put the hurricane shutters up. You weren't working too hard when we got there. And then you used us as an excuse to get out. You said you were going for a soak. But later you said you went to your room. The video we saw shows you coming down from your room via the lobby stairs."

"So I prefer stairs to elevators. Heart healthy isn't a crime."

"Not at all. It's a darn good idea. But here's the thing. When you came out from the gym, the video shows you bypassing those stairs. I thought at the time it was because you were headed for the hot tub. But the hot tub was the other way."

"There were other stairs, nearer to my room."

"So you say. There are also cameras in the elevator lobbies on the room floors. That's where the lobby stairs come out. But you took the north staff stairs."

"So?"

"So, those stairs can't be opened at ground level without a staff key card. They are designed for emergencies, to get guests down, not up. You stopped at the check-in desk to say hi to Miss Taylor, but what you were really doing was stealing her key card."

"Oh, I'm a pickpocket now."

"I did lose my card around then," said Emery.

"Yes, you made one for me and one for Detective Ronzoni, and one for yourself. And Deshawn used yours to take the staff stairs to the mezzanine. Where the ballroom is. Shania told me you had a game of tennis in there, and then took Sam and her through Pilates."

"Pilates is a crime now?"

"It's a crime the way I do it. But you did it in a little space behind the ballroom. Near the staff stairs. The door near the boutiques goes up there. Just near where you walked out of shot on the video. And from that little area on the mezzanine you can go through the ballroom and down the south emergency stairs without being seen."

"You are really clutching at straws."

"I often do. But you get enough straws you can build a palapa hut, and that's the best place to sit after a hard day's work. Which Ron and I did in the gym, putting up shutters with no help from you or Paul. I bet when we left the gym you were right behind that door to the stairs, waiting for us to go. And when we do you go back into the gym. Maybe you convince Paul to lift, or maybe he's in the rack already because I goaded him into it.

"I figure he's got the safety bars in place. He's a lifter, he has a process. But you offer to spot for him. Maybe you're talking about making a deal with him. He thinks he owns you, so he says fine, spot me. But a spotter stands at the head of the bench. From there it takes just a little push to knock the safety bars out of their hole in the rack. If he's lifted the weight up, you could knock the safety bars out on each side before he knew it. And he'd have to push the weight back up into the racks to get out from under it. Plenty of time for you to push against him. Plus gravity and three hundred pounds on your side."

"Like Shania said, you're certifiable."

"On many levels, but not the one you're on. See, you had to push down with your palms. You know the weight will come down on his chest if it falls straight, so you drive it back toward yourself, right onto his neck. And you push until he's dead. Then you take a gym towel and you wipe down each of the safety bars and hide them behind the barbell racks. That will make it look like Paul was stupid and didn't use them, or at best didn't know they were there. Then you wiped down the bar that crushed Paul. And then you left."

I waited to hear something from Deshawn but he said nothing. In the circumstances it was the smart play. Most people who open their mouths to police just get themselves in trouble. Especially when they're guilty. But Shania spoke.

"This is all ridiculous," she said. "You are slandering a good man. Tell him, Deshawn."

But Deshawn went with silence. Shania looked at him and then at me.

"He might have gotten away with it too. But for one slip. Deshawn knows how weights work. He knows that Paul would be gripping the crosshatched section of the bar, where there would be no prints left. So he knew that his palm prints would be on the smooth section of the bar. He wiped them down. But he forgot something. When you press down with force on a bar, you don't naturally do it with an open hand. You grip it. You wrap your hands around it. So you wiped the top of the bar where your palms were, Deshawn. But you forgot the underside, probably because Paul was under there, dead. You left eight perfect fingerprints under the bar."

Deshawn dropped away from Ronzoni's hands. He wasn't making a break for it. He looked deflated. Shania spun around to him.

"That's not right. Say it's not right, Deshawn. Tell him."

But Deshawn didn't tell me. He looked at Shania. What I saw was shame. Not shame in what he had done to Paul. I got the feeling he was going to find a way to live with that. But shame that he had let Shania down. The knight had fallen from his steed.

"He was going to come after you," he said. "Don't you see? I'm not rich. Not like a professional tennis player. He'd want more. It was inevitable. He said if he couldn't get what he wanted from me he'd get it from you. He'd take you down. I couldn't let that happen."

"But . . . My dad?"

Deshawn dropped his eyes. He couldn't look at her. I didn't blame him.

"I'd do anything for him. I'd do anything for you."

"You did," I said.

CHAPTER THIRTY-NINE

The rain stopped within the hour. It took ten more hours to get out of the hotel. The lake around The Mornington showed no signs of abating, but eventually it did. I was gone before then. The Palm Beach PD arrived in a rubber dinghy, puttering along the streets like it was Venice. Ronzoni had locked Deshawn and Sam in separate utility rooms. They couldn't go anywhere. Hotel doors could be used in prisons, except they don't let enough light in, and that's against the charter of human rights, or some such. With hurricane shutters on the windows the rooms were safer than the city lockup. Ronzoni collected them one at a time and deposited them in the dinghy, one officer at the rear working the throttle, one behind the prisoners, Ronzoni at the front, facing back. He was back in his suit and looked like Ronzoni again.

He sealed the gym and the hot tub hut with police crime tape, and then he asked if I wanted him to come back for me and I told him not to bother. The officers said despite the work on Flagler Bridge the city had been able to open it, and although they weren't yet letting folks back onto the island, it was the best route off it. I told them I'd give it a shot. I watched Ronzoni putter away, the clouds breaking and the sun beaming down to warm the water like a bain marie. He glanced across the parking lot and saw his car with the palm tree sticking out the windshield. He stood in the small boat and looked back at me and yelled something but I was too far away to hear it. It made me smile anyway.

The coast guard came for the remaining guests. Rosaria the maid and Chef Dean went with them. Neville and Emery remained on board like the captain and executive officer of a sinking vessel. The evidence and the bodies would be collected the following day in a Florida National Guard Humvee.

I left my borrowed linen suit on the bed in my room and reclaimed my laundered shirt and shorts. My SUV had clung tight to the embankment around the hotel, and despite a good deal of water running through it, it started the first time. I threw up some thanks for Detroit. Cassandra rode out on my back. Ron waded out with their luggage. Cassandra demanded to be taken home to their apartment. I was confident it would still be there, but I wasn't sure what kind of shape it would be in. The gardens were a lake and the subterranean parking lot was subaqueous. The elevators were out of action and the doorman was MIA, but Ron said the stairs would be fine. I tried to convince them to get off the island but Cassandra was having none of it.

"This is my home. And we've got a lot of work to do."

I drove at walking pace out onto the South County Road, and gradually made my way onto Flagler Memorial Bridge. The water was still high and moving quickly but it had lost its gray pallor and twinkled in the midday sun like a mischievous child.

I stopped by Longboard's. There was a pond in the courtyard, and the surfboard that was attached to the back fence had come loose and was floating around on the water, looking for a way back out to the ocean. The palapa was gone. The bar underneath had been soaked. The indoor bar looked bashed but not beaten. I stood in calf-deep water and took it in and was thankful that Ron wasn't there to see it. It would have brought a tear to his eye. Mick was stoic as usual.

"Look," he said. He pulled one of the beer taps and the amber liquid flowed out onto the bar and mixed with the water on the ground. There were no glasses to be had, but the sight of flowing beer made Mick smile. I didn't. I couldn't say why. Sure I was sad that half of Longboard's had been blown away, but it wasn't the first time and it wouldn't be the last. We would clean up and Mick would rebuild and life would move on. It always did.

"I'll drop by tomorrow. We'll get her shipshape," I told Mick.

He nodded his thanks and then turned and waded into the darkness of the bar.

I drove Route 1 home. It was a mess. There was debris everywhere. Homes with no roofs, roofs with no homes. A donut truck was lying on its side opposite the Good Samaritan Medical Center. It took a long time to get to Singer Island but moving slowly felt appropriate. Funeral processions rarely get booked for speeding. By the time I got onto Blue Heron Boulevard the sun was out and steam was rising from the wet ground. The houses on the Intracoastal looked mostly in good condition. Lawns were a mess but homes were new and built to code. Some of the houses further from the water weren't so lucky. There were a few flattened here and there, bug-proof cages had collapsed into swimming pools. People were already sweeping the debris from the stores and restaurants along the beach.

My place looked like it was in one piece. It was a single-story rancher surrounded by two-story McMansions, and I figured the McMansions had taken the brunt of the wind. The sandbags at the front had held and let only minimal water through. I pulled up into the driveway and stopped. I didn't get out for longer than was necessary. I wasn't ready. And then I got out anyway.

The back of the house wasn't so lucky. The Intracoastal had made itself at home. Many of the sandbags had been picked up and deposited inside, through the sliding door that was supposed to be hurricane-proof. No doubt the manufacturer had a caveat about raging water. The shag carpet inside was like a mangy dog. The sunken living room had become a sort of indoor hot tub, and that thought made my mind flash back through the previous night to confirm if it had actually happened as I remembered it. I figured it could be worse. I could be Deshawn or Sam. I wasn't convinced they were evil people. A case could be made for the opposite to be true. But when good people do evil deeds they no longer hold the right to claim to be good. No doubt their defense counsel would suggest they were the victims in all this. Paul Zidane and Carly Pastinak weren't around to argue different, so I wondered if their voices would be heard at all.

I felt at a loose end. I didn't want to go, but I didn't want to stay. There was much work to be done, but I hadn't the faintest idea where to start, or if I even had the heart to try. I didn't want to howl or scream or wail, but I didn't want to stay silent. The world had turned upside down on me, and I wasn't sure what it would take to right it again.

And then I knew. I turned from my sorry-looking living room toward the mass of dead sandbags outside and I saw the answer. The answer to everything. Whatever questions I had, whatever questions were raised, the answer would lie there somewhere. She was in a gray t-shirt with FDLE emblazoned across the front, and long blue shorts. I don't know what she had on her feet because they were under water, but she leaned on one leg with her hands on her hips.

"Nice place you got here," Danielle said.

I nodded. "It's a unique fixer-upper opportunity."

She smiled. It was a perfect smile. Not flawless. It was lopsided, just a little, turned up more on the right than the left, but it was perfect to me.

"What are you doing here?"

"Governor called a state of emergency. We're here to help."

I waded out of the living room and onto the sandbagged patio. She looked freshly showered and smelled like jasmine.

"You're here to help with what?" I asked.

She smiled again.

"Anything you need."

GET YOUR NEXT BOOK FREE

Hearing from you, my readers, is one of the best things about being a writer. If you want to join my Readers' Crew, we'll not only be able to keep in touch, but you can also get an exclusive Miami Jones ebook novel, as well as occasional pre-release reads, and other goodies that are only available to my Readers' Crew friends.

Join Now:
http://www.ajstewartbooks.com/reader

ACKNOWLEDGEMENTS

Thanks to Marianne Fox for the editorial support.

To the betas—especially Carole, Wayne, Andy, Celeste, Bob, Debbie, Peter, Colin and Jim—I am in your debt.

As always, any and all errors and omissions are mine, especially but not limited to running around in a hurricane wearing nothing but a poncho. That's a real lack of planning, that is.

ABOUT THE AUTHOR

A.J. Stewart is the author of the USA Today bestselling Miami Jones Florida mystery series and the John Flynn thriller series.

He has lived and worked in Australia, Japan, UK, Norway, and South Africa, as well as San Francisco, Connecticut and of course Florida. He currently resides in Los Angeles with his two favorite people, his wife and son.

AJ is working on a screenplay that he never plans to produce, but it gives him something to talk about at parties in LA.

You can find AJ online at www.ajstewartbooks.com, connect on Twitter @The_AJStewart or Facebook facebook.com/TheAJStewart.

Made in United States
Troutdale, OR
05/29/2025